RUSKAYA BEND

T. C. GIBIAN

ISBN: 978-0-615-24662-8

Warning:

This is a work of fiction. Dropping one hundred twenty-seven feet into twenty feet of water may seem to be the grand gesture, but it would probably get you dead. Do not try it.

Disclaimer:

There is no such town as Ruskaya Bend – you won't find it on the map although the Russian River does exist in Northern California. This imaginary place may resemble several real towns; some of the characters may seem like actual persons, living or dead. All purely coincidental.

Advice:

Legas et Fruaris
(May You Read and Enjoy)

ACKNOWLEDGEMENTS:

GARY "DOV" GERTZWEIG –
> Constant encouragement
> and inspiration

RAFAELLA DELBOURGO –
> Perspective, compassion,
> long and treasured
> friendship

REID GIBIAN –
> Critical appraisal and
> support

SCOTT BROBERG –
> Cover Art providing
> substance to a dream

TOD CAREY –
> Proofreading and critical
> evaluation

This work was prepared using Kubuntu,
OpenOffice, and Gimp.

Chapter One

James McCanna took stock of the image in the mirror before him. A rugged face, with almost seventy years of contest and struggle portrayed in grand relief – a face to intimidate, to command. With a sharp look, he turned away and went out the door into the hall which led to the City Council chambers. He entered in his accustomed, mayoral style. With a word to the City Clerk on some matter and a nod to the other Council members, he took his seat and surveyed the crowd.

There were the usual hangers-on, gadflies, and sensation mongers, scattered in small groups. He knew that each of them would use his two minutes of public comment time to deliver some self-important declaration about nothing. A few also-rans from the last election sat off to one side, grumbling among themselves. A bored reporter filled out the cast of perpetuals, a luckless hack who probably had pulled the short straw at the office. The engineering staff was passing papers of obvious importance back and forth. The City Attorney fidgeted and looked bored. Each of these characters performed his part of the grand play like a cheap toy freshly wound up. Only Jeff Heit, the City Manager, seemed still and purposeful as he scanned the members of the Council, planning his part in the evening's events. And, as usual, Howard Keller occupied his accustomed seat in the front row. His face showed no emotion as he followed the Mayor's movements.

The City Clerk was reviewing the agenda and making notes next to each item as about fifteen residents of Turner Canyon marched in through the rear door. They seemed a bit out of place as they settled into seats near the aisle. Looking nervously at each other for a moment, they slowly turned to face front in silence, arrayed like a phalanx about to charge the dais. Dee Carella was with them. She was not smiling.

McCanna grunted quietly to himself. *The canyon rats are*

here. His glance toward them was sharpened by the recollection of past aggravations. *What time is it? Two minutes to go. Hell with it. Let's get this damn thing going.* Mayor McCanna straightened up and leaned forward. In tones that were intended to command unquestioning respect, he spoke into the microphone.

"The July nineteenth meeting of the Ruskaya Bend City Council will come to order." The Mayor smacked the gavel down briskly. "The City Clerk will call the roll."

A motion outside on the street caught the City Managers eye. He idly followed it.

"Council member Ryan." . . . . . "Present."

"Council member DelOstro." . . . . . "Present."

In the avenue outside the council doors, a beige VW bug crept down to the stoplight at the corner and stopped. The car paused past the turning of the light to green, expressing the driver's uncertainty.

"Council member Goetz." . . . . . "Present."

Slowly the car eased into the intersection and began a left turn toward Rosie's bridge.

"Mayor Pro Tem Williams." . . . . . "Present – I'm here."

"Mayor McCanna." . . . . . "Yes. Present."

The car disappeared from view.

"The first order of business is the consent calendar." The Mayor had his faults, but a weak voice was not one of them. Every syllable echoed throughout the hall. "Without exception, all items will stand for approval by voice vote."

"I have one item that . . ."

"Yes, Laura." The Mayor slowly turned to face her with bored condescension. His use of her first name was not intended to convey affection. "The chair recognizes Council member Goetz."

She smiled and continued smoothly, " I would like to see item four removed for discussion and a separate vote."

Mayor McCanna was obviously not pleased. He shot a glance into the back of the audience and finally growled, "Very well."

Laura sneaked a look at Dee Carella who was smiling, but

just a little. Howard Keller was scowling in his chair, shooting angry glances alternatively at the Mayor and "that damn woman." The City Manager had the look of a kibitzer watching a chess game where one player had just made an interesting move. The rest of the City Council seemed confused or bored.

"The chair will entertain a motion."

"I move that we accept the consent calendar excepting item four." Laura was quick to pin it down.

"Seconded."

"All in favor say 'Aye'."

A chorus of approval rose from the Council.

"All opposed? . . . The motion carries unanimously."

The gavel slammed down.

"Staff will describe item four."

Will Hansen, head of the Planning Department, rose to address the Council. "Item four is a routine geological report for The Cliffs subdivision proposal, prepared by Halley, Merrick, and Davis, a firm from San Francisco." He went on to describe the scope of the project, the nature of surface and subsurface investigations, and finished with the conclusions developed by the firm. "H, M, and D further sees no serious problems with overall stability on the project site." He sat down.

McCanna swiftly jumped in. "The chair will entertain a motion on . . ."

"Excuse me."

Laura Goetz was not going to let the door slam shut so easily.

"Yes, Councilmember." He turned stiffly toward her as if it was more bother to face her than it was worth.

"Public comment is allowed for all individual items before this body, isn't it?"

The mayor paused for just a moment. "Members of the public will have two minutes each to comment on this item." The gavel struck again.

Dee Carella rose to move toward the podium, but Howard Keller rushed his pudgy frame to stand before the microphone before she could get there. She shrugged and took a seat just behind him.

"Howard Keller. Ruskaya Bend." Everyone knew that the man did not live in town, but they let it ride. "Mayor McCanna, members of the Council. This is a routine matter, hardly deserving this level of fuss." His hand fluttered in a dismissive wave. "Halley, Merrick and Davis are a renowned firm who have done other work in this town. Uh, you should just vote this in and get on to some important business."

He sat down looking very self-satisfied. He had told 'em how high; now let 'em jump. But Dee was approaching the microphone.

She was a diminutive, raven-haired woman known for wearing colorful clothing and for chewing gum. About fifty, she still had a pleasing look to her, and she was the delight in many a man's eye. As she spoke, she framed her words with extravagant hand gestures, something that Howard Keller found very irritating. In fact, most things about her irritated him. His dour expression was counterbalanced by the look of expectant admiration on the faces of her neighbors at the back of the hall.

"Good evening, members of the Council." She never included the Mayor separately in her salutation. "I'm Dee Carella, 247 Turner Canyon Road. I won't waste your time. I have only one question of staff regarding a matter of procedure." The Mayor flipped his hand in their direction, but Dee had already turned toward their table and started speaking.

"Tell me, who selected the firm that prepared this geological report?"

For an instant no one moved, then Howard Keller turned bright red and looked as if he were about to speak, but did not. Mayor McCanna blew a little colder, if possible. Most of the Council seemed as if they had just woken up. The Mayor turned to stare at Will Hansen.

"Umm . . . the proponent selected the firm."

"Well, then." Dee continued before anyone could stop her. Her words were sure and sharp as a rod striking the surface of a pond, radiating a series of ripples in all directions. "According to S.B 1094, which was signed into law by the governor of this state last year, the proponent may not select the geological firm for his project if it is more than a four lot subdivision. That selection must be made by staff from a list of approved geological firms. Apparently this law was passed to deal with irregularities which occurred in Santa Rosa and other communities over the past few years." She knew very well that Howard Keller had come from Santa Rosa and had been involved with some of the "irregularities."

"Now, it would seem that, in order to conform to the letter of the law, this report should be rejected. Staff should generate a list of qualified geologists, and one of them selected to do the appropriate investigations on the subject . . . ."

"Thank you, Ms. Carella." The Mayor did not want to let this get too far out of hand. "The proper course of action will be decided upon at the proper time. The Council . . ."

Howard Keller could not hold back – he saw the moment slipping away and jumped up. "You could just take a provisional vote and sort this all out administratively at a later time." He rarely blurted out from the audience, but he had to try to get this thing back on track.

Dee leaned forward to the microphone and filled the hall with her firm voice.

"Members of the Council. As you know, there is no such thing as a provisional vote in a matter that is clearly a violation of state law, however inadvertent."

McCanna glanced at the City Attorney who gave an abbreviated nod. "Very well, the Council remands this matter to staff to take appropriate action and report back before the next scheduled meeting."

The gavel came down, and a roar of approval rose from the back of the hall. Dee made a gesture as if sweeping dust from the podium and turned to join her exultant friends. As she walked back, many eyes followed her expressing admiration or loathing. Only one pair had no strong emotion. The City Manager followed her gliding gait down the aisle with a reserved amusement. *Not bad . . . you are a quick study. But let's see if you can keep it up.* Howard Keller slipped out the door like a breath of steam evaporating into the still air.

The Mayor used the gavel freely, trying to thunder the audience into a mannerly silence. He succeeded, but only because Dee and her neighbors left the hall. With concealed pleasure Anna Ferrier, the City Clerk, completed writing a synopsis of the previous discussion, made a few additional notes, and turned her attention to the next matter.

Over the next twenty minutes, the Council's time was filled with the usual interval reserved for public comment. Several familiar faces rose and addressed the Council, some with praise, some with criticism. Others were primarily interested in the spectacle value of the moment, cherishing their own amplified voice, the captive audience, their appearance before the camera which televised the Council meetings. Most of the Council drifted into mild torpidity, hoping it would end soon. Only Laura Goetz even tried to look interested. The Mayor scribbled notes and the City Manager was bent in conversation with the City Attorney.

They had a long regular agenda to push through.

Dee and her gang of smiling faces wandered across the street to The Plum Branch, Ruskaya Bend's beloved watering hole, to hash over the recent events. As they settled into the chairs around one of the large, oak tables, Dee tried to bring them down gently from the perilous heights of exultation.

"Now remember, this is just a small victory. We will have to win several more, and we still can't afford to loose a single one."

"What does this mean, really?" Aurelia Salgado lived up the street from Dee and was always quick to get to the heart of the matter.

"Doesn't he have to start over?" inquired Bob Henley.

"Not necessarily."

The waitress came, took orders, and departed.

"The steamroller which Howard Keller has aimed at us is definitely parked in neutral now, but he hasn't had to turn the motor off yet." Dee paused to let the point register with her audience. "City staff will rush to develop a list of sanctioned geologists, but they never hurry very fast. This will take a few weeks. Most likely at the top of the list will be H, M, and D, the very firm retained by Keller. The crunch will come when they try to approve his geological report in retrospect. Sometime before this occurs . . ." She permitted herself a slight expression of fiendish glee. "I will wander down to City Hall and have a chat with Will Hansen – on other business, of course. I will inquire offhandedly whether the City has signed a contract with any geological firm regarding this project as a part of the official selection process."

After a pause Bob inquired, "Is that all?"

"For right now. They will be put on notice that we know the contract signed by Howard Keller will not satisfy the requirements of state law, and the City will have to develop its own contract with H, M, and D. Those bandits will probably be eager to see a new contract as representing a new job with a new check to follow. Negotiation will take several weeks. In the end, the City or Keller will have to grease the skids with a modest amount of cash, the geologists will retitle the original report and hustle it off as if it were brand new, and it will be accepted in a rush by the full Council."

"So, what have we gained?" Bob and the others seemed a bit crestfallen.

"Maybe two months. They will surely miss the next Council meeting, and perhaps the one after that too. Remember, the key to all our strategies is November fourth." She leaned forward to bear down on this point. "The delay will break Keller's momentum for a while and bring us that much closer to election day. Getting a new council is our only way out of this. McCanna and his buddies love this project as much as they despise us. They have the votes, and they're like a coked-up quarter horse lunging at the starting gate. We have to keep them from taking a vote before the election."

The assembled neighbors murmured their understanding.

"What do we do in the meantime?"

"Well, a little electioneering, a little obstruction, a bit of publicity. Nobody here in town really knows what is happening –

we have to change that.

"Perhaps a few well penned letters to the editor of the Ruskaya View," suggested Aurelia. "The editor might provide a forum for us."

"Yes! Roy Butler will surely help us."

"The South Wall Neighborhood Association is having a meeting next month." Carl Fish hadn't had anything to say up to this point. "The chairman Greg Tyson is a friend of mine. Maybe he will give me a few minutes to address the members – let 'em know what's going on."

"Great!"

Ruth Frazee was frowning. "There's nothing I know to do."

"Ruth, you know more people in this town than any three of us together." Dee was almost laughing. "You can get on the phone – I know you like to chat – see if you can find some sympathetic ears." She turned to face the group as a whole. "Remember, McCanna is the target here. He has already stepped on more than a few toes with some of the outrages he has run through the Council. Hammer on the man."

The group relaxed visibly. Their purpose was still before them.

"Dee, where did you learn how to do all this?"

"Oh, Ted was a good teacher. He taught me that small town politics is the art of the possible. You just have to find it. A lot of folks think that you can't fight City Hall, that they always have all the cards, but it is just a matter of finding where to put in the lever to flip them over."

"But where did you find out about that law, SB whatever?"

"Oh. Well, you see . . . There's this lawyer who happens to be an old boyfriend . . ."

She didn't have to say any more. The crowd burst into laughter.

Howard Keller was drinking alone in his office. He was having a problem with the "little people" again. He poured his anger into his scotch and drank it down.

Damned Lilliputians! Every time I make a move, these worms come up out of their holes and try to trip me up. What attitudes these people have! Don't they know that I have the land and I can do whatever I want with it! They can't stop me.

A second shot followed the first with a measure of loathing in it.

That woman! I should do something about her. Cut the head off, and the whole animal dies. I should fix that little bitch — she'll think twice about coming up against me.

The next shot was laced with contempt.

That fool McCanna doesn't have a clue what he is doing. The whole bunch on the Council wouldn't know the ass end of a mule if there was a sign on it.

He poured another one and stared into it.

Got to do something!

Chapter Two

At the height of the last Ice Age, the land that would become Ruskaya Bend was an undistinguished portion on the middle reaches of a moderately sized river. Five miles downstream from that point, the flow entered the ocean on the west coast of a great continent. The river was flanked by narrow bottomland covered with spruce, fir, and some redwood. Each year the snow fell into the valley and stayed for a third of the year. A hardy band of migrants traveling down from the north had discovered the region and explored the course of the river nearly a thousand years before, naming it "the place where you see bears." They knew themselves only as "the People." They passed through that particular spot frequently, considering it a good location for hunting large game, but never stayed long. They knew about the sweet-water spring that issued from a narrow canyon on the north side of the valley.

The People were not there when the south valley wall fell. Months of rain had seeped into the slopes above the river, and when the earthquake came, thousands of tons of rock lost its cohesiveness and crashed onto the valley floor, creating a giant natural dam. Those of the People who lived at the mouth of the river saw the flow decline to that of a small creek. Exploring for the cause, they found the beginnings of a lake forming behind an obstruction of rocky debris. Since the fish from the river and game migrating up and down the valley were critical food sources, now gone, they made the decision to migrate south to more favored lands, fighting other tribes for a place in the sun. They never returned.

It took several years for the lake to fill to a depth of forty feet and overflow the obstruction, restoring the full strength of the river in its rush to the sea. A new group traveling south along the coast, searching for lands to sustain them, came across the river and its renewed food resources. They stayed and prospered.

They called themselves "the Ocher People" after their favored color of face paint. The Ocher People knew the area around the lake, which they called "Still Water." They hunted on its banks and often lived camped out between the giant boulders of the rocky ridge which dammed the river. The winters were not so cold as they once had been – snow was seen for only about a month, and in some years not at all. The spruce and fir were claiming the formerly bare mountain peaks. Oak trees were becoming common in the bottomland and slopes, providing an important new food source. Often the Ocher People lived near the lake from late summer into the fall, harvesting and preparing the acorns for winter food. They came to rely less on the large game, not noticing that the great animals were now becoming rare.

They also didn't notice several changes which were altering the lake and establishing its subsequent future. Annual deposition of silt and sand were slowly making it shallower, creating a wide flat bottom extending beneath the water east of the dam for nearly a mile. At the same time, the north side of the dam, where the overflow occurred, was being worn down. Every violent, winter storm season saw a deepening of this notch, resulting in a lowering of the lake's water level. The day arrived when the Ocher people returned during a hunt and found the lake was no more. Instead, a soggy mud flat had taken its place. During the spring, the river's waters spread out, trying to reclaim its lost domain, but in the fall, it would shrink back into a narrow channel. The time of the Meadows had begun.

The new land first sprouted a coarse grass, and then a few trees began to grow in the rich soil. The Ocher People favored the oaks, planting acorns in likely spots and burning the area each year to destroy the pines, which were constantly trying to crowd out the more productive oaks.

Over the years, the river continued in its attempt to cut down to its original level. For a time a series of rapids extended westward below the notch in the dam, running past the small canyon with its spring; but as the river cut deeper, the rapids disappeared. The channel across the meadows became well developed, and floods issued from it only rarely, during winters when the rain would not stop. The river pressed against the north wall of the valley in a meander, which became more pronounced as time passed, due to periodic collapses. A broad sandy beach began to form along the south side of the bend.

The Ocher People had never gotten along with their neighbors. They had a different culture and language and competed for the ever-scarcer game. Raids back and forth became more common, and the Ocher People were feeling the pressure. They talked of migration, but the pull of the land was strong. For two thousand years, an eternity for them, they had walked these trails and buried their dead along this river and lived among these trees. The land had sustained them graciously, and they chose not to leave it.

The warfare lasted for two generations. In the end the Ocher People were no more. Their enemies had suffered such great losses in overcoming them that they themselves were soon destroyed by a tribe from the great lake to the northeast. For a time the land at the great bend rested quietly with no people to cherish it.

The Lake People slowly infiltrated into their newly won territories, and a group of them found the area around the bend in the river to their liking. The levels of game had rebounded, and an extended oak forest in the wide flatlands just upstream. They settled on the rocky ridge, which jutted out into the bend, and they prospered. The years passed, and this band came to know themselves as "the River People." They maintained contact with their relatives near the lake to the east, joining them in festivals twice per year; but as time passed, they noticed that their lake relatives became harder and harder to understand. They did not speak the pure language, said the River Folk, but they nevertheless embraced them as distant cousins.

One family of the River People had taken up residence at the mouth of the river, living off the products of the sea and trading dried fish and fresh abalones to their kinsmen for acorns.

They were usually called the Storm People for the many powerful tempests which struck at them from the northwest.

One afternoon this family rushed into the village at the great bend with startling news. A giant rock, looking like a snowy peak, had moved across the ocean and stopped offshore from the river mouth. In a small craft, a group of what looked like men had traversed the distance to shore and debarked. At this point the Storm People had fled.

The leader of the River People, called Ducks-in-Flight, quizzed the refugees carefully. What was the nature of these men? Did they speak a human language? Did they seem to have aggressive intent? How many were they?

None of the Shore Folk had been able to hear any of these strangers speak over the rising wind, and none could guess their intent, but the twelve or so men did have a very odd appearance. They had clothes entirely unlike that of the People. They wore bright colors, some in patches, and odd head garb. Most of them carried a black stick, which they treated with some reverence. The strangers were of two kinds. One sort had long, black hair and resembled the River People, except for their clothing. The other had the most amazing features. Their skins were paler than new buckskin. Several of them had hair growing from their faces! This gave them the appearance of bears, and they looked truly fearsome. One was even seen to have hair the color of dried grass. The Storm People knew nothing of their numbers.

Ducks-in-Flight resolved to investigate this mystery but thought it wise to take a group of well-armed men with him. In the past his band had fought to protect their lands from marauders from the south. This didn't sound exactly like a war party, but it was prudent to be cautious. They passed down the valley toward the coast without a sound.

Hidden in the scrub brush near the beach, Ducks-in-Flight saw that all the news was true. Surely, these were very peculiar looking men, but they clearly were men. As they moved objects out of their small boat, he could hear them speaking an unfamiliar language. He resolved to hail them. After deploying his men to concealed positions partially surrounding the strangers, he rose up. Stepping forward with his bow at his side, he held up one hand and called out.

The reaction was immediate. The strangers took up their black sticks and clustered together, chattering excitedly. They held up these sticks to point in his direction, but made no other move. One of them, one of the hairy ones, spoke in a commanding tone to his fellows, tipped his stick back over his shoulder, and slowly walked toward Ducks-in-Flight who told his men in the brush to remain still but ready.

The two men approached each other across the sand to stand ten feet apart. They sized each other up in silence. Then the stranger spoke. His language had a rumbling, gargling sound to it, most peculiar to Ducks-in-Flight; but the man seemed sincere. He spoke for a time, and then stopped. Then Ducks-in-Flight responded, telling the man that this was the land of his tribe, and that no one was allowed to cross it or to hunt without permission. He asked about the intent of these strangers and where they came from. The man before him seemed to understand not a word.

Breaking the impasse, the stranger turned and called to his companions, issuing some order. One of them went to their boat and pulled out several objects and then brought them cautiously to drop them before the two men. He then retreated quickly to stand with the others. Ducks-in-Flight recognized some of the objects immediately – the large one was a skin of inferior quality from a medium sized bear, and the other was the pelt of a sea otter, still stiff and unprepared for use. The other objects were unlike anything he had ever seen before. He took these to be some sort of gift offering, and reluctant to be obligated to this stranger, made to refuse them. The bear-faced one laughed and started a curious skit, with many hand gestures, apparently trying to communicate something. Presently, Ducks-in-Flight thought he understood. This odd fellow wanted more of these kinds of skins. He offered the other objects lying on the sand in trade for them.

Ducks-in-Flight examined these goods more carefully. One was obviously an ax with a wooden handle, but the head was made from a cool, dark material like stone, but yet unlike it. The next was a knife with a blade of the same peculiar material, which was very thin but strong. The third was a mystery at first, having the shape and size of a very rounded, black skull, but the stranger indicated that it was a cooking pot. The last objects had been laid carefully on a piece of soft leather, and his eyes grew wide as they looked them over. These were beads, but unlike any he had ever seen. His own people had beads made from shell and certain rocks, even large seeds, but nothing like these! Each of these glistened and gleamed with a flashing light and brilliant colors. They were hard, like stone, but he could see through some of them. He could certainly please his wife with these.

Ducks-in-Flight liked what he saw and considered that if these strangers only wanted dirty, old pelts for them, the River People would be getting the best of the bargain. He nodded his understanding. The stranger was obviously pleased and then did something which was thoroughly startling. He made a gesture, sweeping off his head gear, crossing his chest with the hand containing it, and lowered his head. Ducks-in-Flight was astounded to see the reason why this man had hair on his face. It had fallen off the top of his head which was bare! From this moment, this individual would be known as "Fallen Hair". Ducks-in-Flight strained to keep from laughing so that he would not insult a man with whom he would make a bargain, merely nodding and speaking his goodbyes.

As he was about to enter the brush and rejoin his companions, Fallen Hair called out to him. As he turned to face them, one of the other men brought his black stick up to his shoulder. There was a flash near his face and a puff of smoke, then a larger puff from the other end of the stick. A sound like a very angry hornet whizzed past Ducks-in-Flight, striking the limb of a nearby tree and severing it in a shower of wood chips. Immediately came a loud, deep sound like nearby thunder which echoed from the cliffs behind him.

He stood still briefly and then issued careful instructions to his nearby clansmen. On his signal they all fired a volley of arrows from their hidden locations. The strangers were caught by surprise since they were looking toward the sun, so they didn't see the flight of missiles until it passed over their heads, striking the boat behind them. At the echoing thud, the strangers fell to the sand, fearing the worst; but there were no more. Twelve arrows protruded from the wooden hull, two penetrating it.

Ducks-in-Flight stood silently at the edge of the brush for a moment before disappearing.

Fallen Hair's people called themselves "Lushki," as near as the River People could tell. Their language made the mouth sore to pronounce it. The others, who somewhat resembled the People, were called "Aliu," and they were a vicious lot.

These Aliu considered that the right to hunt the sea otter was exclusively theirs, and when they caught some of the Storm People preparing otter skins, they caused their black sticks to spit hornets at them, killing two. Before long, the remnants of the shore folk retreated up the canyon to live at the big bend with their kin. At the first meeting for trade, Ducks-in-Flight saw that Fallen Hair had brought several of these murderers with him and he loudly demanded that they be expelled. Fallen Hair seemed to understand and sent them back to their camp. From then on, the River People and the Aliu attacked each other whenever chance brought them together in the woods. An uneasy peace remained with the Lushki.

Ducks-in-Flight found that the Lushki worshiped the bear, as this was a totem for them. They gave much in trade for large skins, and soon there were very few to find in the woods. The River People used a pass over the mountains to travel to the coast south of the river, seeking sea otter. The tribe who lived in those parts was understandably possessive about their territory and game, and there always was the risk of a fight.

Not far to the north of the river mouth the Lushki built a large encampment on the coastal plain. For it they cut a wealth of pine logs and set them into the ground in a rough circle. At one location it was possible to move some of the logs and gain entry. This was where the River People and other tribes went for trade. It was forbidden to fight there. Even the Aliu had to observe this rule. It was there that Ducks-in-Flight's people found about the burning water.

The strangers had a dark, bad-smelling water which they drank during celebrations. It made the Lushki quiet and thoughtful when they drank it, but the Aliu became loud and offensive under its influence. At first, the River People thought that the gods were at work here, and tried some of the water, but it had a bad end. One of Ducks-in-Flight's cousins began to stagger around, crying incoherently, and stumbled into a fire where he was burned badly. After that, any of the tribesmen were forbidden to drink the burning water, a pronouncement which was hard to enforce. The burning water brought trouble.

At one trading session, the River People were waiting patiently to present their goods, when an Aliu, smelling strongly of the burning water, shuffled over to the People and started shouting, pointing at the otter skins they had. Without any warning, he pulled out a knife and lunged at an uncle of Ducks-in-Flight, cutting him badly. He screamed as the knife entered his flesh, and the People leapt to deal with the attacker with knives of their own. He shrieked and ran off with several wounds, and the People fled with their clansmen and their goods. The uncle died two days later.

Ducks-in-Flight had not been at the log encampment during this trading session and he pondered what to do. Perhaps the Lushki would turn their faces away from the affront since the Aliu had started the fight. He counseled patience and restraint, but circumstances took control away from him.

Two sons of the murdered man organized an ambush on a party of Lushki and Aliu who had entered the forest seeking deer to hunt. They caught them in a narrow defile between two cliffs and killed two of them, including one Lushki, but several got away. Hearing this, Ducks-in-Flight knew that there was no going back and he made his preparations. He sent out scouts to watch for movements from the log encampment. He broke camp, moving it from the ridge at the bend to a place farther up the valley. He devised a battle plan and briefed all his clansmen. They prepared their weapons, spoke to the gods, and waited.

Ducks-in-Flight knew that the "thunder sticks," as they were called, were powerful weapons. The little, round hornet they spat out could easily kill a man, but there was a weakness. After the puff of smoke, the strangers had to turn the weapon around and talk to it for a while before it could spit again. Some thought that they used magic substances on it, but one thing was clear – at least twenty heartbeats would pass before the weapon could spit out another hornet. Ducks-in-Flight had the tribe's women gather old clothes.

In the morning three days later a group of fifteen Lushki and Aliu left the log encampment and proceeded down the coast to the river mouth. When the scouts brought the news, Ducks-in-Flight nodded, knowing that the sun would be in the faces of his enemy at the correct time. He dispatched about one third of his men, ordered the women to start some smoky fires in the new camp, and waited. Soon word came that the enemy was moving up river, that each man had a thunder weapon, and they were on the north bank. He frowned and asked whether they were below the ford – they were. He waited. Then the word came. The enemy had crossed the river at the ford to the south side and were approaching the great bend. Ducks-in-Flight dispatched another third of his men to their positions and started leading the remainder into the oak forest near the east side of the bend. His brother East Wind, stationed above the cliffs at the bend, could see him for signals; and all the rest positioned in the woods at the southern base of the ridge could see signals relayed by his brother. They all waited.

Ducks-in-Flight knew that Fallen hair would send some of his men up the slope at the west side of the ridge only to find that the village was gone. At this point they could see the smoke from the camp up the valley and would most likely be ordered back to the main party. The whole group would want to take the easiest route upstream, following the beach curving around the great bend on the south side, sandwiched between the river and the low bluff at the end of the rocky ridge. In the middle of the curve, they would not be able to see upstream or downstream and the land would tower above them on both sides of the river. He could now hear them approaching.

On an alert from his brother East Wind, who was observing from the cliffs, Ducks-in-Flight gave the first signal to attack, a high screeching yell which reminded the People of a hawk's cry. With a shout, one group of the People rushed out of the woods behind the strangers and ran up the beach from the west, setting up a position to cut off retreat. Ducks-in-Flight sent one group from the meadow up onto the ridge to attack the enemy from the bluff to the south of them, while he led another body from the east along the curve of the beach to complete the trap. East wind and his companions fired directly into the enemy from atop the cliffs to the north. Immediately a roar of angry thunder echoed through the narrow passage. To Ducks-in-Flight it sounded like the shuddering voice of rage coming from a cornered bear when the first arrow had struck him. The tribesmen sweeping in from both sides along the beach were instructed to press the enemy but to keep a certain distance, letting the hornets strike the water and the rocks. Ducks-in-Flight counted the booms. Five, six, seven – eight, nine. There was a pause. He gave the next signal.

Suddenly the four groups of tribesmen held up manikins which the women had made from old clothing. The heads were sections of buckskin stuffed with grass, some painted with fearsome expressions. They had painted hair and some carried old bows. These were moved up, down, and sideways in a lifelike fashion, and once again a roar of thunder was heard. Several of the manikins disappeared in an explosion of buckskin scraps. Ten, eleven, twelve, thirteen. Ducks-in-Flight gave the final signal, rose, and led the charge westward down the beach as his clansmen did the same from the other side. The other two groups on the ridge and the cliffs fired their arrows in unison.

As Ducks-in-Flight ran down the beach toward the enemy, he saw a Lushki kneeling down. It was Fallen Hair and he was talking to his weapon! Those who still had hornets spit them out hurriedly, and one clansman running beside Ducks-in-Flight fell, but the remainder of them cut into the enemy like an eager fire burning into dry grass. Ducks-in-Flight closed on Fallen Hair with his spear held high, screaming his war cry, but the Lushki had one more surprise for him.

There was one thing about the thunder weapons which the River People never had learned. They came in two sizes. From his tunic, Fallen Hair pulled out a small one and fired it. The hornet struck Ducks-in-Flight in the chest and knocked him down, but he rose and, spitting rage and blood, he ran three more steps and tore out the Lushki's throat with his spear.

With a gurgling shriek, the Lushki collapsed into a pool of his own blood. Ducks-in-Flight stood for a moment, swaying and coughing up his life until he collapsed. They died there on the sand next to the river.

There were two prisoners. One, an Aliu, was prepared to fight to the end, but he was clubbed from behind and trussed up quickly. The other, a Lushki, got down on his knees and begged for his life with a deep-throated, warbling moan. He was knocked down and tied up as well.

The Aliu would probably have preferred to go down fighting. During the night the River People skinned him alive. They took their time at it, and in the morning they hung his flayed body from a tree for the ravens to eat.

The Lushki listened all night to the screams and was sure he was to follow. East Wind, who was now considered the leader, wanted the Lushki's skin for the death of his brother, but several of the other men presented the argument that he might be more valuable as a trade item if kept alive.

In the end the Lushki was made a slave. He spent his nights fastened to a tree and his days with his leg tied to a large rock, dragging it around as he hauled water and firewood to the village while the women shouted insults at him. He seemed to accept his fate until one night he chewed through his bonds like a wild animal and escaped. Such was his eagerness to gain freedom that he left a tooth on the ground next to the parted rawhide straps. East Wind picked it up and hung it around his neck on a cord as a trophy.

For many years the River People sang about the battle at the bend in the river – certainly a great thing to tell the gods and ancestors about.

Nearly a whole season passed with no further appearance of the men from the log encampment. The River People had accumulated two perfect bearskins and would normally have traded them for many fine goods, but could they now? The battle had been an honorable one, with many losses on both sides. Were the strangers the sort of people to hold resentments indefinitely? East Wind resolved to find out.

He and several others took their weapons and some accumulated skins and followed the trail to the log encampment. Standing a safe distance away, East Wind held up one of the bearskins and called out to the men inside. At first there was no response, then the wall moved open and one man came out. All could see that many thunder weapons protruded from the top of the wall. As the man approached, East Wind observed that it was the Lushki whom they had captured. He stood a short distance off and spoke in his muttering growl of a language while he set a blanket down with trade goods on it. As East Wind examined the offering, he noticed that the man was missing an incisor. There were no axes or knives, and the cooking pot, the bright cloth, and the mirror were things only a woman might want, but it all seemed good enough. The exchange was made, and the Lushki started backing away with his bearskins. He did not take his eyes off East Wind for an instant, and the tribesman spoke one last thing to him. "Remember that you are my slave," he called out, holding up the tooth. The Lushki gave no indication that he understood.

Trade continued on an uneasy basis for several years, but there was no more fighting. The River People had noticed immediately that all the Aliu had disappeared from the log encampment and never returned. Probably the ravens had told them about eating their kinsman. Whatever, they were well gone! A bad sort, those ones. The Lushki were a little crazy, but you could do business with them.

One day in the fall, the River People traveled to the coast with skins to trade and found the encampment abandoned. The entrance was ajar and several buildings inside were destroyed by fire. The People then living on the coast said that the snowy rock had come and gone, taking the Lushki. The River Folk considered this departure with mixed feelings, but they were now rich in axes and beads. They wondered whether they would ever see these curious, pale creatures again. In a generation they had their answer.

The new people were called "Melika," and they came from the east. They were pale also, but more had the hair of dry grass color or even the red of the setting sun, and fewer grew it on their faces. There had been word of trouble with these people, tribes wiped out or driven from their lands. Unlike the Lushki, these people were less interested in skins than with the land itself, and they fought hard for it. They had thunder sticks too, but a different kind, smaller, which could spit many hornets in a short time. Another difference was that they had women and children with them. There seemed to be no end to these people, and it was just a matter of time before they appeared in the valley.

They made it clear to the River People that they wanted the oak forest. The tribe had been much diminished by the spotted disease and the bloody cough, so the vast food resource was no longer so important. These new people seemed to covet the flat land where the forest grew. They offered small rectangular skins with images and designs on them, black and green; but the People would have none of them. Then they reluctantly brought forth small disks, some of a substance colored like the afternoon sun, others the color of sea foam, with images of eagles and women on them. The River People had seen these before, and they were so soft that it could not be used to make anything useful. They rejected those too. Finally a deal was struck with a shovel, a long handled ax, a bolt of red cloth, a worn kitchen knife, four blankets, an old violin, and a rusty bell. The River People established a permanent camp one hour's walk downstream at a favorable spot near a tributary.

Immediately the Melika began to cut down the oak trees. They stacked up the pieces in piles and used a large, slow animal to pull out the stumps. This same beast pulled some sort of tool through the earth, breaking it open, with no regard to who might be buried there.   Then, as the River People watched from a distance in amazement, the new people laboriously planted grass. From that time the new people were sometimes known as "Grass Eaters", and they were thought to be probably of unsound mind. The River People had legends about their ancestors eating grass, but only when they had been starving. The Melika had destroyed an abundant food source which effortlessly yielded enormous amounts of acorns so that they could work endlessly to grow grass. It was hard to see the wisdom in this. Later the People found that this grass produced many large seeds, and food could be made from it, but they never liked the taste of it.

Over the years the River People moved several times toward the coast as new groups of Melika arrived and demanded flat land near the river.   They sometimes traded for it, and sometimes not.   They enforced their will with thunder weapons, and the People thought it wise to make the best deal they could and move on. Every year there were more Melika and fewer of the People. Finally they wound up in two small camps near the river mouth when men in black clothing came to take away the children. They said it was for education – the old people wept for their loss. Slowly the heart fell out of the people.   Some years later a few of the children returned, but they were not easily recognized.   They no longer spoke a real language, but only Melika.   They wore Melika clothing and lived in Melika houses. They never walked the forest seeking game, never collected the acorns, never sang the old songs.   Some even married Melika women. They had abandoned one tribe for another.   In this way The People survived and perished, both at the same time.

Chapter Three

The City Manager of Ruskaya Bend was a man who would always come directly to the point.

"What can I do for you, Howard?"

Howard Keller was one of few men the City Manager knew who could look both humble and arrogant at the same time.

"Well, Jeff. It seems that we have this little problem with the geological report. Heh, heh. A small thing, really. We should be able to deal with this in no time. Don't you think?"

"Howard, the City has procedures to be followed. We don't have a lot of discretionary latitude here. State law is clear."

"Yes, yes, of course. But it shouldn't take very long, should it? A matter of paperwork, eh?"

The Manager paused. *What a thoroughly irritating man this is. Always trying to shovel someone out of the way – with a borrowed shovel, no less. Oh well – best to humor the fool. He has the favor of the Mayor, for the moment.*

"Let's hope so."

"Yes, yes. I know you are the perfect man to take care of it." Keller stretched forward, trying not to look too eager. "You know, I think we may have a problem with this Turner Canyon business."

Here we go. "In what way, Howard?"

"Well, of course, that place is a dump – a firetrap really. It should have been abandoned long ago. How can anyone live like that? But, you see, I think they may be . . . ."

The manager's eyes narrowed.

". . . may be violating the conditions of the planning study – the moratorium. As set forth by the Council, that is."

"How, precisely?"

"Well . . . they seem to be doing a lot of construction without permits." Then he added hastily. "Strictly prohibited by the terms of the planning study and a violation of City ordinances, as you know."

He looked like a poker player who had just been called and had laid down his hand, only to have sudden doubts that he had the winning cards.

"Well, Howard, as you know, enforcement procedures regarding construction violations are complaint driven. Do you have grounds to file specific complaints against specific properties?"

"Oh, well, uh. I'm sure it's the whole bunch of them" He was beginning to look like a man having his head squeezed in a vice.

"All of them?"

"Well, actually, I can hear hammering and sawing from down there all the time. Who knows who is doing what. They've all got something going, surely. You really should get some enforcement in there – straighten things out. Can't just let 'em scoff at the rules. Enforcement."

Now the Manager leaned forward. "What do you have in mind, Howard?"

To the Manager, the man before him looked like an old frog, croaking an evil spell.

"You should get some teams down there – you know, Fire Department, Police, and . . . and building inspectors. Have 'em go door to door doing inspections, find out what's going on, put a stop to all this."

Now that you've spit it out, do you feel better?" "Well, let's see. That would be something we would have to take before the Council for their approval. Have you discussed your ideas with any of them yet?"

"Well, no. Not yet." He was doing his best to look ingratiating. "Everybody knows you are the one who gets things done around here. With your support, I'm sure the Council would go along."

There was some astuteness in this observation. The City Manager controlled the day-to-day functioning of the City. All members of staff were his employees. All policy was implemented by him. The Council relied heavily upon his presentation of the issues before them, and most usually deferred to his advice. It was a position of considerable power.   However, there could be something risky in Howard Keller's most recent attempt to use City authority to hammer his chosen enemies.   Unseen implications. Backlash, perhaps. Nothing must reflect on the Managers office.

"Well, Howard, you may have something there – the inspections, that is. But we can't rush into a thing like this without being sure of our legal position. I want to run it past Don Colesco before I work up a presentation for Council. As City Attorney, he should have some valuable insight."

There was a pause before Howard Keller realized he had just been dismissed, whereupon he jumped up looking like a man who just realized he had left his hat somewhere.

"Yes, Yes.   I'm sure that this matter is in the right hands . . . only you could do . . . " His voice trailed off.

He backed out of the office door, and as he scuttled down the hall, the Manager couldn't help thinking how much more pleasant his office was with that man gone. He sighed and tapped the table slowly with a pencil. Picking up the phone, he entered the code for the City Attorney's office.

"Don, hi. Are you going to have some time available in the next half hour? . . . Fine . . . no, just yourself . . . OK, see you then."

The door opened to an unrecognized woman's face. Two inquiring, blue-gray eyes viewed him carefully.

"Ah, you must be Jason. I saw a car . . ." His beige VW was in the driveway. "And I thought I would stop by. You are Ted's son?"

She could see that he was from the shape of his face and his mouth. The same thick hair, but reddish rather than Ted's black. A thinner version of his father's tall frame. The same body english, smooth, sparing gestures. He had the look of someone dragging his past with him. *He's how old – what did Ted say – twenty-eight?*

Jason Brandt stood before a diminutive woman with long, wavy black hair, who was enthusiastically chewing gum. Looking about twice his age, she seemed an attractive woman. Her hand danced over a stack of papers stapled in groups of three and cradled within her left arm. The seeming nervous manner of her jaw and her hands was belied by the steady gaze of her eyes. She seemed to be looking for something in his face.

"Yes, I am. Have we met?" He felt awkward at being at the disadvantage.

"No, not actually. Not yet, that is. I'm Dee Carella. I live two doors up – the brown house.

"Oh, how do you do." Jason hadn't anticipated meeting any of his father's neighbors.

"You're up from San Francisco and you're an industrial artist for Shaw and Richetti. Oh, I'm sorry. Too forward, I know, but your Dad spoke about you often." Her hand reached forward to touch his shoulder in a reassuring way. "It's like I know you."

"You knew him?"

"We all did here. He'll be missed." She stopped working the gum for a moment. "Sorry about his passing. A good man. He stood by us when we needed him."

"Thanks." Jason didn't know how to respond. His father was someone he had scarcely known over the previous ten years, but this woman seemed to have a high regard for him. In the pause that followed, he heard the call of a hawk curving high in the sky above the canyon behind them.

"Well . . . This is what I came to bring you. It's the Neighborhood Association bulletin. All the news on the project and the Council meeting last night." She looked at him intently. "This is your house now. Were you planning to live here?"

"Oh, I hadn't really thought about it." He didn't really want to tell her the exact truth. "I never have considered living in Ruskaya Bend before."

"Just Ruskaya, honey. Nobody around here ever calls it Ruskaya BEND, only the outlanders. They both measured each others eyes briefly, then started to laugh.

"I'll remember."

To Jason her eyes seemed as if they had found something.

"You are a lot like Ted. He had a good sense of humor, too."

He found this mildly disquieting and moved to change the subject.

"The place needs a bit of fixing-up. I'll be around for a while, then we'll see."

"Well, welcome to Turner Canyon. I hope you decide to stay. The place can grow on you. Your house has a very nice patio in the back." She turned to go but paused adding, "Don't expect anything from the City."

He listened to the slap, slap, slap of her sandals going down his walkway, and at the pavement she turned to smile at him. With a jaunty step she proceeded to the next neighbor down the street, greeting her warmly. They stood beneath one of the several large plum trees in the neighborhood and chatted.

Jason looked down at the handout she had given him. The logo at the top contained the acronym "TCNA." Farther down the page this was proven to stand for "Turner Canyon Neighborhood Association." The document seemed to be the product of a home computer, neat enough, but hardly slick. The first page outlined the results of a recent City Council meeting. He started reading it as he passed through the front door into the living room.

This woman Dee seemed to be a local activist, as well as the author of the newsletter. In a matter-of-fact way the article described some sort of confrontation at City Hall, resulting in a fellow named Keller suffering a setback. The underlying conflict was not clear. The second page contained an article about a weekend outing with pictures of the participants. Below that were a few recipes contributed by neighbors.

The last page seemed out of place. It contained a technical report outlining output of water in gallons per minute, storage capacity, and surpluses on a monthly basis. A column of dollar figures was totaled. Apparently, a certain quantity of water was being divided monthly between the forty-seven houses in this canyon. Each resident was using some variable portion of his allotment and selling the rest. It was all being handled by . . . yes, here it was . . . the Turner Canyon Water District. Jason resolved to ask Dee about this when he saw her again.

First things first, he told himself. After bolting down a sandwich, he set off for town.

"Thanks for stopping by, Don. I appreciate it your time, as always."

Jeff Heit wasn't really grateful, but it was always politic to seem so. The City Attorney owed his job to the him, and knew it.

"Of course, Jeff. What do you have?"

Don Colesco looked rather more like an undertaker than a lawyer – thin, with a narrow face, dressed in a conservative, dark suit.

The Manager sucked on a tooth reflectively. "It has been brought to my attention that we may have some non-permitted construction in the moratorium area of Turner Canyon. I was wondering what latitude we would have in addressing this possibility."

"Have there been complaints submitted to the Building Department?"

"Umm, no. Suspicions only. My question is: Would the City have the authority to implement area wide inspections, looking for safety issues and code violations?"

"You mean house to house inspections based on suspicions?"

The Manager could see where this was heading. "Yes."

"Well, something like this was done a few years back in a small, Southern California beach town." Here he frowned. "They were having . . . ah . . . trouble with a certain neighborhood, and sent in teams from Fire and Building. The problem was . . . well, you see, a complaint filed against a specific property is no problem. The inspection would be strongly supported by law, but against a selected segment of the community where there are no official complaints . . . Well, the whole program collapsed into a flurry of legal actions. The judgment came down that since it was not being carried out on a town wide basis, it represented unequal enforcement of the law and had to be discontinued. I would say that a moderately good lawyer could find all this out, and the result would be the same here."

The Manager rubbed the side of his jaw with a forefinger. "Don, thank you. As always, I appreciate your wisdom."

"Anytime, Jeff."

After the attorney's departure, The Manager sat slowly tapping the table with a pencil.

Well, Howard, you're going to have to fry your own fish today.

Chapter Four

California, they all said. In California the land was good. There was not the gold to be found of a generation before, but the true wealth was in the soil. It never snowed, they said. Corn and wheat grew like no man had ever seen. Just throw the seeds at the ground for a bounteous harvest. A man could hope to attain something in California.

For Jacob Hobbes, life was hard work. He had never expected any different. His childhood had been one chore after another until the war with the South had begun, just after his seventeenth birthday. Fighting at Shiloh and Fredericksburg, he had survived the devastation and had returned to tend to his dying mother in Ohio. His father had never come back from the conflict. Inheriting the farm near Gilead, he sought out a wife – her name was Sarah – and they struggled to begin a family. The blizzard of '77 came close to ruining him, killing all his cattle but one sorry-looking milker. His previous corn crop had been poor, so rather than fight the ungenerous elements for one more season, he looked to the west.

After selling his land and most of his other possessions, he loaded a nearly new Conestoga wagon with a few selected items of furniture and the tools he would need to begin again. Laid carefully among those tools was a new Winchester repeating rifle. His intermediate destination was St. Louis, where all the wagon trains would collect before plunging across the Great Plains. Taking his last look at his own birthplace, he urged the oxen forward gently but firmly. Tethered to the back of his wagon was the shabby milk cow.

The journey to St. Louis was tolerable. He fell in with a few other families eager to find the new land in the west. They were abandoning broken lives in Ohio, Illinois, and Tennessee for the dream of something better. Most of them had also heard the stories about California. They all seemed secretly anxious and unsure. Some talked fearfully of "wild injuns," going on about attacks on wagon trains, corpses full of arrows, scalping, children taken as slaves, men tortured to death. Before long, the wagon master put a stop to this sort of talk.

Jacob Hobbes was a man who took what he got and made the most of it. He had his doubts and fears as well, but he determined not to let them get the best of him. His wife and two children looked up to him with a confidence that gave him strength. He was not nearly so worried about "injuns" as his not measuring up to the challenge. He was determined not to fail.

Of the hardships suffered by those who dared to cross a continent, the Hobbes family had their share. All their furniture was lost when they had to abandon it in order to haul their wagon up a sheer cliff. Illness plagued them, and especially the children, but they never considered turning back. Once, in Kansas, they were nearly set upon by a large band of Indians, but the wagon master instructed all men to hold the barrels of their rifles in the air to be seen as he fired off several shots from his Winchester in quick succession. The show of firepower, actual and potential, conveyed the appropriate message, and the danger passed.

They descended from the last of the major mountain ranges, the Sierra Nevada, into the great central valley of California just as snows began to fall behind them, filling their tracks. Pausing to recuperate and learn more of their new surroundings, they heard word that land was available in several parts of the state for homesteading or purchase. Word was, north of San Francisco some land might be obtained from Indians willing to sell. "Indians". The word brought dread to the family, but no, they were told, these were pretty peaceable, being accustomed to white men for some time. Reprovisioning for this last part of their trek, they headed north to avoid the swampy Sacramento delta, then northwest into the coastal mountains.

They threaded their way over the passes and down the valleys, looking for the right place. Many fine locations were already settled by hardy families who didn't relish company. They moved onward. They kept their eyes forward and told the children, "When we find our place, we will know it."

They crossed one more pass into the valley of a river that a previous group of homesteaders had called the "Russian River" supposedly after a group of "Roosians" who had built a fort north of the mouth several generations before. They followed the bottomland southward and around several broad curves, which brought the course of the river to run nearly due west. The flat land narrowed as it penetrated a series of hills, threading its route to the sea, but they pressed on. After a bit over two days' journey, they broke into a moderate plain on both sides of the river, covered with a stand of mature oak trees. At the west end of this area was a rocky ridge that forced the river to make a large bend to the north. As the river passed through a gap, steep cliffs overshadowed both sides, much higher on the north. No one stood to oppose them. Their bedraggled cow paused and lowered her head to eat the grass. This was the place.

Exploring the area over the next few days, Jacob found that the soil was deep and rich, and the size of the plain was more than enough for several families. River water was cool and refreshing, but even better was the outflow from a spring issuing from a small box canyon on the north side of the river, just west of the cliffs. There seemed to be plenty of game in the forestland rising up the sides of the mountains. He was telling his wife of the things he had found when she started and froze, looking intently over his shoulder. They were not alone.

A half dozen Indians started walking down from the ridge toward their encampment, and Jacob got his Winchester, sending his wife and children to shelter behind a fallen tree. The men approaching him were armed with bows, and he suspected that they had great skill with these weapons, but these were slung over their shoulders in a non-threatening way. Jacob resolved to make the best start that he could with these people and set his rifle on his shoulder, holding the weapon with the stock up and the barrel casually pointing at the ground, available but not in firing position.

As they came close to him, Jacob was surprised to see that most of them wore furs against the morning chill. They approached to within ten feet and stopped, obviously seeking the measure of him. Jacob saw that they were not very tall, but seemed quite capable. One of them glanced quickly over to where Sarah and the children were hidden and then began to speak.

Jacob could not understand a word, but most of the man's statement was clear. This land was part of their territory. He pointed to the earth beneath them, the river, and the hills, speaking for quite a time. When he stopped, Jacob gave a respectful pause and began his own declaration, with appropriate gestures from time to time. He spoke of his home in the east, his family's long journey, his dreams for a better life. He waved his hand around to encompass the land around them and finished by picking up a handful of earth, setting his rifle down as he did so, and holding the rich soil next to his heart.

This set off a flurry of discussion among the Indians. Some seemed excited and waved their hands around, others were more pensive and spoke more temperately. Finally, the one who had spoken first made a statement to the others bespeaking authority, and turned to face Jacob.

It was not the words that mattered – Jacob could not understand them – but the intended meaning was clear. Wait here and we will return. As they turned to go, they caught sight of the tattered cow walking slowly through the grass. They went over to examine this odd beast, and as they stood around talking among themselves, it gave off a sudden moo, shaking her head and ringing her cowbell. At this the Indians laughed heartily, and the leader turned to speak a few last words to Jacob, pointing at the source of their amusement.

Jacob and his family spent an anxious few days.

A high-pitched call from the ridge alerted him that the Indians had returned. This time eight men strode down the slope onto the plain, marching directly through the oak trees to stand before his encampment. Once again their bows were slung over their shoulders. As they approached, Jacob considered rushing to get his own weapon, but thought better of it. Without any preamble, the one who had spoken before began a brief dissertation. He gestured to the land beneath their feet, the river, and the hills beyond. Then on a signal, one of the others spread a blanket on the ground between them. Mistaking the intent, Jacob sat upon it, to the consternation of the Indians. Rising again, he began to realize what was intended: what would he put on the blanket in trade for the things the man had pointed out.

Calling to his wife, he asked for her to bring him the little cash they had left. Reluctantly, she came out of concealment and did so. He put it on the blanket and soon found that a vigorous side-to-side shaking of the head meant "no" to an Indian as well as to a white man. Another request was made to Sarah, and their few gold and silver coins were reluctantly set down, but they met with the same lack of acceptance.

Jacob realized that if he were to make this bargain, he must find something which these men would find useful. He went to his wagon and brought out some of the treasured implements that he hoped to use to build up his farm, a shovel and an ax. Sarah prudently added a bolt of fine, red cloth, which caused much excitement among the Indians. She also brought out one of her kitchen knives, but not the best one. Jacob added four woolen blankets.

This clearly was not enough. The Indians talked among themselves and looked at Jacob expectantly. Suddenly one spoke up, saying something that sounded like, "Nock-shownah-weyshaw MOO."

He knew what would satisfy them – they wanted his cow!

Jacob contemplated this loss with reluctance and dread. This poor animal had followed him from Ohio through everything. It was the last of his original herd and the only hope for milk for his children. How could he part with it, but the Indians seemed adamant. Suddenly an inspiration came to him. Walking to the wagon, he brought back an object none of these men had ever seen before. He tucked it under his chin and began to play a placid melody. It was his father's violin. It lacked one string and was hard to keep in tune, but it had a sweet voice. Would it be enough? He put it on the blanket.

Five of the men seemed ready to accept the offering, but

three argued against it, including the one who originally had called for the cow. Jacob was desperate. He was so close to achieving his dream – what could he offer now? On an impulse he left he men and walked into the meadow where the cow was grazing. He walked back carrying something. Standing next to the blanket, he waved it up and down, and it made a resonant clunk, clunk, clunk. The cowbell! He tossed it onto the blanket hopefully.

A great sound of satisfaction rose up from all eight men. It was a deal! Jacob stepped forward and offered their leader his hand, not sure he would know the custom, but he did. The men raised their joined hands up, then back down, and it was done.

Jacob produced a cloth and showed the Indian leader how to wrap the violin and keep it from the damaging elements. He lifted it up and, placing it under the man's chin, showed him how to coax a few pleasant notes from the instrument. In the best way he could, he offered to show the man how to play more if he came back again with it. Oxoneshewa, as Jacob later learned was his name, nodded his understanding.

The Indian who had wanted the cow seemed to be satisfied with the bell. He had seized it up and, every once in a while, clanged it loudly and laughed. The men took up their new goods and turned to go. As they traced their way back across the meadow and up the ridge, Jacob periodically heard fading into the distance a clunk, clunk, clunk followed by a laugh.

Quietly his wife and children came out to stand with him, looking into the setting sun.

"Daddy, is it really ours?"

"Yes, it is."

Jacob and Sarah Hobbes were the first white people to live in the vicinity of the great bend on a permanent basis. He immediately set out to find suitable pine trees to cut and drag down onto the plain for making a small house. He also started cutting the huge oaks, turning his holding into an open meadow and burning the wood in his fireplace. He left only enough of the giant trees on the south side of the river to provide an occasional island of shade to refresh himself and his stock, but the north bank he left untouched. Oxoneshewa seemed somewhat irritated at this destruction of the oaks, and he tried to explain to Jacob something about the acorns, but his words were not accepted. Jacob considered acorns to be food for squirrels, and nothing more.

Over the years the Indian leader came several times with his violin to learn how to set free its wondrous sound. He eventually learned to play several songs Jacob taught him and adapted a number of his people's melodies as well. When a string broke, trial and error taught them that raccoon gut would serve for a replacement. They never learned each other's language more than just a few words, but they rarely had any trouble communicating. When Oxoneshewa died, Jacob mourned his loss as that of a friend.

In the next few years Jacob and Sarah produced four more children, making six in all. The sons grew up strong in this new land, running the woods for game like the Indians and tilling the fields with their father. All agreed that the girls would make fine catches for suitable young men. Only the youngest son, Edward, was made of a different material than his parents. He developed devious ways and avoided work, but his mother cherished him as her youngest child.

Little by little, the years changed things as insensibly as summer changes into fall. Jacob and Sarah's strength slowly ebbed as their children drifted away to new lives. First she then he went to their reward, leaving Edward as master of the land.

When Oxoneshewa's people learned that both of them were gone, they mourned the loss for three days and nights. The Indians had considered them a bit eccentric, but good-hearted, as few white men were.

After many years, the cow died of old age.

Chapter Five

Dee answered the knock on her door and found it was Jason. He seemed to be in a bruised mood.

"Jason! Good to see you. Have you eaten?"

He slipped right by this question and blurted, "Can you tell me what's going on here?" He immediately seemed regretful that he had been so abrupt and rude.

Dee accepted his blunt manner without reaction. "Do you mean here in this house, or here on this street, or here in this town."

"I'm sorry. I'm being really thoughtless. You must be eating. I could . . ."

"You could come right in. Please. I suspected you'd be coming around sooner or later." He entered shyly and sat on the sofa facing the window. She continued, "So which is it?"

"The last two."

"Ah . . . now I deduce that you either went to City Hall and got the door slammed in your face, or you talked to a real estate agent and got the runaround."

"City Hall"

"Building Department?"

"Right."

"And they sent you to the Planning Department."

"Yes." Jason was beginning to feel a bit transparent.

"And they showed you the door, perhaps not very politely."

"Not at all politely."

"Well, I'll tell you. The whole story is long in the telling." She stroked her cheek reflectively. "Say, let's eat. Everything goes better after some food. You like Italian? I whipped up this killer ravioli – from scratch, and we really ought to try it out." She looked to him for assent.

"Cheese or meat?"

"You're being picky?" She assumed a mildly petulant expression. "It's cheese."

"You're on."

She had been right. Food softened the anxiety and disappointment, and Jason discussed his afternoon at City Hall.

"I went in to the Building Department. I really think my father's house needs a new kitchen and bathroom – perhaps some electrical work – and I wanted to see what kind of plans would be required and fees they would expect. When I mentioned the address, they shunted me to the Planning Department. On the way out, I nearly tripped over some fellow I took to be the Mayor. Not a good way to introduce myself to City Hall."

"What did he look like?"

"Umm, not real tall, dark hair, dark eyes. A very purposeful stride to that man. He was followed by a retinue of people packing papers and charts."

"And the look he gave you?"

"Indifferent. Looked right through me."

"Well, you were almost trampled by the City Manager, not the Mayor. That man is someone you will always have to be careful around. He runs City Hall and the whole city, too. A dictator – benign, if you're lucky. The Mayor is taller and bald." Dee puffed herself up in imitation of someone obviously too sure of his position, waving her arms in grand gestures as she spoke. "He styles himself as a modern day William Jennings Bryan. You'll know the voice when you hear it. He has a lot of teeth and smiles so hard you would think they would crack. Not nearly as great a personage as he would like to think he is."

Jason smiled at the caricature and wondered why he felt so at ease with this woman whom he had just met.

"Isn't the Mayor in charge?"

"Ruskaya is a General Law city, sort of a state-sanctioned cookbook variety of local government. The Mayor is not much more than the presiding officer at Council meetings, and the Council is chiefly a policy body. The real power is exercised by the City Manager." She could tell that he had never heard any of this before. "Listen, I don't know if you will hang around, but if you do, you will find that politics is a necessary survival skill in a small town. But . . . excuse me. What happened next?"

"Oh, so I went to the Planning Department where they scuffed me up with this talk about a moratorium due to some planning study. A fairly huffy bunch."

"Yes, they are."

"After that I was an unperson, a target for scornful looks, so I left."

"Did you go to see a Real Estate Agent?"

He looked as if she had caught him in a compromising position.

"Why would I do that?"

"Oh, it's the usual one, two, three." She ticked them off with her fingers. "Fix up the house, sell it, drive away. It's the logical sequence. If you had seen one, you would probably have heard something like this." At this point she assumed a deep, gravely voice and with a slightly pompous delivery, seeming to imitate some person she actually knew.

"Well . . . Turner Canyon . . . Hmm . . . You see, that area would be somewhat . . . uh . . . problematic, with the . . . planning study and all. It would be . . . difficult to obtain a suitable . . . ummm . . . buyer."

Now he really looked nonplussed.

"Oh, it's all right. You don't have any roots here. It's to be expected that you would be anxious to return to your life in San Francisco. But . . ."

She looked at him for a long time before she spoke again.

"You have inherited more than just a house. In fact, you have dropped right into the middle of a war, and I am sorry about that."

For a long while, neither spoke. Finally, he asked her, "Can you explain it to me?"

"Let's go for a walk. We could catch a great sunset."

He realized that she wasn't merely avoiding his inquiry, so he nodded and they rose to walk out of doors. She began:

"Any powerful conflict with strong emotions and high stakes doesn't come from nowhere. It has a history, a trail of events, and each event is explained by its antecedents and it causes what follows. Understanding this sequence through time will allow you to understand what is happening now. So I have to ask you – do you want the short version or the long one."

"It seems I don't have anything else to do. Shoot the works."

"Then there's someone I would like to accompany us. He should be done with dinner now. He lives right up the street. Henry Turner."

"This canyon is named after him."

"After his grandfather."

They proceeded about ten doors up the street and crossed it, stopping at a well kept, two story green house with a large plum tree in the front yard. Walking right up to the door, she started to pound on it loudly with the flat of her hand.

"Hey you drunken bum! Get your pants on – I have somebody for you to meet!"

Jason was a bit surprised at this jeering announcement, but he kept his silence. Presently an upper window opened and a head thrust out.

"When did they let you out of jail, Carella?"

"Just quit flapping your toothless gums and get down here."

"Strumpet."

"Cretin."

"Hussy!"

"Degenerate!"

He disappeared inside and she turned to Jason saying, "He does so love those Shakespearean terms. He must stay up all night finding them."

Presently a rather tall man of about fifty-five opened the door. He stepped forward, and Dee and he embraced. He looked down at the top of her head.

"Didn't you use to be taller?"

Dee jumped back. "Oh, you . . ." She looked like she was about to kick him.

"Hey!" Jason had realized that these two probably didn't

loathe each other as much as it seemed, or else one or more of them would have wound up dead before now. He did think it prudent to break it up just in case this might prove to be the time when they got serious.

"Oh yes, Henry, I want you to meet somebody. This is Jason Brandt, Ted's son. Jason, meet Henry Turner."

They shook hands and Henry leaned forward to say, "Jason, I am really sorry about your Dad. He was much respected here."

Jason was becoming slightly more used to hearing this adulation expressed for a father for whom he had so many hard feelings. He judged that they knew a different man than he did, and that was all.

"Henry, Jason needs to hear about all that business with the Water District and the City, to clarify things for him. He has already gotten bounced out of City Hall."

The older man smiled and nodded reflectively, as if he had been called again to recount a favorite story. He had an open, straightforward way about him.

"I'd be glad to. I trust you have eaten already. Dee always shoves food into anyone who gets near her.

Jason chuckled and indicated that it was so.

"So just let me grab an apple, and let's walk up the street a ways."

Soon they were strolling toward the end of the road which terminated where the flat bottomland ceased and the steeper canyon walls began. Slightly up the slope was a fairly large water tank painted green, nestled into a small gully. They left the road and started up a well-traveled trail through the scrub brush, following it up to a small knoll overlooking the tank. Jason could see that slightly above the tank was what looked like a small cave blocked by masonry. Through it passed a pipe, painted green, which ran down to penetrate the upper part of the tank. There was a bench made of large boulders shoved together, and they took a seat. Henry looked down the canyon toward the town and started to speak.

"Ruskaya Bend has not always been here. My grandfather

and great-grandfather once farmed this land . . . ."

Chapter Six

One year before the beginning of the twentieth century, John Nicholas Turner and his family had made the long passage from Illinois across harsh and dangerous country to claim land in the central valley of California. Nick, as he was always called, filed for his quarter section along the Kings River, southeast of Fresno, and set about to master the skills of irrigation, a practice he had never used before. The land was desert, but made wonderfully fertile by the application of water, and each claimant along the river had his own canal bringing the precious fluid to thirsty crops.

But water was the gold of the day – wealthy and powerful men coveted it, and California was soon embroiled in what came to be called "the water wars." Men fought and died for the substance which made the difference between worthless desert and rich land, between dirt and soil, between want and wealth. Nick Turner found that the most vicious wars and the most desperate battles are fought in mahogany-paneled rooms with pieces of paper for ammunition. In this struggle, he lacked the support of influential people that others had, and the watermaster parceled out all the available water to large landowners upstream from him, leaving him and his neighbors nothing. He watched as the river dwindled away, and his land returned to a parched waste.

Nick Turner had a choice. After working the land for five years, he had managed to save a few dollars. Should he stay and expend what he had, fighting for a better judgment in the court system, or should he move on and start again. He knew that the same influential men had sway in the halls of law. He weighed in his mind the years of work spent building up his holding, perhaps gone for nothing, against an uncertain future. He talked to his family and made his decision.

The man who came to pay nearly nothing for Nick's

holding was openly contemptuous of him. Nick suspected that this was an agent of the upstream property owners and soon water would again nourish the land they were standing on, but he kept to his resolve. He had a cousin in the region north of San Francisco — he would seek his fate there.

In spring of 1905, few people had automobiles. Nick Turner didn't quite trust them anyway. He loaded his family and his belongings into a flatbed wagon pulled by horses and set out. By summer they were at the cousin's farm near Healdsberg where he heard of a parcel down river that might be for sale. A good farm had fallen to a worthless reprobate of a son who was drinking up his patrimony. If Nick wanted to approach this man, he should be careful because he was in the habit of wandering the property with a shotgun, blasting limbs off the fruit trees his father had planted. Word was, he had borrowed as much as he could on the land, and a passable offer right now might bring results. Nick resolved to look over this possibility.

It took one day by horse to reach the place described. As Nick headed west into an extended meadow leading down to a large bend in the river, he saw nothing but neglect. No hand had guided a plow on this land for years. No stock grazed in the lush grasses, now turning brown. He found a house on the property and observed that several windows had been blown out. He called out, but no one responded. Eventually he found a disheveled man passed out in an old corncrib, cradling a shotgun. As he approached, his shadow passed across the man who started and struggled into consciousness. His hand was on the weapon.

"I don't mean any harm," said Nick. "I wanted to ask . . ."

"What? What? Who are you?" The man seemed frightened, worried, and embarrassed, all at the same time.

"I just wanted to ask . . . I understand that there might be some land for sale around here?"

"Land. Uh. No, there's no . . . Oh! Land. Well, maybe. Right here. I might have some."

Nick gestured around them. "You mean, this land?"

"Yeah, maybe."

"Could we look around?"

Over the next hour the two of them wandered the property, examining what it held. The buildings were not much, badly in need of repair, but to Nick the land had promise. From what he heard from the owner, the rainfall never failed, the river never dried up yet never flooded, the soil yielded more than a man could sell, the game would wait at the door and beg to be eaten. Nick heavily discounted what this strange, little man had to say and still liked what he saw. He decided move toward making an offer.

"If you were to sell, what would you consider a fair price?"

"Oh well, this is fabulous land, as you can see. A man could grow rich by sitting around doing nothing here. The wheat grows up to your chest, and the cows . . ."

"Would you take four hundred dollars in gold now, one hundred next year after the harvest and another hundred the year after that."

The man screwed up his face and made a pretense of considering the offer, but Nick was sure what his answer would be.

"Done!"

"Good. I will return tomorrow with the money. Will you have the deed ready to sign?"

"Yeah, sure." Edward Hobbes seemed to be in a hurry to be gone. They shook hands to seal the deal, and Nick mounted his horse to depart. As he was leaving the meadow, he noticed Hobbes settling back into the corncrib.

The following day, Nick returned with twenty gold pieces in a small bag, half expecting that Hobbes would be drunk again. To his surprise, the man seemed alert and fairly well dressed. Bringing a small metal box from the house he produced the deed, which he signed over to one John N. Turner. Nick produced a paper which specified the terms of the sale, signed it, and counted the gold pieces into the man's hand. As each one fell with a metallic clink, Hobbes' eyes got wider and wider. He clearly had an appointment with a bottle somewhere and was in a hurry to be on his way. Mounting a beat-up mare, he bid his goodbyes.

"Have good luck."

"Say." Nick had noticed several items still in the box, among them a woman's comb and a man's watch. "Don't you want these things?"

"Are they worth anything to you," Hobbes said with a sneer.

"Not really. But don't you . . ."

"Then throw them into the river." And he was gone.

Nick Turner contemplated the day and what it had brought him. He looked at the box, then up into the hills. Searching through a shed, he found a shovel and carefully buried the box and its contents in the meadow not far from the door to the house. He felt that he owed the Hobbes family this last symbol of respect.

Edward Hobbes was intent on getting far away before his creditors found out he had sold the farm. He killed his horse driving her pell mell toward San Francisco. The last of his evacuation was on a gelding freshly purchased in San Rafael which he abandoned in front of a bar on his arrival in the big city. The next few months were spent throwing money at every amusement he could possibly find. While it lasted, he had the companionship of women, and men tipped their hats to him. He accepted it all with condescension. His fortune was nearly gone, and he was sleeping off his most recent alcoholic stupor in his room in the Mission district when the clock reached 5:12 A.M. The great earthquake of April 18, 1906 leveled his shabby tenement, turning a once proud city into piles of rubble as a thousand kerosene lamps and kitchen fires leapt up to destroy the debris. Hobbes lay trapped and moaning in the ruins for half a day, and in early afternoon the fire swept through his part of town and incinerated him alive.

The first few years were not easy for the Turner family. Edward Hobbes had skipped out on his debts, which had been secured by the property, so Nick had to work especially hard to pay off the liens. He concentrated on cash crops and put off a number of his plans for the future. Edward Hobbes never returned for the rest of his payment.

After three years, Nick and Ruth could look forward to being entirely their own masters, and they flew at the tasks before them. Nick put his skills with irrigation to profit by throwing a low dam across the river upstream from the meadows and using a canal to bring water to the upper portion of the south meadow.

The meadows were not of a consistent level, but stepped in terraces down to the river, three in all. The lowest had high enough ground water that truck crops could be raised almost without effort. The middle one was excellent for wheat or corn, but the highest needed irrigation in years of scanty rain. Here he began to plant fruit trees, starting with apples and cherries. This is when he made the acquaintance of a plant breeder from Santa Rosa.

Luther Burbank had come from New York State where he learned the ways of farming on his father's land. One day something unusual and rare happened that changed his life. Potatoes generally flower but almost never set seed. One plant in the field under his care produced a seed ball from one flower for Luther to wonder over. He extracted a number of seeds and planted them, and most of them went on to yield very inferior tubers, except for one. These promising ones were large with a rough skin and they cooked up delicious. They were very clearly superior to the variety of potatoes grown at that time. Cutting up the rest of his meager yield and replanting the following year brought an abundant harvest. This potato would eventually become a supremely important commercial variety.

Intrigued by this success, he considered a career in the systematic improvement of food plants, but he knew that the severe climate in New York presented a great handicap, removing half the year from any work schedule. He, like so many others, found his future in the west.

Settling in Santa Rosa in northern California, he began to work on every variety of fruiting bush or tree and every flowering plant that the temperate climate would allow. Apples, pears, cane fruit, cut flowers, and plums felt his guiding hand, especially plums. The techniques he used contained several novel methods developed by him. Taking stock from all over the world, he cross bred them and planted the pits from the fruit produced. During the next winter he grafted promising whips to the limbs of two ancient plum trees on his property and waited to test the fruit that was produced. At each step he discarded the inferior stock, first in the field and then on the branch. He went through four million seedlings to find the one that he considered perfect. He named it after his adopted community – the Santa Rosa.

One of the ways he tried to recoup on his massive investment of time was by selling budwood. During late winter he would shear off a shoot with six to eight buds on it and sell this to an orchardist. The purchaser would carefully slice off the buds and graft them to suitable rootstock. In a few years he would have his own trees bearing the new type of plum. Unfortunately for Luther Burbank, that man was free to cut his own shoots and graft more trees since the law of the day made it impossible to patent a new plant variety. Nick Turner also grew his own budwood, but each time he cut a shoot to graft more trees, he sent the fee to Luther Burbank. He was the only one to do so.

The Santa Rosa plum prospered in the environment of Turner Bend, as it was now called. The production was heavy and demand was high. He planted all of the highest terrace south of the river, and then the middle terrace, as well as in the small canyon with the spring. The riverfront terrace on both sides was retained for truck crops. The upper terraces on the north side were left in oak trees, which he found yielded huge quantities of acorns to fatten his hogs. The rocky ridge protruding into the bend was put to hay and wheat.

The next twenty years were joyfully spent caressing the land for the bounty it gave them. Of his three children, one son and a daughter found their own lives nearby, and his oldest son, Benjamin, planned to assume his father's duties in time, despite the fact that he had been badly wounded in the Great War.

One day a stranger rode up on horseback with a lot of odd gear, asking to speak to the owner. This man was an artist from San Francisco looking for the perfect place for a retreat. He stood on the bluff at the end of the ridge and declared that it was the most beautiful spot under heaven. He wanted to build a house there.   Nick considered that the man might be mentally unbalanced, and he had heard of these "artistic bohemians," but fifty dollars in gold for a quarter acre of worthless rock seemed an attractive prospect. He shook the man's hand.

This artist had friends, and during the dry season they could be seen with their paints and easels, stroking their vision onto canvas. At times it seemed that you could not take a step without tripping over one of them. But Nick generally liked them, even though they preferred to drink wine rather than whiskey. They were a peaceable folk, seemed honest, and Nick even appreciated some of their work. He didn't let on, but he was secretly very pleased when he was presented with a painting of the meadows and his house. After negotiations, a few more artists built homes on the ridge, but it seemed all right – Nick was rarely using that land for any crops these days. Everything went well, and that business of nude sun bathing on the beach only happened once. It was the new road that made the big change.

There had been a dirt road up the valley from the coast, which crossed the river on a low bridge just before the bend. The road continued up onto the ridge and passed into the forest south of the meadows, following its way upstream. The bridge had often suffered from flood or fire, so it seemed appropriate when the California Highway Commission planned to make improvements, including a new higher bridge and a paved roadway. Nick was of divided mind about these changes – he could see the need for an up-to-date road, but he knew this would make possible a giant onrush of strangers to trample through his peaceful world, gawking and picking flowers. He didn't relish it. The artists were one thing; there were only so many of them, and they weren't that bad. But who knew who might drive up that road now! Despite his concerns, he knew the matter was out of his hands.

This was the time of the Roaring twenties, a freewheeling, madcap era of excess and excitement. Everyone was on the road, and some of them found Turner Bend and liked what they saw. Pressure mounted to sell more land, so Nick and Benjamin felt they had to make a decision. The father was getting older and not so fit for long days working the land, and the son's war injuries were troubling him more and more. They resolved to let go the land least fruitful for farming, the ridge jutting into the bend of the river.

Using the state road as a starting point, they drew a tract map for submission to the County Land Agency. The automobile was here to stay, and so they allowed for wide avenues and larger parcels in the areas set aside for commercial enterprises. The residential areas had lots with broad frontages and alleys behind them. In the center of their budding community they outlined a boulevard circling around a giant boulder in an open space where four main roads came together.

They had no thought of founding a town – there were many unincorporated communities throughout the state, and their vision was to make Turner Bend a combination artist community and vacation get-away for rich city folk. Already many visitors were showing interest in the beach on the south side of the bend as a recreational venue, spending pleasant afternoons sunning themselves and swimming in the river's cool waters. As soon as the subdivision request was approved in 1922, the lots sold as fast as they could print deeds. Nick Turner had been right – the road brought changes.

For the next six years the little community on the ridge spread and developed an identity. During those times there were money and ambition overflowing for any likely prospect, and almost every day someone brought these two ingredients to Turner Bend, intent on starting some new enterprise. Garages and service stations, a hardware store, a farmers market, a laundry, and many other concerns were established – there was even talk of a bank. Houses were in a constant flux of construction. There was one thing missing, some said. There was no City Hall.

When the proposal to incorporate Turner Bend was made, the Turner family opposed it. They saw no benefit that would come from the increased taxes they would all have to pay. County government had served them well up to then, they said. Why change things. But prominent members of the young community argued for this "great step forward". They would have their own voice, they said. They would be free to chart their own course.

They could determine their own future.   These seemed to be persuasive arguments.

When the vote came, the ayes had it, and the town was formed. The first meeting was in a small church and one of the first agenda items was concerning the name of the town. It was thought that "Turner Bend" didn't quite have that sparkle the new age required. Reaching back to the time of Russian presence, the new City Council puffed themselves up and rechristened their domain "Ruskaya Bend."

The Turners never used this name, calling the community on the ridge "Town." Nick Turner came to feel that he had breathed life into a bad child who had grown up to disgrace him.

The incorporation area included the meadows, an area then still owned by the Turner family and still in agricultural production. But Nick had a fear for the future of the land. The new City Council members had already spoken of extending the new town in that direction. He didn't know how long these pressures could be withstood. He made his plans.

One portion of the Turner family holdings had not been included in the incorporation. North of the bridge crossing the river, the small canyon filled with plum trees where the spring flowed had been overlooked. Perhaps it was an oversight, or perhaps Nick had maneuvered toward this end result. Nevertheless, here, at the mouth of this canyon, he built a new home and retired to it, leaving the main house and the farmland to his son. For three more years he lived there, drinking the sweet spring water, tending to his plum orchard, and greeting warmly anyone who walked across the bridge to spend a pleasant afternoon with him. He drew up a plan, subdividing the canyon behind him, but he did not sell the lots. He also visited an attorney to take care of a particular issue regarding the property. In 1931 he died and was buried at the back of the canyon near the source of the spring.

His son, Benjamin was managing the farm when the Stock Market crashed. At first, this seemed a distant, inconsequential event, but the stench of economic decay soon spread everywhere. The fledgling bank failed in 1931, and its patrons lost their savings.

Homeowners and business keepers who were severely in debt were consumed by the monster of repayment and lost everything. As life shrank to a lower level, people learned to live with less, to hope for less, to cherish a job, a meal, a kind word. The City Council no longer talked of expansion, but fretted about paying the police and fire departments. A dusty wind began to blow through the town.

Benjamin Turner saw the spreading misery and, knowing that most of those suffering had not caused their condition, he resolved to do what he could. He brought the farm up to full production, even knowing that prices were low. Concentrating on the crops that local people would consume – potatoes, corn, tomatoes, cabbage, and root crops – he offered jobs in his fields to any individual who would walk to his front gate. He learned quickly never to pay the men directly in cash because they would surely drink it up. He would pay their wives weekly in produce and a few coins. Bachelors were paid wholly in produce. In those days many former merchants and tradesmen learned the way of the soil, laboring long hours in the hot sun in the meadows, and they were mighty glad to have the job. In time two widows with families were accepted into the work crews, sharing long hours of toil with the men.

As the years shaded one into the next, men were gradually able to find jobs and drifted away, being replaced by youngsters from Town. His own sons were two of them. No longer needing to feed half the community, he shifted progressively to more lucrative crops and sold into the thriving markets. It seemed that, at last, normal times had returned to the land – until late 1941.

Almost no one seemed to know where Pearl Harbor was. "They" had attacked us there, and the call went out. Almost overnight, his labor force was gone, and Benjamin's fields lay fallow for the first time in more than sixty years. For the next few years he contemplated the empty space that his land was becoming. The women from Town continued to help him work the soil on a reduced level and he could hire migrant workers from Mexico, but he was in his fifties, and his old injuries made it difficult for him to walk. He had a lot to think about.

Returning from the war, his sons showed no interest in

continuing the family way of life. One settled in San Diego, and the other took a job in Town, living a half mile from his father but seeing him seldom. When the City Council, goaded by renewed economic prosperity, started pressuring Benjamin to sell part of his land for development, he reluctantly had to admit that an era had ended and decided to make the best of it.

In 1947 he moved to the home his father had built just outside of town at the head of the small canyon. From there he guided the subdivision of the old farmstead and sale of parcels of about twenty acres each for home construction. Every few years another would be made available, and about eighty homes would shortly be built. The boom times following World War II brought an increased reliance on the automobile and improved roads. Freeways were being built. Many couples found the open vistas and the clean air in the meadows to be perfect for raising their families, and a man could drive to Healdsberg, Santa Rosa, or even San Francisco to have a good job. Times were good again after so many years of disheartening struggle.

During the last years of Benjamin's life he formed a strong relationship with his grandson, Henry, who was born in 1950. Typical of many families where an intense bond skips a generation, the two spent many long hours talking about the history of the Turner clan and the community they had founded near the great bend. In this way, the continuity from the past into the future was maintained and enhanced.

Benjamin also sold most of the forty-six lots in the canyon behind his home, but he chose the purchasers very carefully. They had to show a certain originality and spirit of independence, and as a result, the houses these people built presented every conceivable variation of style. These contrasted with those built by developers in the meadows, which showed almost no diversity. Without telling him, he set aside one fine lot for his grandson as well as a fund to pay the property taxes. Another was given to Aron Salgado who had been his majordomo on the farm for many years. A man looking toward the end of his days was clearing the books.

In 1955, Benjamin woke up unable to get out of bed. His

speech was slurred, and his left side was paralyzed. A stroke, the doctor said. He may live, but he will not recover. His daughter, Margaret, came from Arizona to care for him with a singular devotion. Henry was distraught at the fall in his grandfather's health. Benjamin could not form the words to speak any more, but Henry realized that his "gampa" could still write with his good right hand. Assiduously applying himself to the task, he taught himself to read and write a year before his peers by studying his older brother's spelling words. Soon the flow of communication was reestablished. Henry had a thousand questions and learned the art of patience waiting for his grandfather's replies.

In 1958 the tide went out, and Benjamin Turner passed from the earth.

Chapter Seven

Jason looked over this man who was the descendant of pioneers in the area. He seemed rather ordinary at first glance, but as Henry spoke, Jason saw a gravity and dignity arising from a long acquaintance with the land. His voice was measured and sure, and he illustrated his description with calm gestures of his ample hands. The generations spoke through him with a clear voice. Jason saw much to like in him.

"My great-grandfather had seen his land in the central valley made valueless when he lost control of the water which irrigated it, so he took precautions that no such thing would happen to this little community when he created it."

He gestured toward his left to the houses lining Turner Canyon Road.

"He established a water district, with each of the forty-seven original parcels owning one share of the district and having one vote. For years this meant merely that water was free if you lived here. The natural spring at the back of the canyon supplied more than enough for all, and the rest flowed down the creek and into the river. Then the City got into trouble."

Henry's brow rose in wrinkles. "It was their own damn fault, really. About fifteen years ago the Council had foolishly decided to pass up buying into a water project that was to get supply from the headwaters of the Russian River. The City had always drawn its water from local wells a short distance from the river, and that was good enough until about four years ago."

"They almost got shut down," Dee interjected with a laugh.

"Yes. Over the years various contaminants and pollutants had crept into the river water, and when the State upped the standards for potable water a few years back, the City was found in violation and had to do something fast."

"But where does all this stuff come from?" To Jason the

river had looked pristine.

"Well, that's the problem." Henry shot a glance down the canyon. "It all comes from distributed sources. Agriculture gives off fertilizers, insecticides, and other chemicals. Industry adds a bunch more to the mix. Cattle ranches shed urea and bacteria. It all adds up. The polluters have a lot of clout in Sacramento, so the burden was laid on each city to provide clean drinking water by whatever means necessary."

Dee harrumphed. "You should have seen them squirm! The townspeople swarmed on City Hall, screaming about having to buy bottled water, cancer risk, skin irritation from showering. It was murder!"

"Dee is only pleased when the mighty are humiliated. I am satisfied to see them retired into obscurity. But to continue . . . What were they to do. Filtration and various methods of water treatment would have been extremely expensive. The public was already in a mood to lynch somebody. The State Water Quality board was about to condemn Ruskaya's water supplies entirely. Desperation. Then some shifty soul in City Hall suggested that the crisis could be resolved by blending water from a pure source with the outflow from the wells, pushing down the levels of contaminants into the range permitted by the State.

"Then all eyes turned toward this canyon. They wanted the water."

Dee took the handoff. "The snakes first tried to force an annexation, but they couldn't get the votes. Then they tried again six months later but this time including a large undeveloped parcel to the north and east of us in the annexation district. That owner wanted into the City. They pulled strings at the County Seat to get the assessments on our homes lowered and the big parcel's raised. When the votes were counted, we lost, and they dragged us in."

"How did that happen?" Jason couldn't see how one parcel could outvote forty-seven.

"Assessed valuation." Henry put in. "They weight the votes by the assessed valuations of the properties. We didn't have a chance."

Dee continued, emphasizing each incident in her memory

with slashing gestures of her hands, as if attacking an ancient enemy. "They then sent us all letters claiming that they had a proprietary right to the water, and at that point your Dad became involved."

"He was terrific."

"He sure was. He had his lawyer send the City Attorney and the Council a detailed letter describing the status of our water district – such districts have a legal existence independent of any municipality, and ours had the same standing as any city. At this point we offered to sell any surplus water to the City at a reasonable rate. They responded by threatening to seize the water rights by eminent domain. We answered that, with the usual pre-trial motions, trial time, appeals, and counter-appeals they would be lucky to get a judgment within four years, and their chances of prevailing were only fifty-fifty. In the meantime the State was threatening legal action. The letter ended with the suggestion that the political ramifieations of such a messy legal wrangle could result in none of the current Council being in their seats for very long."

Dee's smile was almost sinister in its glee.

"So what happened?"

"You could almost hear the screaming from here. Then we were invited to negotiate."

Henry picked up the thread. "We chose Ted to handle our side, and on the first day the City offered to buy out all our shares in the water district and then charge us to use our own water. He laughed outright at them, renewing the offer to sell the surplus at five dollars fifty cents per unit."

"How much . . . "

"A unit equals seven hundred fifty gallons. That's a pretty high price, by the way, and they gagged on it. As he left, he said that he would be back in twenty-four hours, reminding them that in that time period Ruskaya Bend would owe a penalty of four thousand more dollars of the tax payers' money to the Water Quality Board and also two hundred thousand gallons of pure water would flow unused into the river."

Dee was beside herself with glee. "They were cooked.

Those bums shivered to face a political and legal battle at the same time while the State was breathing down their necks. They all met for another few times; the Council growled and threatened, but Ted held firm. In the end they agreed to pay three twenty-five per unit and take whatever surplus water we didn't use ourselves. They got out of trouble with the state, but they have hated us ever since."

The restrained hostility Jason had experienced at City Hall now came into focus. From what he had already learned about politicians, they liked to think that they walked on water. Even though the Council had gotten what they needed at an acceptable price, his father had reminded them that they were all wet up to the knees. Pride is a vicious animal, knowing no rest.

"So now, my boy, you own one forty-seventh of the outflow from this spring, to do with as you please. You can drink it, bathe in it, or let it run down the street. If you use more than your allotment, you have to pay for the overage at the same rate as the City. If you use less, the remainder is sold to the City and you get the money. Basically, they pay you to water your own lawn."

"Sweet deal."

"Your Dad was the sharp edge on the sword that cut it out for us."

"But I have to ask — what is this moratorium thing? They can't just keep you from improving your property just because they are chagrined by your negotiating skills, can they?"

"They probably can, but there is more . . . "

"Say, Dee. . . ." Henry reached forward to touch her on the shoulder, and Jason saw her respond to the touch of his large hand. The years of their acquaintance made it unnecessary to express the rest of his suggestion. With a nod she took a deep breath as the group turned to face west.

Silence spread over their little party, sitting on the stony bench. Jason was fully prepared to be bored since he had never seen fit to spend time on sunsets in San Francisco. It was light; it got dark. He listlessly looked up to notice a thin stratum of clouds draped across the hills to the west catch the edge of the sun's glow. Its color was first gold, then orange, then cherry red. Thin, dark rays extended away from the now invisible sun, and they looked to him like a giant fan extending half way across the sky. Was it opening or closing? Slowly the cloud faded to a dull gray, leaving only a small patch of color beneath it to remind them of the glorious light of the past day. A cricket began a solo presentation, and time passed measured only by the cadence of the cricket as the sky grew dark.

Jason was startled when the others rose. He followed them, walking down the trail by the light of the stars. They strolled casually down the street to Henry's gate where he bid them good evening. A short walk took them to Jason's house and he hurriedly said goodbye to Dee, suddenly remembering his promised call to Tracy.

He entered and turned on a few lights on the way to the study.

J ason stood hunched over the phone as he dialed, jabbing the numbers. Tracy had wanted to hear from him as soon as he knew anything about the house, and he had meant to call her before sundown. It rang once . . . twice. A sudden change in the background noise and he was speaking to her.

"Tracy? Hello, darling. How are you?"

Her voice seemed to come from a greater distance than there was between them. She passed the amenities casually.

Jason began with a brief description of Ruskaya and its environment, in which she seemed to have only passing interest. The house, its condition, the sale possibilities, perhaps renting it out during the moratorium – these topics she acknowledged with an indistinct murmur. She wanted to know when he would return to the City. She was worried about the security of his job, even though his firm, Shaw and Richetti, had granted him a three month leave of absence. His six year term of service spoke well for him.

"I'm not worried about my position with them. Peter Shaw told me to take as long as I might need. Say, Tracy, why don't you come up for the weekend? An outing in the country, some fresh air."

"I don't think so. You know how I am in cow country. Too much like where I came from. Why can't you come back for a few days?"

"Are you sure you wouldn't like to give it a try?"

"I'm sure."

"Well, maybe you are right – I could come down on Friday evening for the weekend. By the way, how is Crash?"

Jason's cat had exceeded his usual level of mischief. To hear it said, he broke into the bathroom, maliciously attacked some of Tracy's underwear drying on a towel rack, and reduced it to threads and patches all over the house. He promised to make it up to her as soon as possible. No, he still didn't want to get him declawed.

"He'll grow out of it."

"I might not."

For a short while they both listened to the background noise in silence.

"Tell me what's happening with you. How is work going?"

With this cue she embarked on a detailed exposition of the last few days at the brokerage firm where she worked – who was aggravated at whom, who was now teamed up together, who looked good or bad. Jason was always amazed that she almost never cared to talk about the work that was being accomplished. It was as if intrigue was the stock in trade. He knew that the firm wrote a small mountain of policies per week and was vastly successful, but he never heard about this from her. Her voice seemed to fade as she spoke.

The communication passed into the usual conversation-end murmurings of affection.

"So I'll see you this weekend. Love you, Tracy. Bye."

"Bye, Jason."

He had always liked the lilt of Tracy's voice, even over a phone line, and he was glad to hear from her. They had been together for nearly two years, and they had scarcely been separated except for those retreats she went on. Oh well, the weekend wasn't so very far away. He would do something nice for her to make up for lost time, certainly buy new lingerie. She could be awfully high maintenance at times, but worth it. He was hoping that this business with the house wouldn't drag on too long.

Being here reminded him of his father, and at times that could be uncomfortable. The rooms were full of things Ted had used, and Jason was ambivalent toward them. Nice things, but not his taste. Seeing them made him think that his father was still here in a way.

He drifted out the back door onto the patio, settling into one of the recliners there. With no lights shining on him from indoors, the stars slowly became visible. He wondered if it would be possible to see the Milky Way from here. You never could from the City. Weren't there supposed to be crickets or bats here, or something? At least coyotes howling.

Relaxing, viewing the stars in the still air, he drew toward him all the thoughts and experiences of the day. His life had been so regular and familiar until now – until that call had come from the hospital. After a moment's hesitation, he had raced to the cardiology ward in Santa Rosa, but his father never regained consciousness. Jason had arrived to watch him die, and now he wondered if there had been more to this man's life that a son should have known.

He had been so angry after his mother's death. It seemed that his father had not cared about her, but had Jason's evaluation been correct? Had Ted held back his grief? For what reason – to be strong for his son? It had looked like indifference, but . . . how could he know now? The moment had passed, and he had turned away, never reconciling. Now he owned his father's house, and it stood like a last communication to him in paint and wood. What did this all mean for him?

As Jason's thoughts wound down into a more relaxed state, he noticed that a strong glow had touched the hilltops to the west. Slowly, the moon, just past full, was rising to assert itself as ruler of the night. The illumination crept down the slope toward his house, gradually banishing the stars from his view of the sky. He could almost hear the light roar its dominance as it broke free of the hills east of him and shone down to the patio. A slow breeze had begun to wander down the canyon toward the river, washing across his body and through the trees. He heard the crickets now.

His mind was at ease.

Chapter Eight

Howard Keller was in a hurry. He bustled into City Hall with an armload of plans and a determined stride, trying to look as if he belonged there. A nod to the Planning Assistant at the counter, a smile for what's-her-name in the Building Department, a murmured hello to the assistant City Engineer. You had to grease the skids to get what you wanted, and Howard always brought lots of grease. Stroke, stroke, stroke, then take it all – this was what he knew.

He hastened down the hall toward the conference room, nearly colliding with the City Manager exiting his office.

"Jeff! How are you? I am afraid I am a bit late, so let's go be late together, eh?"

Jeff Heit drew back to view the man before him. Howard Keller represented merely a pressure to be deflected, a pushy loudmouth with a plan he needed passed – a hack. In his many years as City Manager, he had seen several of this type. They either got what they wanted and they left, or they didn't get it and they left. All they did in between was to spread a lot of ink, talk overly much, wave their arms around describing the grand new world they would create, and act too chummy. The Manager hustled up his best grin for an instant, and let it fade.

"Howard. Good to see you. I don't think we are late, in fact, I know the Mayor has been delayed."

"Excellent. There is a little matter I had wanted to discuss with you."

They turned the corner and entered the empty conference hall. The table was large enough to accommodate twelve chairs, and the one at the west end was particularly large and plush. The Manager increased the illumination, and both men took seats adjacent to the large one.

"What is it, Howard?" He knew very well what was on the

man's mind.

"Well, I was wondering about that matter I discussed with you the other day – about enforcing the moratorium. Have you been able to make any movement in that direction."

The Manager briefly considered telling him outright that nothing would be possible, but he knew that the everyday realities of life did not make a great impression on Howard Keller. The legal implications, precedent, the potential backlash, none of these would dissuade him. He was a man used to shoving his way to what he wanted.

"I am still working on that with Don Colesco – it is a surprisingly complex matter, though. But I will let you know, Howard."

"Fine, fine."

For a short while there was nothing to maintain the conversation, so the Manager busied himself with the papers before him while Howard Keller stared at the wall. Shortly, there was a jostling at the door and it flew open. Mayor McCanna had a way of making an entrance that gave the impression that a brace of trumpets had just sounded a fanfare. He strode in, impeccable in a conservative brown suit and white shoes. Jeff Heit always thought that the white shoes were a bit much.

"James!" Howard Keller jumped up to extend his hand and wrapped it around the Mayor's as the tentacle of an octopus would. Both men ratcheted up their displays of affection to make them commensurate with the amount of money Keller had contributed to the Mayor's election campaign.

"Howard. It's good."

They sunk into their chairs, the Mayor assuming the large one at the end of the table.

"Jeff, how are you." The Manager smiled and nodded in an offhand fashion. "Howard, I'm going to have to offer you my apologies" , the Mayor began, "about that business at the Council meeting. I am sure your report will speedily be approved. Halley, Merrick, and Davis is a highly reputable firm. There is no problem there." He shot a glance at Jeff Heit who nodded briefly. "It's just a delaying tactic."

"Yes, of course, James. But let's hope that it doesn't cause too long a delay."

"Everything is in progress as we speak. But there is another matter that we may have a bit more trouble with."

The Mayor let his words settle in before continuing.

"At the last Planning Commission meeting . . . "

"Ah, they voted that the project was completely in conformity with the General Plan – unanimously." Keller made a quick wave of his hand as if to brush aside all complications unheard.

"Yes, they did. But another matter was raised which will have to be addressed before we get too much further – the issue of access."

"We have gone through this before, James. Access will be from the end of Turner Canyon Road. You know that is the only route I can use. A road up from the Meadows would be far too steep and costly."

"Yes, surely, we do understand your constraints, but the problem lies with certain requirements of State Law. To access a development the size of yours – one hundred and twenty lots – we have to be able to provide a road easement of fifty feet in width. The current easement is only thirty feet wide, and the pavement is a maximum of twenty-two feet."

"So?"

The Mayor frowned. "Howard, it would be strategically more feasible if your project were not so large, say, fifty lots. Then we could . . ."

"No!

"We are talking about just for now. The rest of your project could be presented after a suitable delay."

"NO!"

"Howard, what good would it do to have a single court order shut down your whole project?" The Mayor put on his best "spreading the word of wisdom" look. The Manager watched Howard Keller carefully preparing his response. He looked like an enraged cobra. When he spoke, it was with a low growl.

"You have to get me a fifty foot wide easement."

"Howard, we have looked into that. With the narrowness of the canyon and the way most of the houses are crowding the road, we would have to . . . "

"Tear 'em down. Yes, I know."

"Howard, even though that might be desirable, how could we do it? Where would the money come from to condemn and demolish at least twenty-two houses? Would you provide it?"

"No, and neither would the City."

"But . . ."

"James, you are missing one important point. I need a fifty foot easement for you to grant a subdivision – an easement. These are just lines on a piece of paper. Child's play. Getting fifty feet of pavement is the problem for the next guy, the one I sell to."

There was a long pause while these words were absorbed and the implications strained from them. McCanna now knew that Howard Keller had no long range intentions in this community. The plan behind his plan was to flip the property and run. On the other hand, no one knew better than James McCanna that you could throttle someone just as well with reams of paper as with a rope. The Turner Canyon residents would live with an ax poised over their necks until it finally fell. In politics nothing is more gratifying than to inflict misery on an old enemy, and as an additional benefit, this pest Keller would be gone. Further, eventual condemnation of a majority of the homes in Turner Canyon would give the City control of the water district. The pieces started to fall together in the Mayor's mind.

"If we did as you are suggesting, it would cast a pall over the properties in Turner Canyon . . ."

"So that you could buy them up cheap. They are hardly worth the cost of demolition anyway."

The Mayor sucked on a tooth. "Jeff, you haven't had much to say. What is your take on this."

The Manager leaned forward.

"Well, it certainly couldn't be considered good planning, but it is legally supportable. It would have to go back to the Planning Commission for a vote on the road extension and resolution of the construction moratorium."

Howard Keller narrowed his eyes at the Manager. *Have to keep that man on a tight leash.* "And with a favorable staff report, they should know how to vote."

"Yes." The Mayor thought this particular line of discussion should not be continued. "Yes. Jeff, will you prepare any staff presentations and set up the Planning Commission meeting?"

"Of course."

"Fine. Howard, thank you for coming. Don't be a stranger." The Mayor rose up. Just as he liked showy entrances, the Mayor preferred abrupt exits, and he hastened out the door. With a glance toward the City Manager, Howard Keller followed him.

Jeff Heit sat musing over the previous conversation for a moment and then reached into his briefcase which was sitting on the table. He switched off the recorder which had been the unseen witness to the words just spoken. Reaching forward, he took up his pencil and began to tap its tip on the table before him.

Dee never knocked on doors. She hammered them with the flat of her hand, which would often set them to rattling in their jambs. It befit her style.

"Hey, Jason. Come on – we have to go!"

The door flew open. Jason looked out to see Dee and Henry with another woman.

"What?"

"Come on, or we will miss it! Two young studs are going to jump the Bear! First time in three years."

"Do you still have bears around here?"

"No, no. Not . . . oh, you'll see. Come. Come." She got behind him and started pushing him out the door.

"Wait a minute, Dee. Aren't you going to introduce me?"

"Oh, yes. Aurelia, this is Ted's son Jason. Jason, Aurelia Salgado. She lives just up from Henry. Her family goes back here a long way."

Jason shook the hand offered him and looked into the eyes of a tall, Hispanic woman. Although her long, black hair had

turned mostly white, it was difficult to estimate her age –
somewhat more than Dee, probably. She was still quite beautiful.
She was dressed in a work shirt and a long, flowing skirt. Jason
spoke without thinking.

"*Mucho gusto, Señora.*"

After a second's hesitation, she responded. "*El gusto es
mio.*" Her voice was like the sweet tones of a cello.

Dee seemed to have a bus to catch. "Say, that's wonderful.
But let's go. We'll miss it."

Soon the four of them were hastening down the street
toward the river, and as they progressed, they were joined by
several other groups from the canyon. They all crossed the bridge
and followed the path down to the beach, where Jason turned to
Henry.

"Can you tell me what this is all about?"

"It's a local custom, a rite of passage thing, which goes
back to the years following World War Two. Dwight Harwood, one
of the local lads who had served on an aircraft carrier, had been
trained by the Navy to drop from a flight deck into the sea and
survive. He eventually had put his technique to use, leaping off
the burning deck of the Lexington during the battle of the Coral
Sea. A few years after he returned, he got a little drunk and on a
bet he jumped off the Bear. Now every few years a couple of the
local boys summon the pluck to try it."

"But what is the Bear?"

"All Ruskaya lies in the shadow of the Bear, and there it is
above us."

Jason looked in the direction indicated toward something
near the top of the cliffs north of the river bend. He saw nothing
but rock. Slowly, as his eyes probed for the hidden form, it became
clear – two hollows for eyes, a broad brow, and the muzzle of a
great bear! Standing on the top of this enormous head was . . . a
human form.

"He's not going to jump from there, is he? That must be
more than one hundred feet straight down."

"Of course not, silly." Dee was laughing. "He has to climb
down to the nose so he has a clear drop to the water. You can see

that there is a slight protrusion which creates an overhang. It's one hundred and twenty-seven feet from that spot to the water at this time of year. He will have to take just one step, but a big one."

"That's just plain crazy."

As the spectacle started to develop around them, Jason saw a small motorized rowboat push off from shore and edge out into the river, setting up station just downstream from the dropping point. As the young man climbed down to get into position, the cheer went up.

"All right, Danny, you can do it."

"Yay, Danny."

Dee moved closer to Jason. "Do you see the man over there? That's Danny's father, who jumped the Bear . . . oh . . . twenty-six years ago. He was his son's trainer, too."

"They need a trainer?"

"Are you kidding? From that height? Do it wrong and you could get broken to pieces. A drop like that into water feels like hitting concrete. A couple of guys have broken their ankles. Even when you do it right, he shock goes up through your spine and rattles your brain. Plus, the water's only about twenty feet deep. They have to have to be trained by someone who has done it before. They practice on the ten meter platform at the high school pool. They must go off the Bear fully clothed and cold sober. No diving, no flips or twists – just straight in – and they pick a second to back them up."

"A what?"

"The guy in the bow of the boat, there. See him? He is ready to leap in and pull the jumper to the surface if the impact knocks him out.

"Oh, that's great. But why fully clothed? Why not just a bathing suit?"

"A conventional bathing suit would just rip off on impact, as well as the skin, probably. Even with clothes they can get some bad bruises."

Jason just shook his head. "Isn't it safer to go out cow tipping, or something?" She just snorted at him. On impulse he asked, "Do women ever jump?"

"Buster, you are talking to the second woman ever to jump the Bear."

He finally noticed the legend on her tee shirt. It said: "THE BEAR" across her chest, and below it "127". He quickly recalled that Henry was wearing a similar shirt, partially concealed by a plaid overshirt.

"I bet none of your city friends would have the guts to try something like this."

"I don't know. Jumping on the trolley car can be pretty hazardous, and there are certain parts of town that . . ."

"Piffle! Look now, he's ready."

The young man on the rock stood at attention as the three hundred or so townspeople who had been cheering him on grew silent. He raised his head up to look at the sky for a moment, then elevated his arms into a horizontal position.

In a instant he was in the air. Jason was surprised at how fast he picked up speed. Half way down, an air horn sounded from the boat, and the boy moved his hands into position to protect himself. One covered his crotch and the other covered his face from his chin to above his nose.

Whump! He was into the water with a giant splash. His second didn't wait for signs of trouble and was immediately into the river after his friend. When the two of them raised their heads above the surface, three hundred voices rose together in a cheer of praise and relief, amplified by the reverberation from the cliff. The boy raised up his hand and seemed alright, but did need help getting into the boat.

"That position of the hands – is that usual?"

"You bet. If a boy doesn't protect his manhood, he will be singing soprano for life. The other hand has to keep the water from shooting up his nose and blowing his brains out the top of his head."

She could see that he was mildly appalled, so she kept on the same vein.

"Often the pants split open at the crotch, or the pants legs split open up to the kid's knees. Sometimes the shoe tops separate from the soles and wind up around the his calfs. A lot of guys loose their shirts. And you don't ever want to go off wearing anything like a Saint Christopher medal."

"And this is strictly voluntary?"

"Yes, but very few people even consider making the jump."

"You must have a lot of out-of-towners flocking here to try it – young studs wanting to impress someone."

"Never. We don't publicize it, and Bear-jumpers always go off during the winter when there are no tourists around. It is strictly a custom for locals. Had you ever heard of it before now?"

Jason had to admit he had not.

"And, assuming the victim survives this escapade, what do they get for it?"

She paused for a second and said, "They get to wear a tee shirt like this!" She pinched the fabric of her own and pulled it out away from her body. "And they walk on air for at least a year."

The cheers of encouragement surged up again as a new young man lowered himself down to the nose of the Bear. Jason could see even from that distance that this one's motions were much more tentative than those of his predecessor. He seemed even a bit pale.

"Yay, Phillip!"

"Just one step, Phillip."

Jason could see that that one step was going to be a much bigger one for Phillip than it had been for Danny. He stood at the edge, looking down.

"What if he doesn't go off?"

"There's no disgrace in that. About a third change their minds. Most of them jump the following year, but not all. One kid went up there for four years straight before he jumped." She smiled broadly. "He's on the City Council now."

The crowd was quiet, watching the boy on the rock. His second was in position. Everyone waited. Somewhere on the beach were worried parents, siblings, friends. It was a long way down. After a minute, a few people near Jason looked away as if they thought there would be nothing to see . . .

He was off!

The boy assumed the defensive position immediately and

he dropped like an arrow straight toward the water. The horn blew.

Woosh! This one entered the water with diminutive splash, hit the bottom of the river and pushed off. Before his second could even enter the water, the leaper was back at the surface, screaming in exultation and smacking at the water with his palm as if to punish it for the past moment's fear. Kicking to push his upper body out of the water, he raised both fists up to shake them at the rock above him.

The crowd exploded into a roar of approval and admiration.

Jason found himself adding to the cheers echoing off the cliffs. Leaning toward Dee to rise above the clangor, he told her, "Pretty brave. . ."

She just smiled and nodded.

"But it's still pretty nuts."

The young man, Phillip, swam right past the boat directly to shore and purposefully rose up out of the cool water to embrace a middle aged couple. Jason watched as the boy's mother cried and hugged him and his father patted him on the back, speaking words of praise into his ear. A group of his contemporaries stepped up to slap him on the back and shake his hand.

Jason watched all this and he shared in the sentiment of triumph buoying up the crowd, but a vague feeling of unease nibbled at the margins of his consciousness. He watched the young man and the people around him for several minutes. Slowly people started to drift away in the direction of their homes.

The walk back was pleasant and leisurely, and Jason had a chance to meet several more of his father's neighbors. Most seemed to be working folk, some retirees, and a young family or two raising children. He found nothing to dislike in any of them, and they seemed to have a strong sense of community identity that he was conspicuously invited to share with them.

Jason tried to maintain a certain distance and aloofness in his dealings with them, nodding politely, not making a great effort to remember their names. This all will be temporary. A few months in the country, then back to real life. Real life.

One elderly couple passed near to him, inviting him over for afternoon tea. He nodded his approval. Another fortyish woman offered him part of her abundance of plums since his house didn't have one of the several large, bearing trees in the neighborhood. He thanked her. A teenager on a skateboard glided past him with a cheery "Hiya."

Two thoughts forced their way into his attention: that his resemblance to his father must be more than he had ever thought and that an outgoing manner was the common currency in this neighborhood.

Saying goodbye to Dee at her house, he continued up the street and entered his walkway. For a few moments, he paused at the threshold of the entry, looking back at scattered groups of people making their way to their own houses. They chatted and laughed, several nodding and waving in his direction. They seemed to be drinking deeply of the afternoon's events and the promise of a restful evening to follow. Jason had taken a sip, and he had to admit that he liked it.

Chapter Nine

The morning sun enveloped Jason as he lay on the queen sized bed in his father's bedroom. Seven o'clock, eight – finally he stirred and eased into a pleasant awareness of the new day. The sharp light flowing in around the blinds, the smell of sagebrush and pine trees, the lone mockingbird voicing his endless medley of one-line tunes. He stretched and rolled into an upright position. *What a rest . . . no alarm clocks.*

Rising up, he padded into the kitchen, gathering the ingredients for his first meal of the day. A few eggs, some cooked rice, chopped ham, and snow peas, sliced long. Soon they were cooking in the pan. *Definitely bachelor fare.* A glass of orange juice with it, and he was ready to jump at the day. *Should work on the outside of the house before I leave for the City. Where is that scraper?*

He found his tools and started to attack the degenerated paint on the sunward side of the house. *This place used to be green!* Tan and green chips flew off as his tool found the wood underneath. *A little bondo here.* As he worked his way down to the lower part of the wall, he found the lowest boards damaged beyond simple patching. Looking up, he saw the cause. *No rain gutters. The splash from the eaves has gotten these boards. Hope that lumber yard on Fourth will have this old ship lap stuff. Hate to pay to have them milled out.* He made a mental note to measure how much rain gutter he might need and price it, both metal and PVC.

Several times one or another of his neighbors stopped by to say hello or to introduce themselves. They all seemed to have known his father. A few complemented his endurance or offered the name of a favorite primer/sealer. Before long it was noon, and then it was three; and he had a house scraped and sanded almost completely for his efforts. *Time to shower and get ready to go. Tracy will be home at five thirty. Good that traffic will be going the other way.*

As he was cleaning up, Aurelia Salgado strolled by with two other women. One was a freshly scrubbed lass about fourteen, and the other was a pretty, young woman about twenty-four, as he judged.

"Jason, hello. I see you have had a productive day. I would like you to meet my granddaughter Cynthia and my niece Constancia."

He reminded himself how much he liked the sound of her voice. She spoke English, with a nearly indistinguishable accent, like a touch of seasoning to make perfect the meal. He started to offer his hand to them, but thought better of it.

"Sorry, I'm really dirty."

"Not as dirty as we are," returned the younger one, "we've been planting flowers. Yuck!"

"In that case . . . "

As they shook his hand, both with a firm grip, he noticed that the younger had the same black eyes as her grandmother, like deep, inky pools. The woman more his age had dark brown eyes and a pleasant but reserved smile.

"Connie. It's just Connie," she murmured.

"Connie it is."

They passed a few moments in small talk and they seemed ready to go when Aurelia added one thing.

"Cynthia will have her quinceañera on this coming Sunday. We would be very pleased if you would come."

Jason knew that a young girl's fifteen year celebration was quite an event.

"Isn't that usually just for family?" Jason wished he hadn't said it the minute it was out of his mouth.

"We have decided to invite the neighborhood." Aurelia leaned forward. "That is, if the neighbors care to attend."

"I certainly would! Are you going to have a piñata?"

Cynthia made an explosive puffing sound. "That's just for little kids!"

"Oh, well, if you're not . . . "

"All right, a piñata." Her expression of mock disgust was well laid on.

"I'll be there with my baseball bat."

"I gotta see . . . "

"That will be wonderful," Aurelia interjected. "We start at four o'clock. See you then." She wrapped her words in a smile and a nod, and soon they continued on their way. He followed their progress down his walkway and up the street until they were out of sight.

Shortly, Jason found that he liked his father's taste in shower heads. The water beat on him almost to the point of hurting. Only the need to get down to San Francisco cut short the pleasure of cleansing himself. He hurried down a snack as he considered the road map of the area. *Which is better? Inland to Healdsberg and down 101, or over to the coast and down highway 1? 101 can have some nasty traffic, but highway 1 can be foggy.* He wrinkled his nose.

In a few moments he was traveling down Turner Canyon Road toward Highway 116. With a brief hesitation at the stop sign, he turned the wheel to the right and set his course to the Pacific Coast. The five mile ride took him through agricultural land, mostly put to vineyards and orchards. A few homes and one winery were hidden here and there, and a lonesome tractor plowed dust into the sky. As he approached the coast the bright sunlight turned to haze, then to clumps of low clouds, then to solid overcast. Just before the little hillside community of Jenner, he turned left and crossed the bridge over the Russian River to follow Highway 1.

The road took him up onto the coastal plain, a bench of grassland one to two hundred feet above the sea. Here the land and the sea fought for control of the air, but the battle was witnessed only by cows. At the higher portions of the road, sunlight had baked away the low sheet of fog, but as he descended to cross the canyons, a blanket of gray covered him, and the road was still wet. Isolated settlements slid past – Ocean View, Sereno Del Mar, Salmon Creek. Bodega Bay and its little community of the same name went by just before the road diverted inland for some five miles. Here the full intensity of the sun made the road dance with sparkles of light, glistening off the polished gravel in the pavement.

He made a right turn, leaving Ford Road to continue along Highway 1, and soon he reached salt water again at Tomales Bay where he followed the flooded scar of the San Andreas Fault southeastward. Across the bay first he saw flights of ducks and then pelicans, working their way to some rendezvous with a meal. The traffic was light, and he stopped at the town of Point Reyes Station for gas and a look around. He had driven through here several times in the past, but never really had done more than glance at it. In the block with the gas station were a country market, a nice looking restaurant, a few gift shops, and a hardware store. The enjoyment of his view was only cut off by a thunk from the gas nozzle, signaling a full tank.

Back on the road, he went through Olema and soon was passing Bolinas lagoon on his right. At the origin of the sand bar sheltering the lagoon was Stinson Beach, and a few miles farther found Muir Beach where the Highway departed again from the coast. A winding road took him over the crest of the coastal hills into the heart of Marin County – a community of houses of great price, cars with attitude. In a few miles Jason went from seeing another automobile every minute or so to being surrounded by them as if by a pack of wolves. He was on the edge of the City.

Making the transition to Highway 101, he raced by Sausalito on the approach to the Golden Gate Bridge which he crossed in fairly light traffic. Leaving the span, he followed 101 through the Presidio eastward, turning south on Divisadero. Eight blocks farther and a left turn brought him onto Pacific Street and in seven more blocks he crossed Laguna Street and parked. He trudged up the flight of stairs to the second floor apartment he shared with Tracy and went in.

Crash greeted him by turning sideways and doing his best Halloween cat imitation before scampering off, no doubt to destroy something. The apartment seemed as he left it, except for Tracy's shredded underwear draped over a chair in the bedroom.

The kitchen called for few more items in the cupboards, a pile of magazines on a table next to the TV needed straightening, the curtains were closed rather than open. It seemed like the home he had left a few days before. He found himself on the tiny balcony, enfolded by the afternoon breezes – a whiff of pizza from the Italian joint on the corner, the pungent smell of hot pavement. He found himself wondering whether he could see the moon from there after it became dark.

Abruptly, Crash lived up to his name. A shattering sound came from the entry as the cat himself flew into the living room, trying to escape the scene of the crime. At that moment the key turned in the lock and Tracy entered.

"That damned cat! Oh, Jason, you're here!"

Their embrace was firm and long.

"I don't like it when you are away."

"Neither do I."

"You don't have to go back up there, do you?"

"I'm afraid so, but not right away. Right now I think I have a lamp to repair. How was your day?"

She spoke earnestly about the unusual or frustrating events of her day at the office – the conflict with a co-worker, difficulties with supplies, a balky client. From time to time she shook her head to emphasize her point, and her short, brown hair swirled around her head. Jason worked on the downed lamp in the hall as she spoke, occasionally rising to get a tool from the kitchen. He loved to watch her talk, even about negative things. The tone of her voice and her body english had always held attractions for him.

The lamp was not so badly off. The great clatter as it fell was caused by the metal decorations hanging from the light shade, and the real damage was the shattered light bulb. All the glass had broken off and the aluminum base was stuck in the socket. Jason pulled the plug from the wall after cleaning up the shards of glass. Then he got a screwdriver and carefully pried the base inward away from the socket in two places as Tracy began a testy description of her immediate superior's work ethic. He grasped the bent portion of the base with a pair of long nose pliers and started to rotate the base out of the socket. At this point Crash came to investigate. The base came out and soon a new bulb was installed and the lamp restored to its original position. Crash fled the scene as if a large predator were after him. Tracy was finishing a narrative of her day with a few ripe comments about a couple on the trolley car.

"... and it was all very disagreeable."

"But here you are, and I bet you are hungry."

"Yes, I am. But let me freshen up first."

He followed her into the bedroom. "I was thinking Cioppino's."

Her voice came muffled from the bathroom. "That'll be fine."

Jason changed his shirt and went to set out some food for his cat. Crash had his best "who me?" look as he was chastised for overturning the lamp. He would put up with a certain amount of scolding as long as there was a meal at the end of it. Then Tracy was ready, and they set out.

"Oh, Jason, let's take my car." She never did like his vintage Volkswagen bug, but taking her vehicle meant that she would drive, and she tended to get a bit overamped in city congestion.

"Sure." *Oh well.*

She revved it up and shot into traffic moving down Pacific. A left turn on Van Ness, and they were heading north toward the bay, next making the right on Beach Street, and then into the parking garage under Ghiradelli Square. Except for nearly becoming airborne at the grade transitions, it was an uneventful drive.

It was only a few blocks' walk to the restaurant, but they took their time, passing through the array of street vendors and entertainers. There was the bored looking jewelry peddler, the black saxophonist with his yawning instrument case hungry for tips, an overstuffed fortune teller, someone selling glass dangling things, another selling pipes for consuming unnamed substances. Jason tried his best never to have eye contact with these merchants, but Tracy reveled in the attention she could get from them by admiring their products. She never actually bought anything.

They passed the trolley car terminus with its extended line of anxious would-be riders and walked down to Jefferson Street and the heart of the Fisherman's Wharf area. They crossed the road with a group of tourists, walking past the Hyde Street Pier and its collection of ancient ships tied up at the dock. Shortly, they were at Cioppino's, and as she always did, Tracy stopped to look over the copy of the menu posted by the door.

"Chicken Marsala looks good. What are you going to have?"

"Cioppino at Cioppino's. The best in the City."

She smiled at him delightedly.

The restaurant was large and airy, unlike many in the area, and had a fine reputation among the cognoscenti of San Francisco eateries. They were seated by the hostess near the center next to a large potted ficus tree, and a waiter named Louis came for their order. He was personable and suggested a salad, which they accepted. It was soon before them.

"Do you really have to go back?"

"It's not so bad, and yes, I do. There is a lot of clean up work I would have to do before I could consider renting or putting it on the market. And there is this political dustup I may have to see through."

"What is that all about?"

He paused before answering. "It's just local politics. Dee has told me . . ."

"Who's Dee?"

"She is one of the neighbors there, a friend of my Dad's, and she seems to be very active locally. I've met several of the people there."

She displayed a mildly exasperated look. "I just can't wait till you put all this behind you and things get back to normal."

Their main courses arrived with two glasses of wine, Merlot for him and Chianti for her, and they ate most of the rest of their meal in silence. They both ordered tiramisu for dessert, and she had a cup of coffee before they rose from the table. As they exited onto the sidewalk, Tracy took his hand, and they strolled casually across the street and past the shops, restaurants, and bars that the district was known for. The fading light and still air made a magical time of day for both of them. They wandered through Aquatic Park, pausing to watch a juggler in black and white makeup, a pair of conga drummers stroking a flashy rhythm from their instruments, and, very briefly, an evangelist haranguing a small crowd through an amplifier which was overloading badly.

As fog poured through the Golden Gate, a chill settled in around them, bringing the evening's entertainment to a natural close. They made the short walk up to Ghiradelli Square for the car and set out toward the apartment. Tracy was bantering about one of her girlfriend's romantic entanglements while Jason idly watched the people bustling about on the sidewalks, a family carrying their groceries and herding two small children, an older gentleman traveling slowly with a walker, elegant couples hurrying to the theater, ragged street people resting in a warm spot.

Tracy was not able to find a parking place near to their apartment immediately and became more than a little irritated at having to park so far away, but Jason merely shrugged and accepted it as part of the price of a evening out. The walk to their door was not so far after all.

Later, sitting warm on the couch, Tracy expressed her concern that Jason would spend increasing amounts of time out of town, and he reiterated that if she would come to Ruskaya for the weekends, their separation would not be so long prolonged.

"Well, we'll see. I hope you wouldn't expect me to scrape paint, or whatever it was."

"Of course not. Just to be your natural, charming self. I am sure the work would go faster, certainly more pleasantly."

"Tell me, this place doesn't have outdoor plumbing and a rooster in the front yard, does it?"

He just frowned at her. "Some people have plum trees in their front yards – that is about as rural as it gets. There is a river a short distance away, and red tailed hawks fly overhead. It's quiet."

"It sounds like the place I escaped from to come here. I've

had it with 'country ambiance'."

"It would be only temporary, like a vacation, and we could be together."

She just looked down at the floor.

"You know . . ." He tried to restart the communication on a more favorable plane. "I can think of something to do much more pleasant than talking about all of this."

"So can I."

They stood up and, after kicking their shoes off, slowly started to undress each other. It was part of their love making ritual to caress each item of clothing from the other's body, stroking the then exposed flesh with fingertips and lips. Sometimes they never actually made it into the bedroom, but dropped back onto the couch to join their bodies together. This time he murmured something about the cat getting the clothes, so they gathered everything up and took it into the bedroom, shutting the door.

She didn't like mouth to mouth kissing, but the touch of his lips almost anywhere else on her body was very welcome. They each knew how and where and when to touch each other to produce a rush of ecstasy and took turns driving each other to shivering excitement. He always waited until she begged him to enter her, taking everything slowly to prolong the anticipation. They were joined, gasping their breath together when a faint sound occurred at the door.

On the other side Crash the cat was petitioning for admittance, but no one could hear him.

Chapter Ten

Neither Jason or Tracy heard the distant foghorn begin its lonely bleat as the opaque shroud of marine air stole into the bay through the Golden Gate. Crash stirred from his slumbers briefly at the faint sound, then settled back into the inviting realm of dreams.

Fog crept across the stilled water and settled onto the land at the Marina District, oozing between the town houses in a silent, gray flood. It pushed through Fisherman's Wharf and on down the bay into the Mission District, claiming the business heart of the city. Street people, bundled in for the night, grumbled at its approach and drew closer their scanty protection against the elements.

Yard by yard the white blanket marched up the hills like an army enveloping and overcoming the last resistance. Just before dawn only the white sentinel of Coit tower stood above it. First light showed a city lost in cool dreams, buried as if by a massive surge of the sea, a city to be remembered but not seen.

The lovers awoke to find that once again their world was in a bubble, a miniature realm with an event horizon fifty feet away. In that hazy domain light, sound, even life was subdued and muted. There was no sun; there was no sky; nothing cast a shadow. Standing on their balcony, they drew deep breaths of moist air and contemplated the day presenting itself.

"Maybe it will clear." Her assertion did not carry much conviction.

"We're supposed to have fog for a few days."

"We can still go out. There is a new opening at the gallery on Van Ness, and there is a poetry reading I would like to go to."

Art and literature were not natural inclinations for Jason. He went, he saw, he heard, and he tried to appreciate. Perhaps he was too analytic and lacked the levels of intuition and sentiment necessary to grasp the deeper meanings. Perhaps in time there would be an awakening for him. Tracy was always enthusiastic for the arts, but he had the suspicion that she didn't understand any of it much better than he did. Well, they would go to these events, and he would enjoy being with her.

As they sat down to breakfast, Crash came to wheedle what he could from Jason – he knew better than to try to beg anything from Tracy. He made no sound but sat next to the chair and looking up, tilting his head from side to side with a quizzical look. Presently, his attention earned him a portion of scrambled egg and a bit of bacon. He pounced on the latter with relish.

"Is he growling?" She seemed mildly disgusted.

"It seems he is. The predator thing."

"Well, I wish he weren't so predatory toward my clothing. I hope we can replace today what he destroyed."

"Maybe he just likes your scent. I do."

This brought a sly smile to her face, but it faded as a thought crept into her mind.

"Jason, do you really have to go back there, do you?"

He had noticed this about her. If the response to a question was not to her liking, she would wait a while and ask it again, hoping for a different answer.

"I can't just walk away from it. It will take a month or two to do the minimum repairs I would need to rent it out. Then there is this moratorium thing."

"Yes, what's that all about?"

"There seems to be bad blood between the city and this neighborhood, going back some years. My Dad was involved in part of it. Further, there is some development plan that would require access from our road. The neighborhood is fighting it. Small town politics."

"Thank god we don't have anything like that here."

"You're right. Here if you have a problem, you take a gun and shoot the mayor."

Her blank stare indicated to him that she probably didn't know anything about the assassination of George Moscone. This brought a long pause to the conversation.

"Well, at any rate, when is this reading you mentioned?"

"Not until after dinner. I was thinking we could go to the gallery after lunch, then the lingerie shop is just down the street, and then we could get some fresh coffee over on Polk street."

"Sounds good."

The sidewalk was slick from the fog as they sallied out into the heavy mist. All colors were pastille, sounds were muffled as if heard underwater. They walked in a confined space which traveled with them, passing into and out of view of a familiar street corner, a neighborhood park, a favorite bench now dripping and uninviting. They had chosen to walk since parking was always difficult and the distance was not great. Few people hurried by them, like figures in a dream. Soon they were outside the gallery which was called "Benson's". To Jason it sounded like it was owned by a former butler.

"Whose work is at this showing?"

"I just read about it in the Chronicle, and it has several local artists."

Jason grimaced inwardly – has-been's and wanna-be's most likely. When they entered, he found it was better and worse than he had thought. The patrons were the whole show. Each one was a stylized caricature of an art affectionado, suitable for framing. Jason resolved to have a good time.

Just inside the entrance was a lanky, overage dowager with a cigarette in a long holder. Her clothes looked sprayed on in multi-colored paint, and as she held her hand to her wrinkled cheek, she was expounding about "the movement" to a rotund gentleman trapped in front of her. As Jason and Tracy passed, she shot them a mildly disapproving glance then continued her exposition. The receiving end of this lecture was trying his best to hold up, all three hundred pounds of him. He was dressed in a sports jacket and a polka dot tie, and with his short hair and natty mustache, his head looked like a fuzzy cue ball. He was sweating despite the cool weather.

Farther along was a gaggle of art school students, all buggy eyes and awe struck countenances, raptly listening to a slightly older person who was apparently their instructor. He was standing in front of one of the landscapes and occasionally flipped his hand loosely toward it by way of illustration as he talked. Off to the side was a slight, middle aged man wearing a baggy sweater and a worried expression. Jason took him for the artist.

Next was a faded couple, stylishly dressed and pressed close to a painting which could not possibly be described. An abstract, mostly in blue. She obviously wanted it, going on about the merits of the artist, the many homes and museums where his work was hanging, the fitness of the price. Everything about his body english said, "Not A Chance", but Jason estimated that it would take five or ten more minutes for her to grind him into submission, and she would be taking her treasure home to be deposited in a closet and forgotten. Jason was trying his best to keep a straight face.

At the back of the gallery was the proprietor, standing behind a table with several alcoholic beverages on it. This man was all business. He was intently glancing around through the patrons, looking for a hand to put a drink into and trying to sniff out the likely buyers. After sizing up Jason and Tracy, he condescended to give them both a glass of wine, after which they merited no further notice. They moved on.

A short distance away was a professional looking individual who was scribbling generously into a spiral notebook as he stood before one of the paintings which Jason noticed was a nude. From the look of it he had notes on each of the paintings in the gallery, and Jason got the strong impression that this man was a Police officer. Was he looking for stolen art? Was there an art tax which had been avoided? Had this work gone too far, or not far enough? The possibilities were without limit. Jason could only think that somewhere there was a parking meter fallen to zero and an opportunity to write a ticket being neglected.

Next along they came across a raven haired woman admiring one of the paintings. As she turned Jason could see that she was truly beautiful, full lips, dark eyes, excellent figure, dressed to perfection, any man's dream. When he had been unattached, this was the woman he would have been drawn to, sifting through all his best opening lines, wondering how to get her telephone number. She moved lithely toward them and as they passed, the gorgeous stranger looked once up and down over the body passing her and smiled, liking what she saw. Jason was only slightly surprised that it was Tracy she had been admiring, not him. Jason was prepared to be amused even by this.

As they were about to leave, they saw a skinny, reprocessed street hustler with a paw full of flyers.

"Hiya, folks. Didja enjoy the showing? You, know, we're having another opening at Gargiella's just down the street. Better art, better prices, better booze, even. Try it! Here."

He shoved his handout into Jason's unwilling grasp and turned to assault the next set of departing patrons.   Jason wondered if the shark at the back of the gallery knew about this guy. Was this part of the plan? To get you going from gallery to gallery until you wound up in the next county? The whole thing was beginning to remind him of a Tijuana street hustle when Tracy broke into his deliberations.

"Well?"

"Hmm?"

"What did you think?"

"Oh, it was great. I enjoyed it immensely." He was trying to remember what the paintings had looked like as they disappeared into the fog.

The lingerie shop was about a block away, and he entered it with some misgivings. He preferred not to be mistaken for a fetishist lunging into a crossdressing experience, so he stuck close to Tracy. Crash had evidently gone for the panties, and Tracy pulled out several for him to pass judgment on. One was black and lacy, and another he was sure would prove transparent. He especially liked the thong type and requested that Tracy model it, which she immediately vetoed. In the end he escaped fairly cheaply, all considered.

They then drifted through the fog past the various shops as Tracy savored the commodities within. Occasionally, they would enter and she would examine or try on several items, buying nothing in the end. She seemed to do this a great deal, and Jason expected to find her picture on a poster at the front door with the legend: "Do not admit this woman!", but the shopkeepers seemed to have a high tolerance for this sort of behavior. They had the patient expectation of a fisherman who knows that they have sunk the hook and the fish can be reeled in eventually.

Walking a few blocks more, they were soon on Polk Street standing before a shop from which drifted the most amazing aromas. This small business had sold coffee beans and tea at this location for more than a century and the most delightful varieties were in ancient bins within. Jason didn't actually drink coffee, but the smells of this place were a gift from heaven. Tracy chatted with the proprietor for a few minutes and then requested small lots of three different types – a deep roasted product of Colombia, an Arabica and one from the Kona coast. Jason decided to splurge on a small amount of an exclusive tea from Sri Lanka that could not be obtained anywhere else. The phrase "worth its weight in gold" came to mind, but he knew that his acquisition measured up to it.

They dallied in a few adjacent shops, one that had mainly hand-blown glassware and another with women's clothing not in Tracy's style. The shopping adventure was winding down.

Before too long they were thinking about the evening meal, and they chose a small corner restaurant close by which sported a French cuisine. Gigi's, as it was called, was informal enough so they would not have to change for dinner. The wait was not long, and soon they were seated at a small table surrounded by other small tables full of chatting patrons.

The place was a chaos of sound and smells. The walls and ceiling were painted with enamel, presenting a hard surface which reflected every whisper from the customers as well as all the kitchen noise. The murmuring clatter forced Jason and Tracy to lean toward each other to be heard in their conversation, a posture instinctively adopted by all the other patrons as well. As the chef produced his masterworks the aromas drove into the dining area, making the not yet served patrons salivate in anticipation. Ordering what the chef was currently cooking was common in this establishment.

Jason could not read the menu since it was in French. He knew that he liked the onion soup, but the rest he left to Tracy to pick out with the proviso that she not tell him what his meal was made from. If the French had developed a way to make sandstone edible, he preferred the blind taste test to the revelation of hard facts. He generally liked what she ordered, and this evening was no exception. The dessert was a delightful custardy substance, and they walked away well pleased with their meal. He had always wondered how she came to know about French dishes as she did, but she would never say.

They had about an hour before the poetry reading, so they walked through the fog down to Fisherman's Wharf for a chance to smell the ocean. It was approaching darkness, and the street vendors, already somewhat discouraged by the weather, had mostly pulled up stakes for the night. He dried off a bench with some discarded newspaper so they could sit and enjoy the stillness. Somewhere a ship's bell was idly clanging, and the foghorn outside of the Golden Gate could be heard through the saturated air.

As they turned to go a man in a ragged coat approached them and asked for spare change. Jason did what he always did on such occasions and spoke a few words.

"Gomen nasai."

The recipient of these words froze staring at Jason who then continued.

"Eigo ga dekinai de sumimasen. Wakarimashita ka?"

The man stumbled and looked a bit nonplussed, finally muttering "OK" as he wandered off. Originally Jason had customarily claimed ignorance of the English language in Russian, but one evening he had been caught by a Russian expatriate who promptly tried to start a conversation with him. He had found it necessary to give the man a few dollars to get him to go away. Japanese was the current language of choice for discouraging panhandlers. Safer.

The poetry reading was to be at what was usually called a coffee house, but they would serve you almost anything there but a plain cup of coffee. When they arrived, Jason and Tracy assumed their seats as a classical guitarist worked his way through a gutsy flamenco piece. As he finished, the audience demonstrated its clear approval. *The crowd's in a good mood tonight.* As they ordered something to drink, the announcer rose up to proclaim that the management was honored to present a bay area poet, Reina Disandro from Berkeley, reciting original works.

He described her as a published author and college professor, and as she assumed the stage with reserved composure, Jason saw that she was a small woman with short black hair and a Mediterranean appearance. He thought she seemed unused to public performance, but she greeted the audience with a calm and assured timber in her voice. Since his attention was elsewhere, he didn't actually hear the title of the first piece, but as she started to recite it, his attention slowly focused on the voice issuing from the stage.

Each word uttered revealed its magic and rang like a note in a perfect melody. Together they sang of love and patience, unfolding in a remembered and treasured encounter. Then it was over, too soon. A generous applause filled the small hall which he added to enthusiastically, noting that Tracy's approval was less abundant than his own.

The next poem was entirely different, of unexpected death and loss, a sadder moment but styled in the same perfection. Not a word could have been changed without unraveling the whole. Again the strong response from the audience rose to surround the author who seemed a bit unused to it. Something in her words called to him – *Sappho must have sounded like this.*

None of the poems was long, and three more were read, each a crystallized emotion deftly laid down before the audience, and each equally well received. Then a brisk "thank you" and she was gone.

The last of their espressos was accompanied by a flute and mandolin duet playing some fifteenth century piece. The transition was perfect. Before long Jason noticed that Tracy's eye had a familiar cast to it and he proposed that they find their way back to the apartment. Her sly smile framed a suggestive look.

They gathered their things.

As they passed out into the embrace of the evening fog, it seemed that the dense air had become even more enveloping. Visibility was not much more than an outstretched arm, and Jason's directional sense was put to the test. Other pedestrians would suddenly appear from nowhere and fade away; it was impossible to determine the direction of any source of light; sounds were dull and indistinct. Crossing a street required an act of faith since it was impossible to see any oncoming automobile. Somehow they arrived on their home block to Tracy's great relief.

Their apartment opened to them, snug and warm, and the two embraced at the entrance as Crash the cat loudly demanded a meal. Tracy nudged him with her foot.

The two were not long in retiring to the bedroom. Their lovemaking had not so much of the intensity of the previous night. They took their time in caress, mutually bringing delight to each other in a rhythm which was now familiar to both of them. He was expected to take the lead, offering something to please her, and then she would reciprocate. It was an exchange, a silent conversation where each had the unexpressed intention to drive the other past coherent response, to compel a begging for culmination and fulfillment. Each tried to postpone that moment for as long as possible. The loser in this debate often betrayed an approaching collapse with a sharp intake of breath, a slight convulsive shiver. This time it was Tracy. With a sharp, moaning gasp, she got on top of him and took what she wanted. He arched his body up to touch against hers in that moment that was like death and life fused together. They collapsed together.

The next day started off devoted to domestic maintenance and errands. There were the usual cleanup chores, a sticking window for him to massage into further smooth operation, a minor rearrangement of furniture in the sitting room. They liked to work together and chat about their recent experiences, but Jason let Tracy have most of the air time since she didn't seem to want to hear about what was happening in Ruskaya Bend. It was after her long exposition on several workplace intrigues that he told her that he had to leave the City in the early afternoon rather than Monday morning. She was clearly displeased.

"Why couldn't you stay one more night?"

"I've been invited to a family gathering by a neighbor. I promised her I would come."

"Her?"

Jason knew that tone of voice.

"She is a long term resident there. It's a celebration for her granddaughter, and it would be disrespectful for me not to come."

The stern look of displeasure melted into a pout as he tried to placate her. "I will be back before too long" – he kissed her cheek – "and you know I will be thinking of you all the time" – another kiss – "only of you."

"I can hardly wait until you turn your back on that place."

There was a promise and a threat in her words, and Jason wondered if he could safely cherish one and ignore the other. He knew that she could be self-centered at times, and his absence must be aggravating her. He counseled patience, yet he knew that this was not one of her outstanding attributes. She seemed somewhat placated.

"Well, if you have to go, there is something I would like you to do . . . ."

Chapter Eleven

Crash objected sharply to being stuffed into a cardboard box for the transport to Jason's car, yowling and scratching the sides of his confinement. Jason was reminded of the inmates at San Quentin yelling and banging their cups on the bars. Fortunately, he didn't have many additional items to load up – cat sand, Crash's food and toys, some additional clothing and a tool kit. Tracy hugged him goodbye in a pointedly reserved fashion but then relented and renewed her embrace strongly and smiled, wishing him a safe journey.

The traffic was light until he got on Highway 101 and approached the Golden Gate Bridge. Crash had already broken out of the box and was stretched out on the dash board, sunning himself, as Jason paid the toll and proceeded out onto the famous span. He liked the bridge, the rise of the towers, the graceful inverse arch of the main cables. He liked everything about this classic structure except the color. The rustproofing paint made it look as if it were completely rusted. As he left the bridge behind, the small town of Sausalito slumbered below him on the right, and a few miles further he made a quick decision to continue on 101 northward rather than cutting over to the coast and retracing his original route into the City. He would get off on Highway 116 at Cotati which would take him to the Russian River and then westward through Guerneville to Ruskaya. It was a good plan.

Unfortunately, CalTrans had chosen this particular week to begin long delayed improvements to the highway at Petaluma. Even though there was no work on Sunday, several of the lanes were torn up. Traffic slowed to a walk, then came to a stop for fifteen minutes. The only excitement came when Crash awoke enough to notice a large, toothy canine tied up in the bed of a pickup truck in the next lane. Crash hated dogs. Soon the cat was screaming and pawing the glass and the dog was barking and straining at the leash. the dog owner leaned out from the window of the cab and hollered something inarticulate and probably obscene as Jason reached for his map. Unfolding it, he held it in front of Crash's face, blocking his view, and the fight was over. Not able to see each other, each combatant assumed the other had run away. Soon the traffic began to move again.

Highway 116 was a welcome change. It progressed through Sebastopol and increasingly rural countryside on its way up to the Russian river. Jason had never seen much of this area and was enjoying it. Good weather and light traffic added to the general feeling of well being he was regaining since leaving the 101. He reached the river at Rio Del and soon crossed the bridge and went through Rio Nido and Guerneville. One more bridge and then he entered Ruskaya, pulling up to a small jewelry shop he had noticed the previous week near the center of town.

He had seen Cynthia wearing a charm bracelet and soon he found the ideal addition to it. A gold star with eight points – a star to guide by. It seemed the perfect thing, and he had it gift wrapped.

The house in Turner Canyon received a thorough appraisal from Crash. He wandered around a bit, loudly vocalizing his qualified approval, sharpened his claws on a carpet, and found a sunny spot for a nap. Jason spruced himself a bit, changed his shirt and made ready for the quinceañera up the street.

As he went out through the gate, he noticed a small group of neighbors proceeding up the street toward the same destination. He was introduced around as "Ted Brandt's son, new in the neighborhood" and greeted with smiles and handshakes. The afternoon sun made long their shadows in the street.

No one could mistake the house where the party was being held. The large plum tree in the front yard was draped with Christmas lights, and bouquets of flowers covered the porch, overflowing onto the lawn. Mariachi music, coming from a live band on the back deck, filled the canyon with an invitation to dance. The murmuring roar from inside the home spoke of a large, happy gathering; and greeting all entrants was Aurelia Salgado at her front door, looking like a member of royalty in a long, lacy dress. Each person received a kiss or a hug, and there was a brief exchange in Spanish with a gentleman from down the street who had been introduced as Cesar. Since Jason could understand the language, he was amused to hear them exchange mild insults, as only good friends would do. She then hugged Jason warmly.

"I am so glad you came."

"Thank you. I brought a small gift."

"She will be honored to receive it." This woman's smile could light the darkness, thought Jason. He placed his offering on a table with several others.

Entering the living room, he searched over the crowd for familiar faces and almost immediately saw Henry Turner sporting a cup of punch and a large smile.

"Jason! I want you to meet some people."

He was introduced to a few more neighbors and some of Aurelia's family. As soon as the name Brandt was mentioned, smiles of recognition and acceptance appeared. Before too long, Dee was among them, laughing and talking with the others about some neighborhood gossip. She turned to Jason.

"You're back. I hear it was foggy in the City. They had to shut down SFO." The airport lost a few days each year due to poor visibility.

"Apparently. It was pretty thick where we were." As he spoke with her, he caught sight of Connie on the other side of the room with a silver platter, serving delicacies to some of the guests. Dee didn't seem to notice him briefly gazing at the younger woman.

"Jason, there is going to be a City Council meeting on this Thursday, and one of my informants" – she flashed a wicked smile – "has alerted me that something is up. I was wondering if you would want to come. There should be some action, daggers flying, heads rolling, that sort of thing."

"Oh. Well, what time would this be?"

"Probably during the consent calendar. They usually try to muscle through their off-agenda surprises then. About seven thirty."

"I suppose I could."

"Excellent! I'll be by at ten past the hour. But don't have dinner, just in case. If I'm right about the strategy afoot, I'm buying."

This all seemed cryptic and confusing to Jason, but he let it pass and continued to chat with the other guests.

Cynthia's father Luis was recounting a story about her first adventure riding a horse, one that didn't particularly like being ridden. It had ended with a trip through the air and a sudden impact with the dusty earth.

"And then she got right back on, *que valiente era mi hijita.* She grabbed that horse's mane with both hands" – he gestured enthusiastically with his own large hands – "and she would not let him throw her off." The man's pride filled the room, but he suddenly caught a movement from the opposite doorway. A tall, younger man was motioning to him. "Oh, I must go. She is coming. Excuse me."

At that instant Connie appeared and offered the guests in their little group a chance at the treats on her tray. She looked particularly elegant as she paused before each person, smiling recognition, recommending one item or another. As she got to Jason, she seemed to stand more upright as she presented the tray to him.

"Good evening, Jason."

"Connie, how are you?"

"Fine, thank you." Her eyes briefly crossed his own as she turned toward another grouping of guests. He just smiled into empty space.

Suddenly a hush spread through the crowd as the music stopped. Appearing at the other side of the room was Luis with his daughter in hand. With measured steps she entered, dressed in a flowing, silken pink dress. Her father held her hand forward.

"*Señoras y Señores,* Ladies and Gentlemen. Allow me to present my daughter, Cynthia Morales."

There was a great applause from the assembled relatives and friends, and as it died down, Cynthia stood forward alone. Her black hair was held back with two matching ribbons, and slowly reaching up, she carefully removed them and set them aside. Her hair then cascaded down across her shoulders and back nearly to the mid point. On cue there was a shout of celebration and the band began a lively song. Her father took his daughter out on the floor for the first dance as all applauded.

Before too long a small group of boys about Cynthia's age gathered at the edge of the dance floor, trying to summon the pluck to cut in. No one wanted to be the first. Eventually, one lad, possessing a more determined look on his face than the others, broke from the pack and strode across the floor to tap Luis on the shoulder. The older man turned to survey the potential rival to his daughter's affections with skepticism. Making a show of reluctance, he permitted this lad to dance with her, and it was on. One young contender after another followed the bolder one's lead, crossing the floor to demand dancing privileges. Cynthia accepted the awkward attentions of all with grace, treating each as if he were the only one there.

Before too long, several other couples began to dance. In about twenty minutes the band took a short break, and as they were about to start up, Cynthia strolled over to Jason.

"You are the only one who hasn't asked me to dance." He stared at her somewhat nonplussed, so she continued. "Well?"

"OK. I can take a hint."

They both laughed, and he took her hand. The music started, and he found that she was a surprisingly good dancer, making him feel somewhat awkward. They made small talk for a while. Then she flashed her deep, dark eyes at him.

"By the way, what do you think of my cousin."

"Which cousin are we talking about here?"

"Connie, of course!"

He looked around the room and spotted her talking to a few of her relatives.

"It's hard to know what to say. I don't really know her."

"She is a good person but she's in a funk right now. She's coming off a bad relationship with this guy, a real jerk, so she pretty much hates all men these days. But she likes you."

"And when did she tell you about this?"

"Oh, we haven't discussed it."

Jason contemplated these revelations in view of his own experience. "Is there any chance you might be totally mistaken about this?"

"I would say . . . almost none."

"Does it matter that I already have the love of my life waiting for me in the City."

"Oh. Well, it won't last with her. You'll see."

Jason had pretty well run out of retorts, so he remained silent. As the dance ended, he was wondering what ever happened to that poor horse whose mane she had gripped so tightly.

"Tell me, Cynthia. These young bloods, climbing over each other to dance with you. Are any of them the right one for you?"

"Hey, I'm only fifteen. I get some time to play the field."

Jason was beginning to think that the horse had gotten off light.

Music, dancing, hilarity, and good companionship filled the next hour for the assembled guests, and then came the time for presentation of gifts to the young lady of honor. Jason watched as she opened and accepted one opulent donation after another; each made Jason's tiny package seem the more insignificant. He had a sinking feeling as she held it up, reading the tag and enthusiastically removing the paper. The tiny, gold star was suddenly in her hand as she searched the crowd for his face. Beaming at him, she held up her wrist with the bracelet, holding the star in its appointed position for revue. The relatives nodded their approval. Jason felt he could relax.

At the conclusion of the gift giving, Luis stood on a chair – much to the alarm of his wife Adelita – and suggested that they all adjourn to the rear patio where the youngsters would be given a chance at the piñata. As they reassembled out of doors, they were greeted with a fiendish image suspended by rope and pulley from a huge live oak tree. It looked like a Salvador Dali hallucination in the form of a demonic burro, and at the end of the rope was Cynthia's older brother Henrique, who was usually known as Ricky. As the group moved into positions of vantage, he called out a challenge to them.

"You may think you are strong and fast and smart; but I am holding the rope and I will deny you the prize. So puff yourselves up, step forward and be humiliated."

Most of the youths who had danced with Cynthia pushed forward, along with several smaller children, and they all contended for the head of the line. With some shoving and grumbling, they sorted themselves out, mostly in order of height. On a signal from Aurelia, the first moved forward, received his blindfold and a four foot long stick, somewhat narrower than a broom handle. He was spun around three times and aimed in the general direction of the dangling piñata. Before he had his opportunity, Ricky laid down the terms.

"Three swings only."

The youth started to protest.

"Anyone who objects to the rules gets only one swing."

With a thickly mumbled objection, the first blindfolded combatant cocked his stick and made ready. Woosh. As the wood was flying through the air, Ricky drew on the rope, pulling the piñata out of reach. A sympathetic "Oooh" rose from the crowd. The boy then decided to play it coy. Holding the stick down, he waited, knowing Ricky would not be able to resist taunting him. The piñata came lower and lower until it actually touched his head and woosh, but the prize was already out of reach. One more ineffectual swing and he was replaced by another lad just as optimistic about his own chances. He didn't last long. Four other young men strained at the prize, and four more were retired. Each had stood forward full of hope and retreated chastened.

At last an unpromising looking fellow named Frank took up the pole. A middle-aged woman called out to him, "*golpealo bien, Francisco.*" Positioning himself, he made one mighty swing hitting nothing and then waited with the stick touching the ground in front of him. He had seen the routine and knew Ricky would lower the prize to within reach, perhaps even touching him. He waited. As the piñata grazed the top of his head Frank suddenly raised the stick in an arc, stabbing upward as if with a saber and punching through the side of the paper-maché burro. He quickly slid one of his hands to the middle of the stick and braced himself.

Ricky had seen the stick's movement and hauled furiously on the rope, but Frank's plan was sound. As it rose, the piñata ripped open, spewing its sweet cargo of candies over a large area which was immediately carpeted with small children frantically collecting their share. Frank removed the blindfold, crossed his arms with a flourish, and stood triumphant in the middle of them. His cleverness earned him a kiss on the cheek from Cynthia, to the great consternation of her father, and for the rest of the evening he would bask in celebrity status.

Ricky mounted a half-hearted objection. "He cheated. He's supposed to hit it, not spear it." But in the end he joined in the congratulation, slapping Frank on the back.

"Well done, but do you suppose you will ever be able to beat me again?"

"I dunno. How many more sisters do you have?"

At this they both laughed heartily and wandered up into the main room for refreshments. As the band started up again, Frank asked to be the next to dance with Cynthia, and she accepted with obvious pleasure.

As Jason watched them move gracefully past him on the dance floor, he looked around at the assembled family and friends. The bright eyes, the joyous faces, the exclamations of delight at the young girl's first night as a young woman all pleased him enormously. He knew this was one of those times, those golden moments, which are not marked as they occur, but which remain in memory as an inspiration, as proof of how good life can be. He felt privileged to be present.

The next hour saw Jason paying his respects to Cynthia and her family and to the several neighbors he had met. Dee reminded him of the Council meeting they would be attending. Luis gripped his hand with both of his own, and his wife hugged him as a long lost friend. As he slipped out the front door, the band started up a lively number, and the enthusiastic roar from the crowd indicated that the event would continue long into the night.

There was no street light in front of the Morales house, so Jason's way was illuminated by a sterling moon, nearly full and directly overhead. A faint echo of his footsteps reverberated from the canyon wall, and his path home was accompanied by the roar of a myriad of crickets.

Chapter Twelve

Just before dawn, Crash opened the closet door and pulled several of Jason's shirts off their hangars. He then spilled a glass full of water in the kitchen, making a substantial puddle. At dawn he decided to cruise the mantelpiece knocking several items off as he passed, and each made a clatter as they struck the hearth. This finally woke Jason from an untroubled sleep, but he remained still. It was all part of the game. If he rose, he had to feed the cat, so Crash would try progressively more noisy and irritating things until Jason caved in from the pressure and got up. As the human in this war, Jason postponed the payoff as long as possible, trying to maintain his species' slight advantage. Soon he heard a sound that resembled a refrigerator door being opened.

He jumped up and bellowed, "Where's that cat!"

The chase was on – Jason was out the bedroom door and into the front room where a very surprised cat turned on a dime and raced into the kitchen. They both thundered across the tiles, Jason nearly losing his footing on the wet floor. He almost had the cat's tail as they raced through the dining room into the hall, but Jason bounced off the wall as the cat made a precise, high-speed left turn on the carpet.

"I'll get you."

Crash rocketed through the door to the bedroom and disappeared. All was silent, but Jason knew well where he was. Sneaking into the bathroom, he slowly peeked around the corner into the tub.

There was Crash, sitting with his head cocked to one side with a look which said, "hey – what kept you?" The tub was a safe zone, according to rules known only to cats, but Jason was willing to play along. Someday the human would win this game, someday.

"I suppose you want your food now."

Crash was not a very vocal feline, but he said it all with his eyes and ears. The first widened and the second tilted forward slightly at the offer of mealtime, but he hopped out of the tub and strode past Jason with the self assurance a cat dares to show. Sitting leisurely in front of his bowl, he awaited Jason's offering. In the morning it was always dry food, which he liked, but still he hesitated, giving it a critical review. Finally, he hunched down and began to eat. He had two bites and then rose, striding off as if food was the last thing on his mind.

During the day Jason had plenty of time to continue his evaluation of the house's needs, first getting up on the roof and surveying the shingles. They were old and thinned by age, calling for a total renovation.

One good sneeze and they are gone, plus they are a fire hazard. But what would a new roof run? It is shingles on furring strips right now. I would have to sheet the whole roof, then maybe lightweight tiles or composition shingles. Hmmm. Better measure the surface and start pricing it. In the meantime I could get a few bundles of wood shingles and repair a couple of bad spots.

Later, as he crawled through the space under the floor with a flashlight, he found that the original septic plumbing had been cast iron and was apparently still in good shape. He was delighted to find that the galvanized water service lines has been replaced with good copper not too many years before, but the electrical wiring was as old as the house.

Maybe just a few new plumbing fixtures, but the wiring is that old black romex from the fifties with no ground. Hmmm. New wiring wouldn't be too tough with this crawlspace and the attic for access. Don't have to do anything now.

The electrical panel dated from the late seventies. It was in good shape and had fairly up to date circuit breakers, but it was small.

One hundred amp mains. Only twelve circuits – barely enough for a house this size. Not enough juice for A. C. or an electric range. I could get more circuits with split breakers but there still wouldn't be enough amps for anything big.

He looked over the service drop which swayed out to the pole on his front lot corner.

The service is tiny, looks like #4. But it would be easy to upgrade and underground at the same time. It's a straight run to the pole. No ground rod, though. Hmmm.

Jason was pleased that the structure appeared to be sound wherever he looked. The little bit of termite damage was in the front and already being addressed. Bringing the house up to his own personal standards would require all of his savings and more, and such a plunge could only be justified if the house were to be sold. That meant that major work would require permits, and at present the City was not in a mood to grant them. He decided the safest course would be to continue with minor repairs and see how it went. Putting the house up for rental for a year or two was looking more probable.

A visit to the local lumber yard produced two bundles of shingles, the tongue-and-groove boards he had previously ordered, a few studs, some bondo, and various tools not already in his kit. He also obtained from an electrical supply house a ground rod, a clamp and some #4 bare copper wire. If he would be staying in the house, he wanted to be well grounded.

The afternoon passed swiftly, as time filled with productive work will do. Most of this day's projects were completed as the low slant of the sun's rays reminded him of Dee and the Council meeting. A quick shower was in order. When he got out it was just past six o'clock, and remembering the words about dinner, he had a small snack to cut his hunger. But how does one dress for a City Council meeting? He decided to go casual.

Dee was precisely on time as she knocked on Jason's door. He, on the other hand, opened it minus his shoes and with hair uncombed.

"Step on it, my lad. Plots are hatching."

"Right away. I have to feed the cat first."

"I didn't know you liked cats."

"Well, I used to." He gave a mock disparaging look in the

direction of a back room where, presumably, the frenetic feline was up to no good. Jason's last duties were laid away and they were soon out the door.

The sun was about to set, and Dee suggested that they walk into town. The compact nature of Ruskaya permitted this mode of travel, and Jason had noticed many of its residents on foot, progressing to one destination or another. The evening was warm with a light breeze, and he was game for the adventure. At the head of the street he asked about the small restaurant fronting the highway.

"That's Rosie's diner, a breakfast and lunch place. Rosie is gone now, but her family keeps the business open. It has good food – you should try it. The bridge we are crossing into town is also known as Rosie's bridge, but really the name was applied to the previous wooden structure that this concrete monstrosity replaced."

Jason was content to let Dee chat on about local folklore for a while and then asked, "Are you from here originally?"

"Oh no, San Francisco. I grew up in North Beach – when it was a nice place to live. Just a working class, Italian-Irish family."

"But how did you come to live here?"

The pause before her response spoke more loudly than her words.

"Oh, that's a long story."

They turned a last corner and in the middle of the block was a nondescript building identified by a sign as the Ruskaya Bend City Hall. But for that, he might have taken it for a hardware store. They entered, and pausing in front of a bulletin board, Dee studied the agenda bill carefully.

"OK. It's not here. Good."

"What isn't?"

Dee motioned him farther along the hall, away from an open door. Looking to see if the walls had ears, she spoke in a hushed tone.

"I have gotten word that our illustrious Mayor McCanna intends to pull a maneuver tonight."

"Why is it good that it isn't on the agenda?"

"It means that the old goat is performing according to type. Watch, and you will see how strength becomes a weakness. But first, we have to set the trap."

Jason was increasingly confused by this but realized that Dee took great delight in prolonging and heightening the mystery. He resolved to tag along and see what transpired.

They entered the meeting hall, and Dee guided them to seats in the front row near the aisle. The general hubbub from the audience dwindled down as the members of the Council entered from a rear door and assumed their seats. Last, in great style, was the Mayor. Jason saw a tall, bald man with a manner somewhere between commanding and overbearing. His voice seemed forced a full octave below its normal range as he greeted the other Council members and staff. He completely ignored the audience.

Mayor McCanna called the meeting to order and announced admission of the consent calendar. At this point Dee shifted in her chair, rustling her copy of the agenda, in a manner which Jason thought a bit staged. It did, however, catch the Mayor's eye. She leaned over and whispered to Jason.

"*We should talk about something now. It really bothers him. Any questions?*"

"*What is the consent calendar?*"

"*It is a list of routine matters before the city which are not usually discussed individually but voted on in a block.*"

"*Your item is not on it?*"

"*No.*" She had continually been watching the Mayor's face as they spoke and, anticipating that he would shortly require her to take her conversation outside, she paused. Jason saw her assume the expression of one raptly transfixed by the Mayor's every word. As soon as he turned to speak to a member of staff on some matter, she continued as if nothing had happened.

"*He has tried to slip off-agenda items through on the consent calendar, so we will sit here until they vote on it. Right now we are here to put in an appearance and leave.*"

One item was removed for individual discussion and vote, then the remainder of the consent calendar was passed. At this Dee shot up and, catching Jason's eye, nodded toward the door. It seemed that she rattled the door a few times before opening it, as if trying to make sure their exit was noticed. Soon they were outside, heading across the street to the Plumb Branch.

"What just happened, Dee?"

"Nothing. But it was a very meaningful nothing. We baited the trap, and now we wait to see if we catch anything. How about dinner?"

Entering the restaurant, Dee sought out a table adjacent to the bar, and as Jason sat, she stepped away to have a few words with the barkeep. A smile, a touch of the hand and suddenly the wide screen TV above the bar was presenting the City Council meeting that they had just left. This raised a few complaints from one patron, but the barkeep was firm.

"Do you know the bartender?"

"An old friend." And she laughed.

"Now what do we do."

"That depends on what you like to eat. I'm buying. We just have to kill about an hour and a half."

"Can you tell me what is going on?"

"OK. Mayor McCanna intends to introduce an off-agenda item before the Council calling for the widening and extension of Turner Canyon Road. This is purely to benefit his great pal Howard Keller, and it would mean the destruction of our neighborhood. He is vitally interested in avoiding any public opposition, so he is using a method which is basically illegal to ram his proposal through a usually compliant Council."

"Illegal?"

"Yes. The Council may not introduce, debate, or vote on a matter which affects the value of private properties without notifying the owners and holding a public hearing. Did you receive a notice of this meeting?"

"No."

"So the Mayor will have a forum free of dissent to browbeat, cajole, and con his way to a vote to pass this measure."

"But you said it was illegal. Won't the vote be invalid?"

"Of course. But later when the proper hearing occurs, no matter what is said then in opposition, the members of the Council will be hard pressed to change their initial votes. It would make them look feckless and easily manipulated by the plebeians. McCanna would have all the cards in his hand."

"How do you know he plans this for tonight?"

"I don't, but it is pretty likely." She leaned forward. "My source indicates that he is ready to make his move. Keller needs it now."

"Wouldn't any member of the Council know that this is not according to the book and raise objection?"

"Yes. There is one, but she can't do that without revealing her position." She looked fixedly into Jason's eyes. "You have to keep this to yourself. . . . she is my informant, and if she reveals her sympathies, she can't help me any more. I have to run this action alone."

"So now we wait."

"And eat." Her smile was abundant.

The Council sloshed through the agenda, debating one vital concern after another. Dee and Jason had dinner, then dessert, and were finishing coffee when she indicated that it was time to go.

They passed through the entrance and paused just outside the door to the meeting hall. The Mayor's growling tones needed no amplification, and they stood still as the last item listed on the agenda was wrapped up. They waited. . . and then they heard him continue.

"Members of the Council, I have one additional item for your consideration and vote which involves an issue of civic improvement."

There was a short pause, and Jason heard a feminine voice requesting that the title be read into the record. He judged that this might be Dee's ally on the Council, but he had no idea what the significance of this request might be. Dee hunched over the knob, drawn tight. Another woman's voice read the name of the proposal; Jason didn't hear all of it, but clearly heard "Turner Canyon Road". At this Dee flung the door open and strode directly for the microphone.

The bang of the door startled the Mayor, but only for an

instant. As Jason watched from the doorway, McCanna busied himself with some papers before him and tried his best not to notice Dee. She did not wait for recognition.

"Your Honor, I wish to speak on this matter."

"Miss Carella. This is not the time for public comment."

"I wish to raise a point of order."

The Mayor started to wave her down, but she continued.

"Is this a noticed public hearing? Because if it isn't, these proceedings are illegal."

"I think we know the law better. . . "

"If you don't believe me, ask the City Attorney. That's what he is here for."

The silence in the room was all enveloping. Don Colesco was staring into his lap. Several of the Council members seemed to squirm. The few souls in the audience perked up their ears. She could not resist one more shot.

"It's either him or the State Attorney General."

At this the Mayor glowered at her with a greater lack of control than he would have preferred. He glanced at the City Attorney who was still ardently looking downward, and then seemed to regain his composure as he made a dismissive gesture.

"Very well. The chair will entertain a motion to table this matter."

Dee had anticipated this contingency.

"I'm sorry. You cannot table a matter which you have not legally introduced." At this she made an expansive gesture in the direction of the City Attorney who was still staring downward. "Since you have completed the posted agenda, I suggest you adjourn."

Suddenly one of the Council, whose name plaque read Laura Goetz, spoke up.

"I move that we adjourn."

One of the other members hurriedly seconded the motion, and in the silence which followed, all eyes fell upon the Mayor who sat stock still.

At this point the City Clerk spoke up, her clear voice announcing, "We have a motion and a second."

There was a considerable pause before Mayor McCanna muttered, "All in favor say 'Aye'".

The chorus of Aye's was robust, and the other members bolted from their seats and were gone before the Mayor could even declare the meeting adjourned. For a few seconds he and Dee stared at each other, then she turned and marched out.

Jason met her at the door, noticing that her face was surprisingly calm for the tension of the moment she had just engineered. On the street her walk was brisk, and her manner casual. Jason couldn't help admiring her self-possession.

"Tell me, Dee. Was that fun?"

"Politics is never fun. You do what you have to do and move on. You can't exult too much in your victories, nor despair too much in your losses. Tonight we deflected the hammer blow, but there will be another, and I am already thinking about what it might be. You see, we are in an awkward position. We don't have the votes. We only have the ignorance, greed and arrogance of our enemies to work with. These are truly powerful weapons, but we cannot afford to loose any major battles."

"Do you think it wise to provoke the Mayor like that?"

"In fact, his enmity and arrogance make him our most powerful ally. Time after time we have been able to use his own condescending attitude against him with spectacular results. To answer your question, I have to provoke him into expressing his basic nature because it aids us immeasurably. He has a serious case of the Big Chair Disease."

"What is that?"

"You know, the mental condition you get from sitting in one of those big chairs looking down on everyone else." Then, almost parenthetically she added, "The funny thing is. . . if he had any compassion, he would be very hard to defeat."

This was beginning to make sense to Jason, and his admiration for her grew.

"Dee, did you ever hear of a guy named Machiavelli?"

"I was his political advisor in another life."

They filled the moon-splashed street with laughter.

Chapter Thirteen

The Mayor's secretary scanned the man before her with a practiced eye.

"Mayor McCanna will see you now."

Howard Keller bustled past the secretary without even a glance toward her. He never wasted his time on underlings, and besides, he had a bone stuck in his throat and needed to cough it up. He rushed through the office door without shutting it and started unloading on the man on the other side of the desk.

"What the hell is going on here."

Mayor McCanna rose and slipped over to shut the door, trying to retain his composure.

"Howard. Don't worry. Everything is under control. Won't you sit down."

They both settled into their seats, the Mayor with all the calmness he could muster; the other man resembling bacon frying.

"That Carella bitch tripped you up again."

"No, Howard. But she did make clear a very important fact. Someone is slipping information to her. This is a situation I can and will take care of."

"James, your technical problems are not my concern. Just handle it. I have a time frame here to live within. The option on that property is costing me monthly, and so far I have nothing to show for it. You made certain assurances to me." His manner was increasingly cold. "And I have been very supportive of you candidacy and goals in the past. It is about time that something came to me by way of reciprocation."

"And it will, Howard. I remain convinced of the importance of your project to this town's future. These, uh, canyon dwellers will be dealt with. They have about fired all the shots they have." He could see that Keller was easing toward placation, so he continued in his best calming tone. "We have only a few bureaucratic hurdles in front of us, but the goal is in sight. You can start clearing a place above your mantelpiece for the permits right now." The other man eased back into his chair. "By the way, I know that staff selected Halley, Merrick, and Davis for the resubmission of your geological report. How is that going?"

Whatever calm the Mayor had been able to induce in Howard Keller was gone instantly.

"Those bastards! They want four thousand dollars to re-sign the report they have already done!"

"Now Howard, they have to cover themselves."

"They're covering themselves with my money! He leaned forward in his chair and glared at the Mayor. "James, I don't like how this is going. I want to see some meaningful progress soon."

"And you will. . ."

"I don't want to hear any reasons why almost should be good enough. Progress, James. That's what I want to see. Do you think you are up to it?"

The Mayor felt his own anger rising but suppressed it. *Not now. I still need this worm's help for a while. There are bigger fish to fry. Plenty of time to smack him into place later.*

"Howard, I know you will be pleased with how things go from now on." He rose, extending his hand. Keller slowly rose to accept the invitation to leave, but he knew that his points had been made. The important thing about slapping a politician around was knowing how much was enough.

"I trust so." He turned to go.

As Howard Keller left the outer office, he passed the City Manager coming in. They exchanged pleasantries, and Keller put on his best fawning manner. He knew well that the man who actually ran the City was not one to aggravate. Jeff Heit was typically cool with him, always careful not to slip into familiarity with anyone. The Manager nodded perfunctorily and then turned away to continue in to see the Mayor. The door closed softly.

Ruth Frazee was busy doing what she did best. A tiny, reserved woman face-to-face, she was a lioness on the telephone. Preferring the speaker phone, she then had both hands free to gesture and emphasize salient points for a sightless audience.   Her rolodex bulged with names of friends and acquaintances, and she never forgot anything about them – what year the second daughter was attending at which college, the youngest son's birthday, how the aged father was doing. Eighty percent of Ruth's life was defined by electrical impulses surging to and fro in the two small wires that led to the outside world. Every afternoon, after returning from her job at Ruskaya's local bank, she would work the phone. These days she had a purpose.

Each call would start with a casual discussion of the callee's recent doings. Ruth actually liked the people she knew. They were not mere contacts, and her own unadorned life was greatly enriched by the activities of her friends. It would be easy to consider her a mere gossip, but she never repeated the things she heard, and for this reason her friends trusted her. Soon the conversation would turn to general, civic news and she would have the chance to introduce the problem her neighborhood was facing.

"Yes, dear. He calls it 'The Cliffs' – it would be right above the Bear, and he wants to take access from our road. The traffic would be horrible, but that isn't the worst of it. He needs a fifty foot wide road for a development of that size, and to get it he wants the city to bulldoze half the houses on the street."

Ruth rode out the shocked reaction at the other end of the line and then continued.

"Twenty-three houses, that would be half. You know how narrow the canyon is, but Henry thinks they would have to take both sides of the street at the end of the road where the flat land almost disappears. He calculates that they would need thirty-five to forty houses."

At this point her audience was usually thoroughly outraged.

"Yes, mine would be one of them. I don't know what I would do. They are willing to destroy the lives of so many people to benefit one out-of-towner because they think nobody is looking and nobody cares. And that vile, little man urges them on."

Ruth knew her friends well. Each had a talent which could

be helpful to the Turner Canyon neighborhood and most were happy to offer it. One was a good public speaker, another masterful at writing letters for publication. Many had their own circle of friends about the town and would know how to present the issue to gain support. Ruth gratefully accepted their offers of help and suggested how best they could contribute. She knew that some would not follow up, others would be ineffective, but much benefit could come from the collective efforts of the remainder.

And so Ruth passed many quiet afternoons, renewing old friendships and passing the word. Late one day she called a man whom she had met one year before at the dedication of Vista Park in the Meadows. He had been pleasant enough, with a delightful family, but he was a member of the Ruskaya Bend Civic Association. Generally a pro-business organization, the RBCA most often favored development. However, a mutual friend had encouraged her to call him, and she was pleasantly surprised that Frank Wells was a very different man than she had expected.

"Yes, Ruth, I have been following it. I usually watch the council meetings when they are broadcast live on channel thirty-three. I didn't understand the whole breadth of what was at stake, but you have filled in the holes for me.

"I have to confess that I don't like what is going on. This matter raises for me a concern over what kind of government we should have and what its priorities should be. I moved here from a much larger city hoping that government would be more personal, accessible, and even benign, but I don't see that here. My wife Delia and I have already talked about this sort of thing, and she is as concerned as I am.

"You know that I was selected as chairman of the Civic Association one month ago. . ."

Ruth gulped. "I didn't know."

"Part of my duties is to schedule speakers to give talks on local matters. How would you like to come down some evening to address the Association and bring them all up to speed."

The blood rushed to Ruth's face. "I couldn't. . .well, I'm not really. . ."

"All you would have to do is to tell them what you have just told me. You have been very persuasive."

"Frank, I'm not very good. . . in front of people. But there is someone who would be. Do you know Henry Turner?"

"Of course. His has a famous name here. Would he come?"

"I can't speak for him, but I think he would. Could I give him your phone number?"

"You certainly can. I'd look forward to talking to him."

"Thank you so much, Frank. I am glad I called you. Please give my best to your wife."

Ruth clicked off the phone and sat in the stillness. She had been forced to think fast and had almost offered Dee Carella, but Dee could be antagonistic at times and might have alienated this group of important local businessmen. Henry would be seen as more their peer and would have the advantage of name recognition. She dove into her rolodex.

J ason stood back near the street to survey his handiwork. New raingutters extended across the roof eave, new siding and a fresh coat of paint graced the front to the left of the door, a cracked windowpane had been replaced, the soil which had been allowed to creep up to the siding had been dug out. Minor improvements, to be sure, but each gave a sense of accomplishment and pride. He was using a scrubbing pad to remove the last of the latex paint from his hands as a visitor approached from up the street. He saw that it was Cynthia Morales, and she carried a silver tray with what seemed to be about a dozen plums on it – doubtless the products of the large tree in her front yard.

"Hiya. You like plums?"

"Yes. Of course I do. Are those all for me?"

"If you like." She looked over the front of his house with care. "What have you been doing?"

He described the tasks recently accomplished in a matter-of-fact way, but she seemed impressed.

"Where did you learn how to do all this?"

"I worked my way through college in construction. Roofing, siding, painting, carpentry, electrical – I did pretty much everything. Although I seem to enjoy it more now that I don't have to do it for the money."

She just smiled.

"Why don't you come in."

"OK."

He had a sudden thought and looked around before closing the door. "You came here by yourself?"

"Sure. Why? Do you think I need a chaperon?" She looked at him disparagingly. "You don't look that dangerous to me."

Jason was contemplating some sort of salty response when Crash thundered into the room. On catching sight of a stranger, he jumped three feet in the air and landed in a defensive posture, his back arched with wide eyes focused on her.

"Oh, you have a cat." She calmly kneeled on the carpet and clucked her tongue, rubbing her fingers together to produce that dry, whispering sound so attractive to a cat.

Crash held his position suspiciously for a long three seconds then slowly moved forward to touch his nose to the tips of her fingers. He looked at her intently for an instant then, as she lifted her hand up slightly, he ran his head and body under it in the typical feline gesture of affection and then flopped over on his back for her to rub his stomach.

Jason was astounded. "He really doesn't do that, you know."

"Animals and small kids love me. What's his name?"

He told her.

"Crash? You've got to be kidding! What kind of name is that for a cat?"

"He used to knock things over a lot when he was a kitten – still does, in fact."

"Terrible name. Do you let him out?"

"I hadn't yet."

"Good. Don't. We have packs of coyotes running through this neighborhood even in broad daylight. They would pick him off in a heartbeat. What do you do with him when you go to the

City to visit what's-her-name?"

"Her name is Tracy, and I haven't had to deal with that problem yet. I thought I could just leave out large bowls of food and water, or board him."

"Horrible! You might as well tie him to a stake in the front yard. I'll tell you what. If you wouldn't mind leaving your back door unlocked, I could come to take care of him while you were gone. Just let me know when."

Jason looked at the object of this conversation. Crash was spreadeagled on his back as Cynthia massaged from his belly to his upturned chin.

"That would be wonderful. I would prefer to leave a key under the mat, though."

She nodded.

"I would hope to make it up to you."

"Don't worry about it. It would be my pleasure." She sat down cross legged on the floor and Crash moved over to sit next to her, one forepaw resting on her leg, looking as if he had just had a bath in catnip.

Over the next twenty minutes they passed the time, talking about neighborhood doings and civic affairs. To Jason she seemed very well informed and imbued with many, diverse interests unusual in a high school sophomore. A person quick to express her convictions, she also listened intently to any opinions Jason might have. A certain measure of her words dealt with light-hearted, almost superficial interests any fifteen year old girl would have, but a surprising amount of her thoughts indicated an unexpected maturity.

The conversation proceeded smoothly until Jason happened to ask her whether she spoke Spanish at home. Her suddenly dour expression told him that he had hit a sore point with her.

"I know what they are saying, but I don't speak it."

He suspected that her displeasure was more than merely linguistic, but decided not to pursue it. The conversation continued for another ten minutes on various matters until it was time for her to leave.

"Just bring the tray up to the house when you are done. And don't eat any more than two of those plums per day or you will get the runs really bad."

He gave her a wry smile and paused briefly.

"Can I ask you a question?" Her face indicated assent. "The people around here – do they usually warm up to a stranger quickly?"

Her deep, dark eyes scanned him closely. True to her nature she skipped directly to the point.

"Maybe they think you fit in." And then she was gone.

D ee breezed into City Hall with the assurance of a person who knew where to place her feet. A smile and nod to the staff members behind the counter opened the way into the inner sanctum where Will Hansen had his retreat as director of planning. His secretary glanced briefly at the list of appointments and then greeted Dee with a broad smile.

"He will be with you in just a moment," indicating one of several uncomfortable looking chairs near the door.

As she sat waiting, Dee went over the papers she had brought with her. A copy of the geological report for Keller's project, which she was not supposed to have, was underneath several individual sheets pertaining to various matters. She composed herself.

Presently several business types bustled out of the Director's office and disappeared down the hall. With a nod from the secretary, Dee entered Will Hansen's lair. After observing the customary formalities, she busied herself with inquiries and requests for certain items pertaining to the Keller development, all a matter of routine for the planning director. He was prepared to be gracious in all ways until she requested one item.

"And could I possibly have a copy of the City's contract with Halley, Merrick, and Davis for The Cliffs project."

He was slow in responding. "Of course, Dee, that would not be under the purview of this department."

She knew very well that it was.

"I am sure it is somewhere here in City Hall. You know how it is, Will, I should put a copy of it in my records. You know who would have it – could you make mention that it would be necessary?"

She smiled at him casually, trying to find the right balance between intent and indifference in her words.

"Yes, of course, Dee." He made a show of scribbling something on a sheet of yellow note paper. "I could look right into that."

The rest of her conversation was about routine matters and soon she was saying her goodbyes. Dee had always considered Will Hansen to be a thorough company man, polite, but not voluntarily helpful to her. She found him most useful to work through, using him to put pressure on others or to spread disinformation. City Hall was like a big, gray machine, and one needed to know which of the buttons to press. Occasionally she regretted having to use this man in this way, considering that he was probably a decent fellow in real life, but politics was politics.

Chapter Fourteen

Henry examined the face in the mirror. Not a bad face, overall. The hereditary Turner family eyebrows were in evidence, heavy but now grayed by his fifty-five years. The thick, straight hair with its slight widow's peak still showed some of its original jet black vigor, but much had gone gray also, and the temples were white. The nose was narrow, fitting the close-set eyes. The skin was still virtually unlined, another family trait. Not a bad face. Not exactly handsome in the taste of most, but acceptable.

The Civic Association was likely to be a tough crowd, mainly comprised of local business owners. The construction and real estate professions were well represented, and in almost all conflicts between developers and residents, their support was predictably for the former. Not all, though. This young fellow, Frank Wells, had been most gracious when Henry had called him, seeming an even handed sort. *Might not last long,* Henry had thought at the time, *too nice,* and then he chided himself for his cynicism.

Ruth had been so insistent and optimistic about the opportunity to speak to this group, and you never knew when you might reach a sympathetic ear. Definitely worth the try. Henry finished shaving and wiped his face dry. His mother's pale, blue eyes looked back at him, garnished with a slight twinkle. Yes, he would give it his best shot. Most important would be to avoid highlighting his family's extended history in this area. Others without his long roots might resent the unfavorable comparison. Tact, that's it. This fellow Keller was the target.

The short walk into town took him across Rosie's bridge, and he paused mid-span to savor the early evening air rising from the river. The previous bridge had been much closer to the water, and on a cool evening, warm air had risen from the water to caress

his face, but no more. The new bridge, much resented by Turner
canyon residents, was too far above the water to feel the its humid
updraft, and he missed it. There was still a great view down the
valley of the Russian River toward the sea, not far away. *You can't
lose it all.* He turned and continued into the center of town.

The Civic Association met these days at the Ruskaya Bend
Library.   As the organization had grown, it had progressed
through a series of meeting places, each slightly larger than the
previous one. The attempts to gain new membership had been
overly successful, bringing in a rush of fresh participants, eager to
do what they might for a community which often they had only
recently discovered. The new talent was viewed ambiguously by
the old-guard membership. The new blood was welcome, but
could these bright-eyed neophytes be controlled – you could have
too much of a good thing. The old lions sat proud, self-contained,
calloused, and mildly skeptical while the young turks bustled
around trying to remake the world, secretly somewhat haughty
toward their older colleagues. Into this dynamic stepped Henry
Turner.

Frank's introduction was brief and polite, not prejudicing
Henry's case either way. A project under consideration by the City
would affect an established community, and Henry would
represent that community. He took the podium and surveyed the
group of faces before him. Only about half were actually looking
at him.

"Good evening. First, I want to thank Chairman Wells for
the opportunity to address you on this matter. I will try to keep
my comments brief.

"For those of you who don't yet know, on submission
before the City is a project called 'The Cliffs' which the developer
seeks to build just above the Bear. On paper it calls for one
hundred twenty units, but considering the building code
restrictions already in place regarding density versus slope, it is
unlikely he could get approval for more than about eighty units.
To do better than that he would require variances which have
never been granted before.

"For my community the main impact would be as a result

of access requirements. For even a reduced number of units, a right of way fifty feet wide would be needed, and the proponent wants the City to widen and extend Turner Canyon Road to provide it."

Henry paused, taking a deep breath and leaning forward.

"To accommodate this, upwards of forty of our homes would have to be demolished."

He watched the crowd carefully, looking for reactions. For some members, this was new information, and their faces showed emotions ranging from incredulity to discomfort. These he might be able to reach. Some merely stared at him as if nothing had been said. Some others looked away dismissively. Those were hopeless. He continued with his arguments.

"You may think this would be an acceptable trade off – loose forty to get eighty. You might be considering that you can't get omelets without breaking eggs, but let's examine who owns the eggs and who will have to pay to clean up the mess.

"The developer is in a position of gaining all the profit and avoiding most of the costs. He will have houses or lots to sell, but the cost of destroying our homes will be borne by the City – that means you.

"There is no hope for any Urban Renewal money from the State because the area is not blighted, in spite of the public relations campaign to the contrary. The purchases and demolitions will have to be financed by a bond issue through the City, and all of you good citizens will have to pay that off plus interest. I, on the other hand, will lose a family tradition and the home I love, but I will be compensated by a hatful of your money to start over somewhere else. You will see your property taxes go up for the next twenty years so that one outsider can turn a profit on a land speculation."

He paused again for effect.

"I think that this is not a good deal for the City and its citizens, and it should be opposed. You members have a perfect right to pick and choose from among possible futures for your town, accepting those beneficial, rejecting others not so good. I hope I have made it clear which this project would be.

"That's all I have to say, but I would be glad to answer any questions."

During the next ten minutes, Henry responded to an intense grilling from the crowd. As he had thought, some were sympathetic and pressed for details, but others were openly negative to his cause. One merchant whom Henry knew well, rose to raise a point seemingly intended to undermine opposition to the project.

"Henry, why should this organization take a stand in this matter, one way or the other?"

"Good question, Benjamin. Why should you? I think because this organization is comprised of good folks like you. Everyone knows you; you have lived all your life in this town. Your sporting goods store is right downtown, next to City Hall. A great location, by the way. But what if the City decided that they needed more closet or storage space, and what if they concluded that they would have to demolish your shop to satisfy their needs. They might call that progress, but what would your view on it be?"

At first Benjamin Frist looked as if he had been smacked with a wet sock, and then with a vaguely sharp look he merely said, "Point taken" and sat down.

The questions petered out, and Henry took a seat in the audience while the usual fare of such a civic group was expressed and discussed. Someone thought that there was not enough parking, another lamented the closing of an art gallery due to raised rents, a third pressed for an accelerated trash pickup schedule for the downtown area on weekends. Some resolutions were made, some votes taken. A few announcements and then the meeting was adjourned. Henry found himself near the refreshment counter as Roy Butler approached him.

Roy had migrated from Perth, Australia twenty years before and had debarked at San Francisco where he soon found a job as a cub reporter at the San Francisco Chronicle. Over the years his "down under" accent had softened as he integrated into American society, as so many others from so many different countries had done before him. Fifteen years of saving every penny brought him the opportunity to purchase a small, hometown newspaper called the Ruskaya View, and now he was a proud member of that community. He had learned to be cautious about his editorial policy, presenting all sides evenly in every matter of controversy, so Henry did not consider that Roy could showcase his community's point of view without giving equal voice to Howard Keller. Roy's words surprised him.

"Y'know, I would like to run something about this business in the View, but I might not be able to cover it as I would like." He typically left much unsaid. "But there is someone who might have a freer hand than I, an old mate from the Chronicle, Michael Coursby. He is on the editorial staff and deals a lot with social issues, and this might get his juices flowing. If you mentioned my name, I am sure he would take the time to interview you. What happens after that . . ." His gesture closed the sentence for him.

After touching his friend's shoulder by way of thanks, Henry made a mental note to pursue this opportunity on the following day. This chance could be what he had come for, and he wouldn't let it slip. The rest of his stay was spent chatting with old friends and near-friends. Most of them were non-committal about his talk, preferring to let their conversations run to gossip and other old news. He knew most of them would stay out of the matter, but a few could probably be counted on when they were needed. It was hard to expect more. Henry estimated that he had won over perhaps half a dozen from this group.

Almost the last person he talked to was Frank Wells.

"I thought you gave a great talk, Henry. What sort of feedback have you been getting?"

"Not bad. Some people don't want to talk to me about it, but most seem at least sympathetic. Though, I do appreciate the chance to come and present our point of view."

Frank leaned close. "To tell you the truth, I didn't like some of the cloakroom talk I was hearing about this project and your neighborhood. It seems that some people have a burr under their saddle about you folks."

"Yes, I suppose they do."

"I grew up on a street like yours, one also with a strong sense of community. I would not like to see that get crushed out of existence. I may not be able to do very much more for you folks though . . ."

"You have done a lot already, and I appreciate it."

The walk home through the still, night air was uneventful.

Connie answered the door. Silhouetted against the glare outside, she saw a tall individual.

"Your cousin Cynthia told me to return this when I was done." Jason held a silver tray.

"Let me guess – plums."

"Yes, and they were delicious."

The intervening silence seemed to be going for extra innings when she said, "Would you like to come in?"

"Oh, I'd love to, but I am afraid I would track a lot of sawdust all over your house. I've been repairing part of my roof."

She looked at him closely. "Well, you could just brush yourself off and not worry about it."

"OK. For a little while."

The front room seemed particularly silent, after the joyous din of the last time he had been there. They sat in two chairs with a small table between them.

It was an awkward moment for both. Each had inhibitions and reservations to work around trying to find polite conversation. Jason was well aware that he knew more about this woman than she might like, so he confined his statements to neighborhood matters, but she seemed to want to know more about him.

"So what do you do in San Francisco?"

"I am an industrial artist for Shaw and Ricchetti – I've been there since I graduated from college."

"Is that interesting work?"

"At times it is. Usually fairly routine. Occasionally I get to do a large rendering and so I feel that I am helping to present the project in the best light. It's usually not very creative, though."

"What do you do for creative outlet."

"I sing in the shower."

For a moment the skimpy attempt at humor went over her

head, but then a wry expression crossed her face. Jason decided then to be careful at making jokes with this woman if he saw much of her.

"How about you?"

"What."

"What do you do?"

"Oh, I used to live in Sebastopol for three years." Her brown eyes had a distant look. "Then I moved back here to stay with my aunt for a while. I just work in the variety store on Maple – nothing significant."

"Well, maybe things will look up." He smiled at her.

Jason didn't want to overstay his welcome so he let the conversation wind down, finally rising and muttering, "Well, the shingles call."

They rose and walked toward the door.

"Thank you, Connie." He wasn't sure what he was thanking her for, but it sounded right.

"Of course." She smiled faintly as the door clicked shut.

The grip of both men was strong as they shook hands. Carl Fish and Greg Tyson may have seemed unlikely friends, but friends they were, and each valued the years they had known each other. The contractor who had built or remodeled many of the homes in Ruskaya and the successful accountant had almost nothing in common but a love of golf and a respect for their differences, but these were enough.

Greg had been very supportive when his friend had called expressing a desire to address the South Wall Neighborhood Association. The conflict between the Turner Canyon residents and the City was just beginning to be known to more than the principle parties involved; the hope was to raise the level of awareness, if he could.

Carl was one whose actions spoke for him in much of life. A man of simple expression, he was not a strong public speaker, and he knew it. A personal, one on one conversation was more comfortable for him. On the few occasions when he was called upon to address a gathering, he would seek out a friendly face among the many and address his remarks to that individual, focusing his attention on that one person. On this evening he found a former client sitting in the middle of the group. He brought his energies together and started talking in a smooth, low-key voice to her alone. As he spoke, this woman, whose name was June, took in each word and fed back through her eyes the reassurance he needed to find the next word, the next sentence.

He told her about the history of his neighborhood and its sense of community, which his audience was sure to understand. All this, all could be gone if plans before the city were approved. He and his neighbors would loose everything, and a majority of the Council not only didn't care, but seemed to relish it. In the past, development had brought many benefits to the City, but in this case it seemed that it would only bring destruction. He mentioned no names, but confined himself to what "they" and "those people" were doing.

"If us this time, who's next?"

The audience was clearly restless, and one fiftyish man rose to ask, "It's so hard to know what is happening. How can we find out?"

"Almost all the Council's actions can be seen at the public meetings every other Thursday, but I have to make a confession. I never go. When I get home from a day's work, I just want to take a meal and wind down. Nowadays they televise all the meetings, and so I turn on channel thirty-three and let it run in the background while I go over some new plans or read the paper. Whenever something important happens, I turn the sound up. They are always up to something sooner or later, and often you learn more by watching how they do things than by seeing what they do."

A gentleman in the third row raised his hand.

"What do you think of the mayor?"

"Well, I might play a round of golf with him, but I would double check his score card."

The group's laughter did much to relieve the last of his initial nervousness.

"This fellow Howard Keller, what about him?"

"A very slippery customer. He has already offered to let me build some of the houses, knowing full well that my own would be torn down. Reminds me of a cobra offering a good view of his tonsils."

Another laugh and some scattered applause.

"What can we do."

The money question, the payoff for Carl's effort. He knew exactly what he wanted to tell the man. He ticked off the points with his fingers.

"Make yourselves aware. Those people think we don't know what is going on. Surprise them.

"Have an opinion – it doesn't have to be my opinion – just do the thinking to have one. They figure you are easily fooled and controlled. Disappoint them.

"Talk to other folks you know. Get them watching and thinking too. Those people downtown think they work under cover of darkness, that what they do is not seen, that nobody knows or cares. Make them wrong.

"Make sure to vote. In a few months we will have an election. The only thing those people are afraid of is getting their bell rung on election day. Give them reason to be afraid."

He paused for a moment.

"Those people have the power to make all the decisions so that they will look out for the good of all of us. If they don't want to live up to that responsibility, they should find another job."

As the applause burst out, Carl once again was pressed down by his nagging discomfort at standing before a group of people. Looking around furtively, he caught June's eyes once more. In them he saw the shine of approval, and the confidence crept back into him. *Not so bad, after all.*

The meeting drifted into refreshments and chit-chat for another half-hour before it broke up.

There was a distant, scratchy whisper for a few seconds, and the telephone came to life

"San Francisco Chronicle. How may I direct your call?"

Henry was pleased that he didn't have to negotiate his way through one of those atrocious automated telephone programs. Here was a real person.

"Michael Coursby, please."

"One moment."

The line clicked once and Henry heard the swoop of a busy hand whisking the phone from its cradle.

"Coursby."

Henry started to introduce himself, but this man already knew who he was.

"Roy called me this morning and gave me a head's-up. He briefed me on your neighborhood's problem. Could we get together in a day or two?"

"Of course. Name it."

"Say Thursday at nine o'clock?"

"Fine. Are you familiar with Highway 116?"

"Get up there all the time. Some great wineries there. What's your address?"

Henry gave it.

"See you then." The phone clicked again.

Henry had known enough city people not to be offended by this man's brusque manner. After all, he did have excellent taste in wine. Who knew, perhaps some good would come of their meeting. He made a mental note to call Roy and thank him.

Chapter Fifteen

The breakfast setting was the image of perfection. James and Evelyn McCanna had high standards for their morning meal, and this one appeared to achieve that level. The plates, their finest, were both arranged at the prescribed distance from the edge of the table, with the design in the centers perfectly level. Silverware, set with the ends of the handles in a ruler straight line, glistened in the shine of the September morning sun. Two glasses of crystal stemware, not yet filled, stood at attention in their appointed places. This was a shrine, a temple, not to be violated by imprecision, blemish, or fault.

The McCannas made their entrance together, fully attired. Exchanging their usual muted greeting, they assumed their places at the ends of the dark, oaken table. Beatrice, with a sense of timing conditioned by years of experience, waited carefully as they both settled into their chairs before presenting the first course, mixed fruit in small, crystal bowls. They both ate in silence.

At his subtle gesture, their servant glided to fill one of James McCanna's glasses with water, the outer one. A glance toward Mrs. McCanna yielded no sign that she wished the same, and Beatrice resumed her invisibility. As the Mayor finished the last of his fruit, she readied herself. He reached for his glass, taking one sip from it and returning it to precisely the same spot. As his right arm pulled back, she reached from his left side and removed the small bowl and spoon without making the slightest sound. An indistinct nod acknowledged the fitness of her performance.

At this instant, Mrs. McCanna indicated her desire for water, and her glass was filled. She had finished her fruit, but Beatrice hesitated for a second before taking the bowl. As she lifted it up, a sharp look from her mistress proved the hastiness of this unbid action. The Mrs. could be very particular about details and seemed to like to keep her servants guessing. Beatrice swiftly assumed the proper expression of humility and retreated to bring the next course.

James McCanna liked just one egg, soft boiled. He always removed the shell himself, and his plate contained the accustomed ham steak and hash brown potatoes. His wife would eat bacon and two eggs, sunny side up, which he considered barbaric, but at least she no longer put ketchup on them. They ate in silence.

Mrs. McCanna finished her meal, but her husband always left a portion of his ham. With a glance to Beatrice their plates were removed to be replaced with the morning newspapers. She read the Ruskaya View, a worthless rag in his estimation; and the San Francisco Chronicle was set at his own place. He opened it, arranged it tidily upon the table, and committed an unexpected breach of protocol.

"My word."

Evelyn McCanna was in a quandary. They never spoke to each other until after reading the papers. Should she respond? Was his remark even addressed to her? What could this mean? He then repeated himself.

"My word!"

She thought she saw an invitation.

"What is it, dear."

"Nothing, darling."

His tone indicated clearly that she had responded out of place. His remark had been an event out of the ordinary, ephemeral, like a lightning strike. It was something to be considered not a normal part of the routine, not acknowledged. He put her intemperate behavior out of his mind and read the article highlighted on the front page of the Chronicle. It was about Ruskaya Bend.

He quickly completed the single column on the front page and continued to page fourteen, reading each word intently. His wife thought for a moment he seemed to tense, but she could not be sure. Finishing the article, he stared out the window with a look that she had seen before, but not often. Presently he would tell her what it was all about. He didn't share everything with her, but surely he would pause to explain this matter. Perhaps it was the stock market or some international news, a war perhaps, a disaster. He would tell her what she needed to know. He always did.

James McCanna carefully folded the newspaper into its original form and put it into his left hand. Rising from the table, he paused before saying, "I'm going to City Hall, dear." He left the room without another word, and soon she heard the car going down the driveway.

Mrs. McCanna sat for a while with the briefest of smiles resting on her face. It was disappointing that their usual time for small talk was avoided so inexplicably. Married life had its occasional disappointments, to be sure, but it was all so . . . abrupt, and she didn't dare respond to it in any way. Ah well, she would find a suitable distraction and forget about these irregularities.

She shrugged and raised her spoon, tapping on the side of her water glass to summon the servant.

Clink, clink, clink, clink.

Summer was sweet in Ruskaya, blessed by sun and water. The town was far enough from the sea to be largely untroubled by the coastal fog common during the first half of the year, yet not far enough to be blasted by the heat found in the coastal valleys farther east. A kiss of warmth and a cool afternoon breeze along the river made the climate ideal during the warm months, and many visitors came to enjoy it.

There were several beaches along the river; the longest and widest was on the south side of the great bend, called Battle Beach by the locals, although almost no one knew why. This and several smaller strands would disappear under high water during the winter, and the reappearance of the sand in spring was anticipated by Ruskaya's residents as a time of renewal. As the summer progressed, declining flow in the Russian River would gradually reveal more territory for the enjoyment of all, and by midsummer each square foot was anxiously coveted by the abundance of visitors. As late fall brought reappearance of the seasonal rains, the rising flow erased ever greater arcs of sand from the public domain. Tired of fighting for space, many would glance at the sun which was lower each day in the southern sky and reluctantly surrender their beach activities to the cold weather to come.

To Bob and Ann Hurley, a summer afternoon at the beach still had a trace of magic in it, and for their young son Brian, it was a time in paradise. The family had lived in Ruskaya for only three years, and their sentiments were shifting from surprise and delight at exploring something new to the comfortable joy of familiarity and appreciation. In truth, Bob might not have chosen this town to live in, but for Ann it was an immediate selection. They both had lived all their lives in San Francisco, and when their child was newborn, a quieter environment to raise him seemed preferable. After driving through most of Marin and Sonoma Counties, they happened up highway 116 from the coast and crossed the bridge into Ruskaya Bend, and this was the place. Ann considered it a "delightful village." Visits to real estate agents and inspections of available houses led them to a ten year old home in an area called The Meadows, just east of the center of town. The portion of this area north of the river had attracted them because the roads and lots had been laid out to preserve a number of huge oak trees. Their new home had one of these in the back yard. They set up housekeeping.

Bob still worked in San Francisco as an accountant and commuted each day. During the week his irritation at "road time" would gradually increase only to ebb away each Saturday as he relaxed on his patio, reading the newspaper. At these times he would think, *Yes, she was right about this place.* The tranquility was beyond price, Ann could devote all her time to her home and family, Brian was in a good preschool. There was truly not much to complain about or to doubt. Then one Saturday afternoon he was reading lazily through the newspapers which had plopped on his porch that morning. He had started with the San Francisco Chronicle and progressed to the the Ruskaya View. Here he noticed a letter to the editor describing a development proposal sited down the river from his own home. Something about the letter caught his eye.

The Hurleys had never been politically enthusiastic, and Bob was not yet registered to vote in this his new town. For years he had only gone to the polls when he was displeased at the leadership or the philosophy he saw in the halls of power. The rest of the time he considered his indifference to be a tacit vote of confidence. Ann was socially active, the PTA and a Church group, but largely shared her husbands brand of stand-off political activity.

The letter described a continuing conflict between a small neighborhood and an ambitious developer who had strong backing from the City Council. On the whole it was written in an even handed fashion, presenting the pros and cons of the project; but at the end the author recommended it not be approved due to the high social and financial cost. Bob was intrigued by it.

He knew the area proposed for development, a steep, pine covered slope above the cliffs north of the center of town, not quite visible from his own home. Normally he was indifferent to development – after all, some developer had built the home he lived in now. But something in this article troubled him. He was thinking about learning more on this matter when Brian ran up to him with a broken toy in his hands and a furrowed brow.

"Fix it, daddy!"

Thank goodness for superglue.

J ason was perusing the bi-monthly report from the Canyon water district. It had come with a check for one hundred seven dollars and some change, a substantial sum considering that he had used a good portion of his allotment over the last sixty days irrigating the yard. Moreover, flows were naturally lower at this time of year, and the previous rainy season had been on the scanty side. *Not bad*, he thought. *I used all the water I needed and got paid for it.* He considered for a moment the individuals who had secured this blessing for him, one of them his own father.

The report had the particulars – average daily flows, average percentage purchased by the City, description of maintenance on the reservoir and valves. All very well presented. *Looks like Dee's work.* He was scanning the second page when there was a knock on the door.

Cynthia was right on time. Friday afternoon, four o'clock.

"Hiya, Jason. How's that rogue cat?"

"Up to the usual. I want to say again that I appreciate you taking care of him like this. It takes a big load off my mind."

"Not at all. Sorry about the shower curtain last time."

"Oh, they're cheap. I trussed it up over the bar this time so he can't do a repeat. And I wanted to tell you about the dry food. I had to find another place for it because he started pulling open the cupboard door and helping himself. He seemed to think it was lots of fun to pull out half the bag and spread it all over the kitchen floor. It's now closed up in the upper cabinet to the right of the sink. The wet food is a failure; he hates it so much that he will spend an hour trying to scrape up enough dust off the floor to bury it. And be sure to keep his water feeder full . . ."

"Hey, I know the drill. I've done this four times so far with no complaints from His Majesty. By the way, where is that scamp." With this she began to make a soft clicking sound with her tongue.

Presently, with a swagger that would befit a leopard, the object of their conversation made his appearance. Trying his best to look as if he had not been summoned, he slowly made his way to stand before them, stretched, and began to claw up part of the carpet.

"Jason, I've been thinking. The name Crash – it just won't do. Too stereotypic, too limited, too . . . improvised. I've been thinking about something better for him." The cat sat on his haunches and looked intently up at her.

"Have you now."

"Yes. At first I came up with Jacob, and its a good, strong name, but it is a name for an old man with a beard. He has stripes, but Tiger is so clicheic, so taken already."

"So?"

"I'm working on it. He needs a dignified name, one to clear the space out around him, one to tell the world what he is about."

"I thought he already had a name like that."

She shook her head. "That's a kitty name – I will think of something better. But in the meantime, don't worry about him. He'll be fine." She stroked the now-adoring feline under the chin. "Are you going to spend all weekend with Trixie?"

"You mean Tracy?" Cynthia assumed a wry look at this correction. "You know I am."

She issued an exaggerated sigh. "Well, have a *terrific* time."

Jason let out a mild chuckle. She never missed a chance to take a subdued shot at his "would-be urban hottie." He had quickly learned that there was something very determinate about this young lady, much like her grandmother, and likewise shadowed by a truly compassionate approach to life. He found it easy to tolerate her casting aspersions on his ladyfriend, knowing immediately that it was not motivated out of jealousy.

"Tell me, Cynthia, are you a registered manipulator, or just an apprentice?"

"Who, me?" She looked around for something to change the subject. "So, are you actually reading that water report?"

"They send me money; I think I should pay attention."

"Aw, that water district ruined everything. When I was a kid, we used to have a flowing stream all year round. There was a place behind old Mr. Ferguson's house where some of the local boys and I used to dam up the water to make a swimming hole. On a hot day we would just throw off our clothes and jump in. It was great! Tons of frogs and mud. Good times, but they're gone now. These days they sell the extra water to the city, and the creek is dry except during storms." She made a puffing sound. "Progress."

"I don't imagine you could get away with that sort of thing now, at your age."

"Oh, sure we could. Old man Ferguson's eyesight has gotten really bad. He wouldn't even notice us."

He looked at her for a moment and then they both broke into laughter.

"Well, now." There was an keen look in her eye. "Have a great time in the City. Don't think anything about this cute, little house in a beautiful neighborhood or your cat who misses you or the many neighbors who like you. Don't let those thoughts cross your mind. Just dwell on what's-her-name as you walk those dark streets surrounded by cold-hearted strangers. I am sure you will be fine. I know you won't get mugged or run over by a bus. Have a *wonderful* time."

"Tell me, when was the last time your father gave you a spanking?"

"He never did. He couldn't catch me."

Chapter Sixteen

Howard Keller was a man who knew how to strut. The agenda for the September twelfth meeting of the City Council had his geological report as its third item. Let them try to stop him now! Negotiations with Halley, Merrick, and Davis had been more lengthy and expensive than he had anticipated. They clearly didn't appreciate a man's timetable. Those thieves! He had spent nearly six weeks haggling over a price for a report that he had already paid for! But now, all was well. He had all his ducks in a row, the council was smiling, nothing would stand in his way. Even though that Carella woman and a half dozen of her followers were in attendance, his disdain for them was conspicuous. What could they do now? Even though they didn't look particularly disconsolate, his own aura of self satisfaction could hardly be ignored. He resolved to savor the moment.

Dee had briefed her clan about what was likely to happen – Keller's report would be accepted and they would move on to planning the attack on the development proposal itself. They could afford to relish a small victory because two months had been ground up in Keller's backtracking to have a report accepted which should have been dealt with in one meeting. Two months. Less than that amount of time remained until the election, and she knew that some members of the Council would be feeling the heat. The three up for reelection would not want to leave an unpleasant controversy as the last thing in the minds of the voters as they went to the polls, like a tin can tied to the tail of a dog. They would be playing it carefully from here on out. The Mayor, in particular, would have an assortment of negatives to overcome. Some of his tactics had resulted in critical scrutiny, his attitude toward the general townspeople had not been well received. He had accumulated harsh evaluations which he would need to overcome. He would certainly have to be very cautious. Yes, Dee liked the potentials; the line up seemed good.

The meeting began in an unpresupposing way, roll call, minutes, the consent calendar. Howard Keller turned around in his chair to survey the crowd. The first item was presented, debated and passed. The second was continued for lack of a report from staff. Mayor McCanna's commanding tone smoothed all ripples as he called for the title of the third item to be read. The City Clerk had hardly completed her task when Keller was up out of his seat and at the microphone.

"Ladies and gentlemen of the Council, Mr. Mayor. This is a moment long overdue. If it weren't for the silly, obstructionist tactics of an unimportant minority, this report would have been accepted long ago."

His cocky attitude seemed to make some of the members of the Council uneasy, a fact which Dee noted carefully. She looked up into the upper corner of the hall to the left of the Council dais. She could see clearly the red light on the video camera. *This guy is great!*

"I would urge you to do the right thing now and vote to approve this geological report. I don't know what anybody could say against it."

With a sweeping gesture, he turned to regain his seat, glowering at Dee and her little band. The Mayor called for anyone to speak in opposition, and Dee rose and proceeded to the podium. She did not speak against the report, instead concentrating on the larger issue of the development proposal. She weighed and timed her statements carefully since she was not speaking to the point and could be cut off by the Mayor at any time. She made a brief mention of her neighborhood and pointed out the public cost to validate a private speculation. As the Mayor started to reach for his gavel, she recommended that the Council reject the report and sat down. The public discussion was closed.

It was clear that the Council was in no mood to spend much time debating this matter. Laura Goetz raised a few procedural objections which were batted aside. The motion was to accept, and seconded. The vote was four to one.

Howard Keller immediately rose to thank the Council,

basking in the steady light of victory. Dragging the moment out for more than it was worth, a mild gesture of impatience from the Mayor cut him short and he scuttled off, oozing smugness.

Dee and her little group retired to the Plumb Branch to lick their wounds and contemplate the next battle. She did her best to lift their spirits. He has the big hammer, she told them, so they would have to spend a lot of time dodging. Yes, he has taken another step, but a costly one. With each victory he will have to sacrifice time, money, and favor. We cannot destroy the man, so we must chip away at the ground he stands on, making his position more and more untenable.

"The approaching election will start to dominate the Council's thoughts. All three incumbents will be called upon to validate their past performance. The Mayor particularly will soon start walking with a limp."

"What?"

"From the hot iron we are holding to his feet."

Their laughter convinced Dee that they had gotten over the result of the Council vote.

"Remember, the election is the key to preserving our neighborhood, and the election is not about whether the Mayor is a good leader, or whether four units per acre is better than five. Nothing like that. It is about whether a man like Howard Keller can blast his way into a town like ours and demand a reward for destruction. Men like him are their own worst enemies. We just have to encourage him to do what comes naturally, being obnoxious and demanding. The Council will be more and more reluctant to support such a man's ambition since they will have to live here after the dust settles, justifying their decisions to their neighbors. The only thing politicians consistently fear is the consequences of their actions. We have that high ground to work from. Each day the public scrutiny will become more intense – folks will be asking the hard questions of these people. Some of them should be about the Turner Canyon community."

Several of her group were smiling.

"Are you game?"

She knew they were.

The article in the Chronicle made quite a splash. The business community loved it since it never hurt to have your town so prominently mentioned in a major newspaper. The article was lengthy and detailed, and Roy Butler put free copies of that week's Chronicle on a stand outside his offices next to his own newspaper. Michael Coursby had dug deeply into all aspects of this controversy and presented each side, characterizing it as a David vs. Goliath struggle. The Turner Canyon residents were delighted at this portrayal. Who had ever rooted for Goliath? Most of the members of the City Council were shown possessing the wisdom of Solomon and whose prudent judgments would determine the future of Ruskaya Bend. Since the article didn't preclude their deciding either way, they wrapped themselves in the mantle of authority and tried to look important. The only one of them who was not so sure was the Mayor himself. Yes, it was even-handed, and yes, it didn't put undue pressure or attention on him, but it wasn't according to his plan. The townspeople found the attention bestowed upon their little community to be flattering, even though many of them had not heard of the issue at contest before. The only person actively displeased about the article was Howard Keller, and he was spitting mad.

His whole methodology was clandestine manipulation. He knew from hard experience that the fewer people who know about his program, the better the chance he would have to win the day. The article did not present him as a rapacious destroyer nor the Turner Canyon residents as ditzy tree huggers, but it was all much too much attention for him. Too many eyes, too many voices. It would take weeks for this to all die down. Bah!

Jason read the article while he was in San Francisco for the weekend. Tracy was not interested, but he read it all with interest. The depth of the turmoil which he had inherited with the house was made very clear to him, and a sense of disquiet enveloped him. His was one of the houses which Keller's plan would destroy even though he would be compensated for it. Yet he had grown comfortable there. He did not express his thoughts to Tracy who was busy planning the day's activities. He realized that he had almost no one in this city with whom he could share his feelings.

Bob Hurley had started to read the article with great interest, and soon Ann had joined him, reading over his shoulder. Of course, they were pleased with the publicity and surge of notoriety for their community, however brief it might be, but soon they began to discuss the larger issue. Bob often formed opinions quickly but had learned over the years to respect his wife's slower and more methodical style of contemplation. Many times her insights had opened up his eyes and allowed refinement to his own thoughts. For a half hour they discussed the various points in the article, not developing any strong convictions when finally Ann made a suggestion.

"Let's go for a drive."

They had to cross two bridges to find Turner Canyon. The first led from their own community to the larger, southern portion of The Meadows. Turning right on Highway 116, they progressed through the center of Ruskaya and crossed the river again to find a small diner at the divergence of a lane leading northward into a box canyon. Bob was surprised that he had passed this intersection many times and never noticed the side road. They drove slowly up past small, well-kept houses, and in front of one, on the power pole, was a large, hand painted sign which had a crudely drawn heart and words which advised:

SLOW
Caution Please
Kids
Dogs
Cats

As if to punctuate the advice, a large, brown dog was sleeping directly in the middle of the street. As they drove carefully past him, he stretched and turned over. Ann noticed that this was a community of large trees, like their own. Several grand oaks were interspersed with others which seemed to be fruit trees. Gardens were nicely tended – many homes had no perimeter fences giving a very open, integrated feel to the area. A few children passed them, walking down the street. After about a quarter mile, the road ended at a turn around, and just beyond it they observed a large water tank painted green. Reversing course, they passed slowly down the street, stopping in front of a yard where a woman was watering her flowers. She was tall, with black hair turning gray, and wore a long, flowing dress. There seemed something very distinguished about her. Through the open window, Bob called out to her.

"Excuse me."

She looked up and smiled at them.

"Could you tell me – is this Turner Canyon Road?"

"Yes, it is." Bob thought he detected a hint of an accent in her voice. "Are you looking for someone?"

"No, not really. We are just out sightseeing, an afternoon drive." He thought it best not to mention anything about the article, and then, as if to explain their presence, he added, "We live over in the Northern Meadows."

"Yes, a nice area." She looked into the back seat and met the soft, blue eyes of Brian who was mounted in his baby chair, taking in the conversation around him intently.

Ann, warming to this woman's dignified manner, leaned forward and added, "You have so many magnificent trees here, just like where we live. What type is this one here?"

"It is a Santa Rosa plum, planted over a hundred years ago. A pity you didn't visit one month ago. I could have offered you some of the fruit."

"That's a very kind thought."

The woman nodded and smiled.

"Enjoy your day's excursion."

They took their leave and continued back down the street.

The dog had risen but remained in the same spot in the center of the road, sleepily eyeing the few passers-by. As the Hurley's car approached, he barked several times but stopped as they pulled up even with him. Then he snorted and wandered off the roadway to recline carefully under an ancient ceanothus bush, still keeping an eye on the passing parade of life, barking occasionally.

"Tough job," remarked Bob.

Ann laughed with him at this.

M ayor McCanna's drive to San Francisco was as unpleasant as he chose to make it. He never liked traffic, especially in the City, and the usual approach to the Transamerica Tower was always congested. At last, his car was in the parking garage, and he was in the elevator rising to the thirty-fourth floor. A few moments later he was in the waiting room of A & D Enterprises, a campaign management firm with a strong reputation of success at engineering the election of conservative candidates.

"Mr. Mayor, David is ready to see you now."

James McCanna was always a man to hire the best. Of course, he had a nominal campaign manager in Ruskaya Bend, a hapless confederate from the Chamber of Commerce, but he could not trust his campaign to him. Politics was not a game for amateurs; it demanded top flight talent, professionals with their fingers on all the switches. David Horving and his firm were reputed to have the drive and ability to get the job done, seasoned with a measure of unscrupulousness. He had better get it done – for all the money McCanna was showering on him.

"James. Good to see you." The view out his window expanded across the city up to Coit Tower, and beyond was San Francisco Bay.

"David. You said you had something to report."

"Yes. We have back the results of our most recent polling effort . . . and the results are varied."

McCanna looked vaguely impatient and shifted in his chair.

"We have assayed a fairly broad sample, some five hundred likely voters, and you have a lot of support in certain segments of the community. However, we have uncovered a few negatives, not major, which I believe we can overcome. Tell me now, you televise all the City Council meetings?"

The Mayor indicated that it was so.

"Well . . . " He smiled broadly, the same look a parent has trying to convince a balky child that a bitter medicine will be good for him. "I have arranged for a . . . presentation coach to work with you."

"A what?"

"We thought your video impact might need a bit of refinement. Some of your strongest negatives have come from citizens who have watched the Council meetings."

"And this clown is what . . . an acting coach?"

"Well, James. He does advise actors occasionally. Some of our best clients started out as actors." The scowl on McCanna's face steadily grew deeper. "I am sure his suggestions would prove very useful to you."

The Mayor looked as if he had tasted something unpleasant and was wondering whether to spit it out now or later. Shortly he made a gesture as if brushing away a fly.

"All right, you want me to smile more at the Council meetings. What else?"

"Well, it's really a bit more than that, but I am sure you will be benefited when you meet with our man Nate. Further, I think we need to generate in the mind of the voters an image of you as the man of the people, a man with the common touch. Have you ever used the name Jim?"

"Not since I was in nickers," snapped McCanna.

"James is a good name, to be sure, but you might consider using the nickname when you are introduced. It will make you seem more one of them."

The Mayor didn't like where this conversation was heading.

"You are still going to all the forums and neighborhood association meetings, aren't you?"

"Yes."

"Good. Never overlook a chance for exposure, and chum around with the folks, admire their children, find out what they do, things like that. Some of the feedback we have about you paints you as, well, cold and distant. You can turn that around."

"So you want me to kiss the babies. What else?"

"We want to portray you as indispensable to the continued well being of Ruskaya Bend, a working mayor, one who tirelessly serves the public. You know, a dedication ceremony or two would work wonders."

"Baby kissing and ribbon cutting. What else?"

"There is one other matter . . . What is this Turner Canyon business?"

At this the Mayor snapped to attention.

"What . . ."

"Turner Canyon. We got a lot of feedback on this one item, not much of it positive for you. Is there something going on there?"

"Oh, just a development issue. A bunch of loudmouths, really. They received some press lately, but I am sure it will die down soon."

"Let's hope so. This one issue cuts across all the demographics, and convictions are very strong on it. Whatever you have to do to smooth this one over should be done."

He leaned forward.

"James, I have to be frank with you. Its nip and tuck. The voters right now are forty-five to forty-five with only ten percent undecided. That's not a lot to work with, and clearly you have to make some strong moves to firm up your win."

"But what are you supposed to be doing? What have I hired you for?"

"We continue to run adds and endorsements in your local paper." He listed the points, one by one. "We have mailers going out every other week. The billboards and placards in shop windows are appearing. We will be manning a get-out-the-vote effort on election day. We will be doing everything but cranking the voting machines by hand. But I am telling you that no mistakes should be made at this point. You have to firm up your base and go on to win over the ones who are vacillating. You have the bully pulpit. Make a grand gesture, a stunning announcement. A lot is within your power to obtain.

"But I'll tell you this," he concluded with a flourish, "I am confident of our victory."

McCanna looked the man over carefully. *All polish,* he decided. *Not a fool, but too much the cheerleader. Probably the first to allocate blame when something goes wrong. Oh well, better lame advice than none at all. Turner Canyon . . . damn those people. Why don't they just roll over and play dead.*

"Well, David, let's make it happen."

Both men rose and shook hands. As they moved toward the door, the advisor added parenthetically, "Stock up on plenty of coffee for election night, James. There are a lot of newly registered voters, and the count should continue until early morning."

"Great. That's all I need." McCanna neither drank coffee nor stayed up past ten o'clock.

"And I will have Nate . . . our coach . . . call your office to set something up."

"Fine."

The door clicked shut behind the departing Mayor. *What am I paying this idiot for?*

Chapter Seventeen

Carl Fish and his brother Jim were made of the same cloth, but the cut was very different. They were both grandchildren of the depression – their parents, Jacob and Irma, had grown up during that terrible time, had felt the want and tasted the despair. Even though the bad times had gone, they tried to pass along to their sons the benefit of their struggles in Brooklyn, tried to express the range of potentials that life could inflict or bestow. Both sons heard the stories and took them to heart, but the manifestation of this wisdom was as different within them as fire and water.

Jim tried to make the most out of life while he could – and that was now. He lived well, perhaps better than he should, driven by the fear that it could all be taken away. Carl saw the future not with an undercurrent of dread, but as a page to be written by someone provident enough to have put away a pen for that purpose. He had tried to instill his perspective and philosophy in his children, with some success, and now as his grandchildren came of age, he spoke to them the words his long dead parents had left him: "You cannot assume that life will always be as you see now. You must prepare for any eventuality."

On this day his granddaughter Sharon would have her twelfth birthday, and Carl had two presents ready for her.

The route to his daughter and son-in-law's home took Carl eastward on highway 116. He drove three miles past the center of Ruskaya Bend to the intersection with Ruth Hill Road and made the turn north to enter a narrow valley. Two miles farther along and he turned into their driveway, passing down a lane fringed with large, evergreen oaks. Crossing the bridge over a small creek, now dry, he came to a stop in front of their home, a ranch-style house on a small rise. Sharon had anticipated his arrival and answered the door.

"Grandpa!"

As in many families, the bond between alternate generations was strong, and especially so for Carl and and his granddaughter. Of course, her younger brother Lonnie loved his grandpa also, but it was more a relationship of shared fun. With Sharon there was something special.

"You took so long."

"I was delayed at home, but you knew I would come. Did you save some cake for me."

"We didn't touch the cake."

"Didn't blow out the candles yet?"

"No. We waited for you."

Entering the dining area, Carl greeted his daughter Carrie and her husband Damon. He liked his son-in-law well enough, but the man always seemed a bit reserved toward him. Carrie assured him that was just his nature; her happiness with him spoke well for the man, and Carl was satisfied with it.

Lonnie was yelling a string of inarticulate syllables as he ran by, but the boisterous "HI, GRANDPA!" was unmistakable. His mother settled him down enough to allow Carl to offer his present before the whole family.

"I hope you like it."

The gift was an instant hit — a gorgeous handkerchief of pure silk, decorated in a blue and gold pattern, colors to match her hair and eyes.

"It's so slippery."

"That's what real silk is like, cooed her mother. "Like a gentle breeze woven into a fabric."

"It's wonderful, grandpa." She hugged him with surprising strength.

Accompanied by Lonnie's growing impatience, they lit the candles, and with great style, Sharon blew them out. At last they were all served.

"I have something else for you." Carl's subdued tone implied secrets to be shared, and his granddaughter stole away with him to the covered patio.

"The scarf is for good days, happy days, days when the sun

shines fully on you; and I hope you will have many. But for the chance of a cloudy day when things don't go so well, I want you to have this."

His hand passed across hers and something heavy fell into it. It was a small, velvet bag of deep blue color. She looked questioningly into his eyes and knew that she was to open it. A golden coin slid into her hand. The side facing up had a woman with a peculiar hair style on it.

"Darling, once this was the money that people knew, and you can see that it says twenty dollars on it, even though it is worth far more than that. Nowadays people are content to pass pieces of paper back and forth and call it money. They all smile and nod and tell themselves that the paper has value, but you will notice that they rid themselves of it as fast as they can. Maybe it will never occur, but someday the paper could fail us and return to what it really is. If that ever happens, this gift may be what sustains you.

"This is actually the twelfth coin like this that you have; the other eleven were given to your mother on each of your birthdays for safekeeping. Now she will show you how to put all of them into a safe place to use if you ever need them. There will be more as you get older.

These are not for something frivolous, but only as your last resource. I hope you can live your whole life and never have to sell them, but we don't know what the future will bring, and you should be prepared for anything."

"Does Lonnie have coins like this?"

"Yes. Seven so far, but he probably will not get them until he is fifteen or so. You have shown me that you are ready now."

She turned the shiny object over in her hand and felt the satin coolness of it. As Lonnie came roaring through the patio imitating a jet liner, Carl noticed that she swiftly palmed the coin and he felt gratified by this. They walked over to the window seat and sat down.

"Grandpa."

"Hmm?"

"I was reading the newspaper and there was an article

about your neighborhood. It said they were going to take your house away. Is that true?"

He tried to appear unconcerned, not wanting to instill in her the anxiety he sometimes felt.

"Oh, somebody wants to try that. My neighbors and I are fighting it, and I think our chances are good."

The look in her eyes told him that she would need more reassurance.

"They can't really take my home away, not without paying me for it. And remember, I am a contractor. If it comes to it, I can lift my house up and move it to a new neighborhood."

"Yes! You could move it here. We have lots of room."

"True, but then I would loose something they would not have to compensate me for. They can take away my choices. I like my neighborhood and the people who live there. We have been together a long time and think of each other as family. They could take that away from me."

Sharon was silent for a long time and then said quietly, "I think you should fight them. What can I do to help you?"

He hugged her close. "Oh, dear one, just having you on my side makes me ten times stronger."

Sensing that her concerns were allayed somewhat, he quickly moved to another subject.

"You know, there is something I would like to ask you. You've heard that your grandmother died two months before you were born, so you never had a chance to know her. Your parents were kind and thoughtful enough to name you after her to honor her memory."

"Yes, I know. She was Sharon too."

"From time to time I have wondered whether you have ever disliked having such an old fashioned name."

"Instead of what?"

"Oh you know. What are young girls named now – I don't know which ones are popular these days."

"You mean a name like everybody else has already."

"That's one way to put it."

"I like my name. My friends call me Sher, which is cool.

But at school, there is only one Sharon, and it's me. I don't mind being different." She slipped the coin back into its bag.

How much she was like her, he thought, not physically but in temperament. Spunky, just like she had been. Self assured. He saw life flowing through both of them into the future, and it gave him reason to be assured.

At this moment Lonnie blasted into the patio chasing a radio controlled racecar. He seemed intent on crashing it into everything he could find along his course, squealing with glee at each collision. Sharon assumed a mildly disapproving look.

"He's such a child."

There was an unmistakable tone in the voice of Gene Ryan's wife.

"Oh, Brace."

Councilman Ryan's wife was one of few people who called him by this particular nickname. The original form had been "Curly Braces", in description of the outrageous muttonchops he had sported during his years at college. Gene knew that his wife Lucinda would either be in an impish, playful mood or in a demanding, argumentative one and he prepared for either eventuality.

"Yes, hon?"

"That fellow McCanna called earlier for you. I think you could give him a ring."

"Alright, I will."

He knew that Lucinda didn't like the Mayor, considering him a stuffed shirt. Gene himself thought the man to be a bit overbearing, but as a member of a team, he was expected to play along. After all, McCanna had helped in his campaign.

"It's probably about that Turner Canyon business." She seemed particularly animated. "You know, it was in that article in the Chronicle. It's a shame about those people. It doesn't seem right."

Lucinda would never presume to tell her husband how to vote on matters before the Council, but she did have the knack of leaving a few firm opinions lying around.

"I am sure that the City will continue to develop," she went on, "but is this the best that can be done? It seems so heedless. What if something like this happened to us?"

Gene knew better than to try to counter any of the points she made – it wasn't required, and it wouldn't do any good.

"And that fellow Keller. He seems very unlikeable, at least the times when I've seen him on channel thirty-three. What's your opinion of him?"

He was surprised that she handed the conversation back to him. Usually she talked around the subject, wrapping it up tight and dropping it into his lap. He cleared his voice.

"Oh, he is pretty much as you see him."

"Well, why does he hate those poor people so much?"

This was not the usual type of conversation about politics he was accustomed to having with his wife. Typically, he would hear her out in silence and then go downtown and do what he had to do. He decided to seize the moment.

"I don't think he actually hates them. His attitude seems to be more like . . . say that you are driving down the road and, going around a curve, you have to stop because a piece of wood has fallen off a truck. What would you think about it? You just get out, you move it to the side of the road, and you drive on. You don't hate that wood. He doesn't hate those people; they are just obstructions to be pushed aside so he can move on. He doesn't think of them as people; they are just objects in his way."

She looked at him unblinking for a moment.

"Gene, would you vote for this man's project?"

She never came so close to trying to determine his political actions.

"To tell you the truth, I don't know yet. In a way, it would be good for the City; but in other ways . . . Lucinda, I have to leave office two years from now proud of what I have accomplished. I am not sure I could be proud of this. I just don't know."

They had never talked so deeply about any political matter before, and Lucinda sensed that she should leave off and allow him to reach his own decision in his own time. The rest of the conversation was about more mundane matters, but each knew that the other was still thinking about their previous discussion. He had a thoughtful look on his face as he left to return to work.

T he phone jingled. For a moment Dee considered letting the answering machine take the call, but thought better of it.

"Dee!"

"What is it, dear?"

Laura Goetz and Dee Carella had been on good terms for a number of years, though not often seen together lately. Dee knew that her friend would always keep her apprised of the latest underhanded doings at City Hall.

"It's on. He will present his project at the Council meeting after next."

"Well, I have my work cut out for me. Tell me now, have you seen it on the agenda listing?"

"It is item number three."

"What is the chance that this is a fake-out? Do you think that the purpose is to lure us down there in numbers only to have the item pulled at the last minute?"

"For demoralization purposes? – not too likely. Howard Keller is thrashing like a speared fish, angry that it isn't on this week's agenda."

"Alright. That will leave only five weeks before the election. Can they actually run it through in that time?"

"Ordinarily, yes. He seems to have the votes, but I have a few ideas . . . "

Chapter Eighteen

Returning to San Francisco for the weekend, Jason requested a meeting with Peter Shaw. He knew that this would be the man to present his idea to first.

"It's good to see you again, Jason. we've missed your presence here."

Peter was the business end of Shaw and Ricchetti. He negotiated the contracts, handled the finances, and interfaced with the City. He laid the tracks that the train ran on, but John Ricchetti was the man who kept the machine running. He handled the personnel side, good at schmoozing with the crew on coffee breaks, encouraging the best out of everyone, and keeping everything on an even keel. If Peter had been less wise a man, he would scarcely have appreciated his partner's contribution to the success of the firm, but he had seen how prosperous companies can easily fly apart without the social glue which John Ricchetti provided.

Jason would have to clear his request with both partners, but an approval from David Shaw seemed to have priority.

"I've missed being here. I had taken for granted the great work environment."

"This place you're fixing up – it's where?"

"Ruskaya Bend."

"Oh yes. I've been there. A nice, small town. Great scenery around there."

The pause following encouraged Jason to get to the point.

"Peter, I know my leave of absence is almost up, and I really need to get back to work, but things are not wrapped up with the house in Ruskaya, so I was wondering . . ."

"I have a room I could set up as an office and work there. I would not be able to take on quite the workload as I could if I were here, but nearly. I could put in four days a week on projects and that would leave three for finishing up the house. I have a broadband internet connection now, and we could be in close communication. Of course this would just be temporary."

Peter rubbed his chin thoughtfully with a finger.

"You know, this sounds very plausible." A sudden recollection played across his face. "Kennison Associates has an all distributed workforce now. Everyone produces out of their homes. They just maintain one office and a fancy conference room downtown for impressing the clients. No more commuting, no parking problems, much less overhead. Hmm. Well, I like the idea, but we will have to run it by John and see what he says." He rose from his chair smiling. "Let's go find him."

Presently they were in the corridor, tracking down John Richetti by the peal of his laughter. He was a big man with a laugh to match and he knew exactly how to work humor into the day's routine, stopping someone in the hall to tell a joke and then asking how the project was going. He was a master at keeping everyone upbeat and busy at the same time. They found him in the coffee room, and he listened in silence as Peter laid out Jason's proposal. John immediately liked the idea.

"You will be our first virtual employee!"

"Not virtual exactly, more like remote."

"Of course, but you must come to all the office parties, my boy. We can't be without you, and you must bring your ladyfriend, what is her name? Stacy?"

"Tracy."

"Yes. Bring her."

For a man of his lifestyle, John Ricchetti was extremely thoughtful and kind toward women. Perhaps because his own position was secure. He and his life partner had been together for fifteen years, and he no longer saw women as the competition. Although he never could remember her name, he seemed to honestly like Tracy, engaging her in long conversations in which Jason had no part.

"Of course I will."

"Then it's settled. My goodness, you will be our first long-distance employee."

"Yes, but not for long. As soon as . . . "

"Don't you worry about it. Everything will resolve as it should. In the mean time . . . mocha?"

Tracy was not happy. Her glum expression exactly counterbalanced the encouragement Jason had just received at his workplace.

"I thought you would be back here by now." She could maintain an elegant pout when it suited her.

"Tracy, I need to earn some money. The house is requiring far more than I thought it would. Because the roof leaked, I am going to have to replace nearly all the lid inside – that's the drywall on the ceiling." He could see that she didn't want to hear the particulars.

"I thought this would be over by now. When can you put this all behind you?"

"Hopefully in November."

"November? That will be two months. What's supposed to happen then?"

"Well, there will be a City Council election and we are hoping that this development proposal and the moratorium will be resolved."

Tracy considered politics to be stupid and boring, a fit subject for discussion only by old men playing liar's poker on the weekends, but there was something else in his statement which bothered her. Originally Jason had referred to the people in Turner Canyon as "they." Now it was "we." She shook her head as if she could make it all go away.

"I thought you were going to rent out that house."

"It is in no kind of shape to rent yet. I thought I explained how much it needed."

Tracy considered construction details to be almost as boring as politics. The conversation devolved into uncomfortable silence. Jason tried to distract her with questions about her job and friends, but she was having none of it.

"Jason, I hope you are right, that everything will be back to normal in November."

"That is what I am working toward."

"It just seems that I don't have anybody anymore."

"Tracy, I still love you just as much, and I miss you each minute, but sometimes we have to make a small sacrifice to have a better result in the end."

The look on Tracy's face gave a strong hint that this was not what she wanted to hear.

"That sounds like something my father would say. He just sacrificed and sacrificed and wound up with nothing in the end"

Another silence prevailed, darkening the mood further. Finally, she spoke in a low tone.

"I don't usually wait for things to come to me, I just go and get them. But if you say that everything will come out right before too long, then I will try to be patient."

"That is all I ask." He embraced her in reconciliation, and if there was a slight stiffness in her response, he put it out of his mind.

When Jason returned from his weekend in the City, Cynthia was full of excited narrations of his cat's exploits. According to her, he was brilliant, probably telepathic, and he had hardly broken anything at all. Then she assumed a serious tone and announced that she had a new name for him.

"Oso."

"What? You mean "Bear"?

"Yeah, but Oso has more punch."

"*Creia que no te gustaba el Español.*"

She scowled at him. "Oh, I like it alright, but I just don't speak it."

"Oh, well. Yes. Oso. Hmm. Punch. I see what you mean."

"Oh, shut up. If you don't like it . . ."

"I like it. It only seems right. Crash was his kitten name and now that he is a mature cat, he deserves an adult cat name."

"That's what *I* said."

"I know, and you're right. Oso it is from now on, but what if he doesn't respond to it?"

"Did he respond to his old name?

"Good point."

There was a round of smiles between them when Jason changed the subject.

"Cynthia, do you mind if I ask you a personal question?"

"I might. Are you going use the answer to blackmail me later?"

"No, its not that kind of question. I was wondering – I know you speak Spanish, but why is it that you don't like to?"

She paused before she answered.

"It's all part of that Hispanic thing. I don't go for that."

"Yes, but you are Hispanic, aren't you." Immediately he could see that these were innocent seeming words that had a sharp edge for her. Her voice hardened in a manner which surprised him. It was as if he had been the one to throw one too many rocks into the volcano, and it was going to blow.

"I don't have to like it." She looked toward the door as if she might presently bolt through it and up the street, but she stood firm. "You don't know how it is to live in a society where everyone is beautiful but you, where you are the ugly duckling, where kids make fun of you because you don't look like them. And don't give me this stuff about how Salma Hayek and Penelope Cruz are doing OK. I don't get to walk in their shoes. I have to go to that crummy school and put up with those crummy people."

"Do you mean the people at your quinceañera. Those boys who fought to dance with you didn't seem to hold you in any particular disregard."

"They have to like me. Most of them are relatives. The rest are all *chamacos* and they can't effort to set their sights too high."

"You sell yourself awfully short."

"It pays to be realistic."

"But I was dancing with you too."

"After I pressured you into it."

"Oh, that was just part of my hard-to-get act." He could see that this conversation was not having the desired effect. He continued in a lower and less frivolous tone.

"Let me tell you something, Cynthia. You merely provided me with the opportunity to do something I hesitated to ask for. I felt privileged to dance with the most beautiful woman there, which was you."

"How can you say that?"

"Because I know something you don't know yet. Let me see if I have this right. You look into the mirror and do not see blond hair, blue eyes or fair skin, so you imagine you cannot be beautiful."

Her expression told him that he had reached a sentiment very deeply buried.

"A man I have come to think of as very wise told me that beauty is something you have to achieve, and not anything you can inherit. As long as you look at your reflection and assume that it isn't beautiful, you will be right. You will make yourself so. If you look at what you see and say, "oh well, that's not so bad," it's a different world.

"The main thing is that you cannot renounce your ancestors. They made you what you are."

"Oh yeah? You renounced your own father and wouldn't speak to him for ten years."

His expression told her immediately that these were words that cut deeper than was appropriate, and her hand moved to cover her mouth as if to punish it for its indiscretion. He took a long time to respond.

"I am not proud of that. I acted out of the passion of the moment and I regret it. I don't know how to make amends for it now – the chance for it has passed. That fact doesn't change anything I have told you."

They both looked at the floor for a long time. She broke the silence.

"Do you really think I am pretty?"

"Absolutely. In fact, if you were two years older, your father would probably send a *dueña* along whenever you came here."

"Come on now. Have you ever dated a Hisp . . somebody

like me?"

"Sure.   For two years I lived with a girl named Silvia Cortez. I used to tease her that her ancestor conquered Mexico, an assertion that seemed to make her rather angry."

"So what happened?"

"Oh, you know. Things don't always work out. There was talk of marriage and kids . . . "

"Let me guess. She was yes and you were no."

"Actually, the reverse."

"Oh."

It was at this moment that the newly christened Oso showed that he had not quite grown out of kittenhood. With a clattering roar, most of Jason's pots and pans hit the kitchen floor. Jason's call had more than a slight bit of irritation in it.

"Crash!"

"Now, now. Try this," Cynthia counseled. "Oso, come here," she cooed in tones which would calm any feisty creature.

The renegade cat shortly poked his head around the corner from the kitchen, the very picture of innocence. Jason just shook his head and looked exasperated.

M ayor McCanna held the phone receiver in a sure grip as he stabbed at the numbers. Len Williams would need some guidance; the Mayor would call in some chits.

"Hello."

"Len. James here."

They exchanged the pleasantries, and the conversation drifted to the agenda of the upcoming Council meetings. Len expressed his concern that the bid for the proposed relining of the old sewer mains might be a bit high. The Mayor felt that the Housing Committee report was in order. The Planning Commission would make a presentation on some such matter. And then there was the point of the conversation.

"You know, Len, that important business will come up at the meeting after next. Howard Keller will present his subdivision proposal, The Cliffs; and I hope you feel that this project is as critical to this town as I do."

There was no immediate response, and Mayor McCanna tried to fill the vacuum.

"The growth of the town is our responsibility. We have to be sure to broaden the tax base where we can."

"Yes, James. But this project has attracted a lot of publicity and has become controversial. It no longer seems to be such a simple matter."

"Len, I am sure you have nothing to worry about. I was able to pull you on board two years ago. Your position is secure, and a project like this would be to your credit when you face the voters again."

"I wish I thought the same, James. There is a lot of talk. People are actually paying attention to the issues this time, asking pointed questions at the forums. You have had to face some of them."

"People will settle down once they realize the eventuality of progress; they will see that the Council is elected to make the right decisions."

"But that is the rub, isn't it. How can one make the right decisions if one is not reelected? I am sorry, James, but it is not such a cut-and-dried matter for me. I am as pro-growth as the next man, but this project is a bit hot right now, and I think that both of us should be cautious. Perhaps some sort of compromise would be in order."

"Len, there is a time for compromise, but this is not yet it. There is a deeper issue that you should consider. We both were on the Council when the arrangement with the Turner Canyon water district was worked out. You saw how the City was humiliated by that Brandt fellow. I believe that it is up to us to make that right. This project provides the leverage we need to redress that indignity."

McCanna knew that a proud image was one of Len Williams' main preoccupations. Even though the final terms of the agreement had been fair, they both remained chagrined at how they had been handled by these "peasants". The promise of revenge was a sweet inducement, and the Mayor did not need to press the theme far.

"Hmm. I think I see what you mean. Yes. Now that you have explained it from that perspective . . ."

"Can I count on you?"

"You can, James. Yes, you can. See you Thursday evening."

They said their goodbyes, but the Mayor was already thinking of his next few calls. Len Williams was an automaton and he merely needed to be aimed in the right direction. The others might be more difficult.

He punched furiously at the buttons on the phone. As it rang, he endeavored to arrange his thoughts. What could he promise; what could he threaten.

"Hello."

Chapter Nineteen

All had to agree that it was a magnificent parade. It started with clowns and jugglers and ended with the presence of the candidate himself, James McCanna. The marchers in between began with young lads carrying declarative banners exhorting the crowd to return the Mayor to another four years of service. A well equipped brass band was next in the retinue, blaring the USC fight song as graceful majorettes deftly worked their magic with batons which seemed to float on air.

A group of local matrons dutifully followed the band. They seemed a bit worse for wear considering the heat, but they were game in their plastic, imitation straw hats emblazoned with "MCCANNA" in bright, red letters. A sound truck came next, and a syrupy voice praised the candidate to the skies, with volume that could rival a commercial jet taxiing for takeoff.

The praetorian guard followed, three of Ruskaya Bend's finest on black motorcycles. From time to time one of them would thrill the crowd with a blast on his siren. Last came the august presence himself.

James McCanna stood upright in the back seat of a vintage, beige Cadillac, looking every bit as splendid as a Caligula or a Domitian wending their way in triumph through the streets of Rome. He basked in the pomp and cheering of his supporters.

A crew on foot worked the townspeople, handing out election literature and offered a few well scripted sound bites, intended to uplift the faltering, sway the undecided, and embolden the supportive.

It was a grand parade.

As the Mayor progressed down River Avenue and turned onto Main Street, he saw an abundance of hand-held signs, alike and professionally made, which prompted all to "Reelect the Mayor". McCanna liked what he saw and commended the choice of colors, which had been his own. He nodded and smiled and waved to the applauding citizens standing on the curb as he passed, but he noticed something which gave him brief pause. Although the throng of supporters was eagerly standing forth, a nearly equal amount of people stood away, backed up against the walls of the offices and shops. These did not cheer, nor did they enthusiastically take the campaign offerings. They stood silently and watched the show passing by. James McCanna glanced them over but then put them from his mind, raising his hand to salute the folks standing curb-side.

The Mayor's wife sat at his side, admiring his style in relating to the crowd. He was master of the nod, the smile, the gesture to his admirers. He knew how to bring them close and keep them at a distance at the same time. As with the wives of many powerful men, she was sure that her thoughts and actions resulted in all his successes, and his failures were due to his own initiative. She graciously acknowledged the groundlings like a modern day Theodora, hoping that the parade would soon end so she could get out of the heat.

Since the area in front of City Hall was so limited, the parade snaked its way to a small park in the center of the town. This was dominated by a large rock outcropping resembling a featureless, gray building surrounded by a ring of grass and bounded by a circular roadway. Here the show reached its logical culmination with a rousing speech from the candidate. He roared, he cajoled, he assailed the hapless crowd with a myriad reasons why they should reelect him. Ruskaya Bend had entered a new age with his leadership and must continue in its triumphant, upward march. No one else had the foresight, the experience, the flair to carry the burdens of power.

Each word and phrase echoed off the nearby buildings, giving an eerie, staccato reverberation. The Mayor was in his element, stroking the multitudes with an expert hand, using fear, anticipation, elation, and promise to mold them like putty.

At his last, exultant utterance, he bowed his head, offering his heart and soul to the populace, and the assembly of almost three hundred individuals went wild. What a parade, what a speech, what a day!

Afterward as he tended to some paperwork in his office, Mayor McCanna listened to the occasional footfall in the corridor outside and the murmured words passed back and forth between staff members discussing work related issues. The silence crept in to envelop him as the afternoon's enthusiasm slowly morphed through a mood of somber contemplation and then into resolve.

He must not lose. He must not lose.

Dee heard the distant phone ring once, twice, and in the middle of the third ring a familiar voice was on the other end of the line.

"DelOstro here."

"Patrick. This is Dee Carella. How are you?"

"Just fine, my dear. And how are you?"

Councilmember DelOstro had usually been open and frank in his discussions with Dee. He didn't seem to bear any rancor for the results of the negotiations which resulted in the City buying water from the Turner Canyon residents. In fact, it had always seemed to her that he had secretly admired how Ted Brandt had gotten the best deal for his community. Several times she had seen him go against the Mayor in close Council votes; perhaps he could be encouraged to do the same when the decision was made on Howard Keller's project.

Since Patrick was one of the three Councilmembers running to retain his seat in November, Dee considered that he might want to be careful about making any controversial decisions just before the election. The key here was to find the right angle of approach. Just like reentering the Earth's atmosphere from orbit, too flat an angle and you will bounce off, too steep and you will burn up.

They passed an appropriate length of time chatting about inconsequential matters and town gossip, and then she came to the point. Dee apprehended a mild level of reserve from the tone of his response.

"Dee, you know I can't really discuss how I might vote on a

matter which has not yet been formally presented to the Council."

"Of course, Patrick, and I would never expect you to do that but I was hoping you would weigh all aspects of the project before you make your decision, with particular emphasis on the economic ramifications for the community at large."

"Go on."

"I feel that the benefit to the City will have a very high price tag; perhaps it will be too high. In your professional capacity as an accountant, I would hope you would look at this project as an investment that the City is considering making, with costs and benefits to evaluate carefully."

There was not any immediate response, but Dee was encouraged by this. All she could hope for was for him to consider the issues presented. A snappy retort, a quick offhand phrase in rejoinder would indicate that no thought was taking place and that there was no opportunity for further persuasion.

"Dee." His words came slowly. "I would like to offer you more, but at this point all I can promise is that I will look deeply into all aspects of this project and vote according to what I think will be best for the City in the long term."

"Patrick, I could not hope for more. I have confidence in your judgment."

For a few more moments they passed the time in innocent banter and then bid each other goodbye.

Dee immediately punched out Laura Goetz' number. She would need to consider the next few steps with an insider. The noose was definitely drawing tighter, but whose neck was inside it?

J ason had accepted Dee's invitation to a strategy session at Aurelia's house with some hesitation. This would be the primary planning session for the opposition to Keller's project, and he was not sure his presence was appropriate. Not that he favored the project, but his official stance was that he was just passing through, not going to stay, firmly intending to return to San Francisco as soon as possible, and that local doings didn't have lasting relevance in his life. However, he had completed the rendering he had been working on, he had no good book to read, TV was a bore, and further, his neighbors were pleasant company. If he had nothing significant to contribute, at least he could do no harm.

Dinner came and went. Crash, now used to his new name of Oso, spent fifteen minutes opening and letting clang shut the kitchen cabinet doors. This went on until Jason roared his disapproval and gave chase, with the perfidious cat retreating to the safe zone of the bathtub. When Jason passed out through the front door he noticed the cat knocking objects off the living room table.

The walk up the street was pleasant enough. A stimulating perfume drifted on the breeze, the strong smell of sagebrush and pine. He paused for a moment to compare this aroma to the smell of sizzled car tire and three day old garbage so usual in the City. Of course it wasn't always like that, but . . .

Aurelia opened the door, but it was Cynthia who gave him his greeting. Moving swiftly across the room, she smiled and put her arms around him, embracing him firmly and unhesitatingly. He felt disposed to respond, but carefully due to the curious and surprised looks on the faces of her family. He raised his hands and placed them gingerly on the middle of her back; only then did she release him. As she pulled away, Jason saw bright highlights, reflections of the porch lamp, shining in her dark eyes.

The hand of Luis Morales was in Jason's as he stepped up to welcome him.

"I am so glad you could come, Jason. I think you know most people here. Dee, of course, and Henry. Have you met Carl Fish?"

He made the acquaintance of several other neighbors not yet introduced to him, and in each case the name of his father was the key to an immediate, positive response. There were about thirty people in attendance, most of whom he knew already.

He noticed Connie where she had been standing along a far wall. The look in her eyes was enigmatic but her demeanor was friendly. She smiled and acknowledged his presence with a nod.

The meeting got under way.

Dee gave a brief synopsis of the project with particular emphasis on the access problems and the number of houses which would have to be destroyed to improve the roadway. She outlined the qualified success she and others had obtained in lobbying members of the Council.

"Right now, the vote is too close to call, so we will have to dig down and throw everything we have at it."

"Isn't there something rare on the property?" Bob Henley spoke up. "You know, an endangered species, or something?"

"I'm afraid not," responded Henry. "There is nothing up there but pines, a few oaks, squirrels and a handful of rattlesnakes. The only really rare bird around here prefers more shade and lives on the other side of the valley."

"Well, what can we fight them on?"

"We can raise doubts that this is really a good deal for the City", he continued. "No other development in this town has required the destruction of so many homes to provide necessary access. The development of my grandfather's entire farm required removal of just one old structure."

"Yes, how could they consider doing such a thing?"

"Unfortunately, there are people on the Council who think that our homes would be worth nothing. To them, this whole neighborhood is a slum, hardly worth the fuel for the bulldozer to knock it down."

"Isn't part of their attitude because of that water thing?" Ruth Frazee was quick to see the motives behind people's actions, good or bad.

"I believe it is," Dee continued. "We saved their bacon, but every month they have to pay us for water they hoped to steal. Those sharp business types were bested at their own game, and they've never forgiven us for it, especially James McCanna."

"So what can we do?"

"We have one great thing going for us, the article in the Chronicle which Henry got printed."

"Oh, wait a minute. Michael Coursby and Roy Butler had the most to do with that. I just answered a lot of questions."

"You held your end up pretty well, Henry. But that article

brought the whole issue out of the shadows into the bright lights. The Council cannot just make a decision in a cloud of smoke and pretend nothing happened. The heat is on, and we have to keep it on."

A multitude of nods greeted these words.

"Will letters to the editor of the View do any good?"

"They certainly will. Roy has promised to print any letter on this project, even if he has to put on another page per issue. Of course, he has to represent all sides, but . . . " Henry developed a conspiratorial manner and half whispered to the group. ". . . he told me our contributions should be to the point, not overlong, and numerous. He will do everything he can for us."

"What about the forums, Dee?"

"Yes. Perfect. They often televise forums, and the only thing more revealing than an honest and damning response to a pointed question is an obvious evasion. Either one looks bad."

"Aren't some of these groups holding forums likely to be on Howard Keller's side. The League of Women Voters will be pretty even handed, but the Civic Association would be a tough bunch for scoring points on McCanna."

"They have to let you speak. They will at least pretend to be fair. Use whatever you can get. If they try to shut you up, the TV audience will see this, and you will look as if you are being manhandled by the guy with the gavel."

"Dee, the way you talk, this is all image and presentation."

"You're right. It is ninety percent image and ten percent substance. You saw that parade that McCanna just ran off – it was one hundred percent fluff. If you try to talk substance for too long, you will put your audience to sleep. But if you say: 'Look what they are trying to do to us. Could you be next?', you have an image which may stir somebody to get out and vote. Most people don't, you know. If you add: 'Who does the Council work for – all the people or just one out-of-towner?', you might just get them to vote our way. It may be a sad indictment of our system that most people vote as an emotional response, but it is what we have to work with. We should make the most of it."

As Jason listened to this discussion, he came to see the

strategy clearly. It was political guerrilla warfare at its best. These people could never hope for a knock-out punch when Howard Keller and James McCanna had such strength, but they could hope to prevent that strength from being used. A dangerous game, but one with a chance of success. It was as Dee had been saying all along – they were playing for the election on November fourth. If the Council had the effrontery to pass the project before then, all was lost. What could be done to forestall that vote?

As the meeting broke up and he took his leave, Jason was enveloped in thought. Cynthia didn't hug him again, which was probably just as well, but Luis shook his hand and thanked him warmly for attending.

He walked back down the street with Carl Fish, and partway home, they came across a large, brown dog who barked briefly at them but seemed to recognize Carl. His muzzle was flecked with gray, and his stride betrayed a touch of arthritis in his hindquarters..

"Dodger, we call him. Nobody is really his owner. He just wandered in five or six years ago and set up camp. Several people put out food and water for him, but he doesn't live in their houses, preferring to sleep under an oak tree. Somebody put up a lean-to so he would be dry during rainstorms, but that's it for creature comforts. Nobody enters this canyon without attracting his notice."

"I've seen him before. He is a big dog. How is he with the kids."

"He loves them. When Edie, down the street, had her son Nick a couple of years ago, almost the first thing she did was to introduce him to Dodger. They're great pals now. Nick rides him around like a horse."

"Why do you call him Dodger?"

"That's because he usually spends his days sleeping in the middle of the street, and everybody has to drive around him."

As Jason laughed at this, the dog looked into his face and barked once. Then, turning away, he strode down the canyon to resume his station near the head of the street.

"He just figured he belonged here, I guess."   Carl's

assessment reminded Jason of an old expression.

"*Hic manebimus optime.*"

"How's that?"

"Oh, something said a long time ago – it's in Latin. It means, "Here is the best place to stay.""

"Hmmm. I like it, but I don't think Dodger knows any Latin."

With a good laugh they shook hands and parted for the evening.

Chapter Twenty

Howard Keller had a way with a telephone. He displayed the same grace that could be seen in the sure touch of a concert pianist. After all, he had spent most of his professional career working a phone as the office manager of a large financial establishment. He could use the instrument to press, to entice, to badger, to cajole, to get what he wanted. It was merely a question of laying on the right strokes. He was in his element.

Today, though, not all recipients of his calls were quite as compliant as he would have wished. Qualified assurances stood in for the snappy conformity he was seeking. Hedging seemed to be the norm today. His disappointment had not yet risen to anger, nor persuasion to threats, not yet. It was more his style to present his case and give the other fellow a period of time to see the wisdom in his words. With any subsequent reluctance on a follow up call, he would bring out the hammer.

Of the Councilmembers he had contacted, predictably the Mayor was as positive as Laura Goetz was the opposite. Len Williams seemed inclined his way, but the other two were cagey and non-committal and seemed to have private reservations. Perhaps they were just waiting to see how the wind was blowing. The subsequent series of contacts was intended to generate some wind.

The heads of civic organizations, business groups, and neighborhood associations next received a call – for some a pep talk, for others a bit of fear mongering, for a few a portion of shame. He laid on each what he thought would make the point and draw another tentative supporter on board. He saw himself as working a bunch of rubes, each potentially with a tether around his neck; and the trick was to line them up, all pulling in the same direction.

Some individuals work objects to make their way in life and often they have a particular reverence for those objects. Howard Keller had always worked people, and over the years he had come to have less and less respect for them. A town like this was full of clowns to be whipped into shape. If he could convince them that it was for their own good, so much the better. No further regard need be expended on them.

It had not always been so for him, but each person is tested and conditioned by life's early disappointments, and his had served to harden him. The once easy smile had faded into a cold smirk. The casual glance had been replaced by the penetrating gaze seeking some weakness. Generosity had been supplanted by predation. At each fork in his path through life he had made a choice, and each choice had channeled his being into the man he now was. His character was certain but not sure, offensive and defensive both, implacable.

He had come to express just what he feared others might do to him. He saw his life as filled with the struggle against opposition which had to be overcome for him to survive. He picked and fought battles initially for the thrill of a possible victory, but before long his primary impetus would devolve into fear of loss, fear of injury, fear of failure. His wife had known his secret dreads, the vacuum which filled him at times. She had tried to give him a sense of security and satisfaction in her life with him, but she had died ten years before and left him to stagger on, carrying his private demons as they slowly ate away at him, replacing his substance with their own.

He had become the hand which grasped the phone and the voice which demanded support.

He dialed another number.

The steering committee was putting the finishing touches on the format for the upcoming candidates forum to be sponsored by the Ruskaya Bend Civic Association. Their unanimous intent was to showcase James McCanna and his accomplishments, to minimize any negativity, to shrink wrap the whole affair, sanitized and contained. Their aim was to provide a springboard for the Mayor to vault into a successful second term, for which he would be very grateful subsequently.

But just how was this to be accomplished? One member suggested that the audience could be filled by invitation only, allowing them to pick all the right people. This plan was soon abandoned when it was pointed out that holding a forum in City Hall, a public building, precluded that sort of control. Bit by bit, a plan evolved.

As was traditional, each candidate would be given a brief period to address the audience and state his or her qualifications and accomplishments. The Mayor would be given the final position so that his words would have the most lasting effect. Then, the moderator would ask of the candidates a number of carefully selected, presubmitted questions. These would have been filtered in advance to remove any potential mudballs aimed at the Mayor, and as much time as possible would be taken up by this period of controlled questioning. It was deemed risky to prohibit any questions directly from the audience, so toward the end of the forum, with little time remaining, a brief period of audience participation would be allowed. Since the Civic Association would be taping the event, it would be simple to perform any necessary editing before the video was released for broadcast.

There were smiles and congratulations all around as they voted unanimously to accept the format. This would put their man over the top, they all agreed. It was all in the packaging, and they had the right wrapping paper. Their confidence buoyed them up as they adjourned for the night.

B ob Kelly was chosen to be the moderator for the forum for his no-nonsense, firm handed approach. From the outset he knew that he had his work cut out for him when a substantial group of Turner Canyon residents strode in and took a position in the first few rows. All mentions of The Cliffs project had carefully been removed from the list of questions he would be asking the candidates, but he knew this bunch would be trouble if he let them. It didn't take long for them to make their first move.

"REMOVE MCCANNA" read the banner which two of the Canyon residents spread across the back wall just before the forum was to start. Kelly glared briefly at them and made a move for the microphone.

"Excuse me, before we begin, all campaign banners will have to be removed from this room."

Dee immediately jumped up.

"What about those signs?" She pointed to several "McCanna for Mayor" signs held up by supporters.

"Uh, those are not campaign banners."

"Then, what are they?"

"They are . . . public service announcements."

The peal of laughter at these words was an unpleasant surprise for the moderator. Dee waited until it died down of its own accord before continuing.

"They do endorse a particular candidate for office, just as that banner does. Shouldn't they be subject to the same rule?"

Bob Kelly made no reply but drew back to consult three other man on the podium behind him. He returned to speak into the microphone with as much composure as he could manage.

"This meeting will begin in three minutes." And then, almost parenthetically, "All candidate endorsements will be removed from the room."

Dee regained her seat exultant. With almost no effort they had purged the forum of all visual cues which would have favored McCanna and at very little cost to themselves. The banner would never have been seen since the camera set up by the Civic Association was aimed to cover only the candidates, the moderator, and that portion of the audience which contained the McCanna supporters. Then came the next boil-over.

On a signal from Henry, Carl Fish and one of his nephews, a cinematography student, entered the hall with a video camera and set it up on a tripod near one of the side doors. From this angle they could easily pan the candidates and the most of the audience. Bob Kelly had his back to them but was alerted to their presence and turned to walk briskly toward them. Henry noticed the movement and hastened to join Carl. His friend was a good man, but not up to a sparring match. Kelly spoke first and seemed to be making an effort to keep his voice down.

"We will be filming these proceedings exclusively and we won't require another camera."

Henry had a habit of smiling just before he struck. He was smiling now – he had dealt with Bob Kelly before.

"Bob, this is a public meeting in a public building, and I am certain you don't have the authority to say who can and cannot videotape the proceedings."

For a few seconds the two men glared at each other, then Kelly turned away and retired to the podium. Nothing in his manner indicated that anything untoward had happened.

Most of the audience was unaware of this business, but Dee had been watching carefully and gave the thumbs-up to Henry.

"That's two out of two!"

As the forum began, the moderator guided the candidates through the initial statements. The order in which they were permitted to speak had been carefully chosen with first, third and fifth position going to candidates not favored by the Civic Association. This allowed each subsequent candidate to have the leverage to refute assertions made by the preceding speaker. At the end was to be the Mayor, batting cleanup. It was neat and tidy, and it went completely awry almost immediately.

Laura Goetz had been chosen to speak first so that her words would have faded from memory by the time McCanna addressed the crowd. It was supremely important that The Cliffs project not become an item of debate, and it was understood that speaking specifically for or against a project not yet submitted to the City could be seen as improper and prejudicial. After the usual preliminary discussion of her qualifications and accomplishments, Laura immediately launched into a brief statement of general development policy which might have sounded to some members of the audience like a denunciation of Keller's project.

She dwelled on the trade-offs to be considered for growth in the City, all on a purely theoretical basis. What if, she said, the gain from a development required a substantial material sacrifice on the part of some of Ruskaya's citizens. Was that truly a worthwhile gain? Was it really necessary to destroy in order to create? Should a responsible Councilmember be a party to such a result? The moderator winced as the audience leaned forward in their seats.

She left the matter unresolved, but the cat was out of the bag. All of the other candidates would find it hard to speak without making some pronouncement on development policy.

Patrick DelOstro was next in line and spoke calmly about his accomplishments during the previous four years. The crowd seemed to responded favorably to him and he continued after a sideways glance at Laura.

"General development policy has rarely been an issue during local campaigns although from time to time candidates have commented on specific projects already passed by the City." He took a deep breath. "I believe that each development proposal is like an investment decision which the City would consider making on behalf of the citizens. As a member of the Council, I would find it paramount to evaluate fully the costs and benefits of such an investment before voting on it."

The audience erupted into applause, and Dee was beside herself with delight. *"Patrick, my man!"* She knew that his statement was no assurance of how he would vote in the end, but it did indicate that he might be persuaded to go against McCanna. She enthusiastically joined the applause, and the moderator had to gavel down the crowd before the forum could continue.

The next candidate was Paul Covarrubias, a local merchant whose family had received one of the original Spanish land grants some eight generations before. He had an easy, graceful manner and was well respected in the community, even though he was a neophyte to local politics. He dwelled on his reputation and outlined a future of continued prosperity for Ruskaya Bend, not dipping deeply into specifics. He earned polite applause from the audience.

Ronald Hale was next at bat, and to Dee it seemed that this man was sitting on a tack. For two years he had been groomed by

McCanna for a run at City Council, holding a position on the Planning Commission. Never fully comfortable in front of a crowd, he rocked back in forth in his seat as he spoke, outlining in an irregular cadence his accomplishments of the past few years. Personally, Dee rather liked the man, but he was prone to buckle under McCanna's pressure and vote the company line. He made some vague pronouncement about how development had been good for the City and left it at that. The crowd seemed to share his discomfort, but he received a healthy applause.

Paige Lee was second last. Although new to politics, she had a considerable following, especially in The Meadows where she lived with her husband and her three children. Moving from San Francisco seven years before, she had started a successful gift shop and joined several civic groups, earning a reputation as tireless dynamo, ready to work on worthy, local causes. As a Chinese-American, she felt completely at home in an Anglo world, and talking to others, they soon were won over by this delightful, tiny woman. However, her best qualities wouldn't necessarily play well in the political arena, and to Dee she had represented an unknown quantity. She had held her own in the other forums, but her lack of experience had been apparent at times, and the other candidates had made her seem ill-prepared. Still Dee thought that she had shown promise but had to admit that this forum would make or break her candidacy.

Paige started slowly with a list of her accomplishments as a member of the PTA and charity groups, then she leaned forward and continued in a steady, clear voice.

"I may not have the wisdom or experience possessed by several of the other candidates. They started fresh and accumulated these qualities through their years of service, and I would hope to do the same. But there is one thing which I feel I could bring to the City Council as a part of my being, and that is respect. As an American who is a descendant of an ancient culture, I have been taught to maintain respect for those who have gone before me, for those who sacrificed to create the world I now enjoy. Since I have not lived in Ruskaya for very long yet, pretty much everyone was here before me."

This got a laugh from the audience, and Dee pricked up her ears.

"For those who have resided here over the many years, paid their taxes and contributed to the community with their good thoughts and good works I could only show my respect. I could not consider that their dreams, their lives, or their homes to be expendable. In the many decisions which would come before the City Council, this principle would be foremost in my thoughts."

The Turner Canyon residents stood up and cheered, and Dee noticed with satisfaction that Carl Fish's nephew turned the camera to pan the audience. It took a long time the Bob Kelly to restore quiet.

Then it was time for James McCanna to speak. It was a grand presentation which the moderator lavished upon the Mayor, full of superlatives and excess. As the lights reoriented to highlight him for the audience, Dee was heard to gasp. Both Carl and Henry turned sharply toward her to see what was amiss, only to observe a face filled with mirth rather than shock or distress.

"What is it, Dee?"

"He's wearing makeup!"

"Are you sure?"

"Positive. Rouge. Look at him."

For a moment the three of them stared in amazement at the Mayor, then all broke into raucous laughter. The commotion caught McCanna by surprise just after his name was announced, and he shot a hard look into the audience but the lights blinded him so he couldn't see the source of the laughter. He could only scowl and begin his assessment of his importance to Ruskaya Bend.

His oration was filled with self-congratulatory descriptions of his accomplishments, and when he reached the announcement of how he had "brought water to the thirsty city", the laughter from the Turner Canyon residents was unrestrainable. Dee observed with satisfaction that the camera once again panned the audience. Mayor McCanna's style was somewhere between a revivalist preacher launching a tirade against original sin and a bank president explaining the fractional reserve system.

"I don't know whether I should fall on my knees and confess my sins, run screaming from the hall, or take a nap," Henry quipped sotto voce to Dee who was trying hard to contain her own amusement.

The Mayor finished up with a flurry of hyperbole and sat back with a self-satisfied smile splitting his face. A generous round of applause erupted from the Civic Association membership and its allies as McCanna basked in the warmth of their praise. A few of the banned campaign signs reappeared briefly, but the moderator waved them down, cleared his throat, and launched into the question and answer portion of the proceedings.

It did not take long for the slant to be obvious to the neighbors from Turner Canyon. No question dealt with any controversy, and each was a softball lobbed for the Mayor to hit out of the park. The questions were so bloodless that even McCanna's supporters were quickly bored, the candidates gave listless responses, and Bob Kelly found that he was having some trouble dragging out the proceedings sufficiently. After a half-hour of this dry lip-flapping, he turned and with an look of dismay, expressed his predicament to one of the men behind him. This man passed his index finger across his throat in a quick gesture, and Bob Kelly turned to face the audience.

"Umm, ladies and gentlemen, that concludes this evenings forum presented by the Ruskaya Bend Civic Association. We hope that . . . "

"What about questions from the audience?" Someone wasn't intending to let them off that easily."

"Unfortunately, we leased this meeting hall from the City for a finite period of time which is nearly up. It seems that we won't have any opportunity for open questions."

Dee knew this was a lie. Having looked over the lease agreement, she knew they had nearly forty-five minutes remaining, but there was little to do about this maneuver but to grumble and accept it.

"So on behalf of the membership, let me wish you a safe journey home, and be sure to vote on November fourth." The lights came up, the candidates faded away, and the crowd piled out of City Hall.

On the walk home a dozen Canyon residents strolled through the city streets in the moonlight, discussing the evenings extravaganza. The emphasis was on sifting through the candidates to select the three which they could support. Laura Goetz was an easy choice, and Patrick DelOstro had roused a number to endorse him, but the third choice did not come as easily.

"The Mayor is still hopeless, and I think Ronald is just a McCanna clone."

"Paul is a bit too easy going."

"And we know almost nothing about Paige. What if she doesn't have what it takes?"

It was Carl Fish who broke the brief silence.

"I think I will vote for Paige Lee. She has human quality, and if you have that, you can remedy a lot of shortcomings."

Carl didn't speak very much, but when he did, all listened intently. The scarcity of his words seemed to give them value emphasized by the careful thought behind them. The neighbors looked at each other and nodded – they had their three candidates.

R ennie Hansen had a problem. Two video tapes had arrived presenting the candidates forum recently sponsored by the Civic Association. One was the production of the firm hired by the Association and it could only be described as "slick". From the title to the credits it showed the professionalism that only an abundance of money could produce. Its viewpoint was carefully controlled, highlighting the Mayor and his words. Several times it seemed that a laugh or an applause track had been inserted, and it was heavily edited. There was even theme music.

The other was more of a student effort, and clearly lacked the smoothness of the first. The label indicated that it was produced by Jamie Fish, and it had a few rough edges. Once someone had bumped the camera, and several times the cameraman could be heard talking with someone out of view, but the shots of the audience reactions and closeups of the candidates gave a depth to the work that Rennie liked. There didn't seem to be any editing, and despite its rough appearance, it expressed a liveness that the more professional effort lacked.

But what to do. As station manager the content of Channel thirty-three transmissions was up to him. The Civic Association had always been a strong supporter of the station, but the free-wheeling presentation by the Fish youngster intrigued him. Both productions were obviously slanted to emphasize a select perspective, and yet he had always tried to present an unbiased view of local news.

In the end he ran them both several times, one after the other. He was aware that young Fish's video made the other look staged, and the Association video made its competitor look crude, but he resolved to let the chips fall where they may and take the heat for it.

Over the next few weeks both videos were seen by almost everyone in town.

Chapter Twenty – One

The most important thing a City Manager could ever learn was to count to three. Three votes would put him in his position initially; a mere three supporters from among the five Councilmembers would maintain it for him in the face of all opposition. Convince any three of them, and an issue backed by the Manager could be passed or if opposed, defeated. Jeff Heit was supremely confident in his enumerative abilities, and they had allowed him to hold his position for twenty-four years, through almost two dozen elected Councilmembers who had come and gone like dry leaves blowing down the street. Three. No more was needed.

The Manager scrutinized a work order on his desk which outlined a minor storm drain project calling for the replacement of several inlet grates. He considered the company contracted to do the project, a firm which had worked for the City on several occasions. His signature soon flowed authoritatively across the bottom of the page. His attention then turned to the current agenda bill.

The consent calendar was fluff and should pass in a rush. Items one and two of the regular agenda were routine matters; the Council would gab for about fifteen minutes on each and pass them.

Item three was the Cliffs project, and this was Howard Keller's giant push. This should be the shouting match for the evening, surely not an issue to slip by uncontested. Three. Where would the votes fall? Recent publicity and citizen interest had made this a controversial item. Heads could roll over it. Lots of heat either way.

The Manager tapped his pencil on the desk. *Best to stay out of this one.* Often the weight which a powerful City Manager could bring to bear would make the difference one way or the other, but not tonight, not on this issue. Tap, tap, tap. Let the *Council stumble through this one. Too many unexpected and unpleasant after effects possible.* Tap, tap. *Hard to look good. Best to leave it be.*

The manager turned to consider an efficiency study done on the Building Department. It recommended the usual busy order of maneuvers: fire someone, shift personnel around, offer incentives and present threats, shake the tree again.

He turned the page.

Young Brian Hurley had a new toy. His parents were conscientious about not giving him an excess of playthings so that he would always appreciate what he had, and this gift had been joyfully received. "Odimus Prime" he called it, an eighteen wheel truck which would morph into a robot. He quickly learned to put it through its transformation, and it would sit next to him, in robot form, as he watched Sesame Street. It was fairly easy for life to be good if one had seen only three summers.

Bob Hurley needed a somewhat broader perspective. His family and his friends came first, of course, but he always tried to make the time to find out what was happening in the larger scene around him. This had often been difficult while Living in San Francisco. He scarcely had come to know any of his immediate neighbors in their apartment building on Sacramento Street, a busy, skittish people they had seemed. But moving to Ruskaya Bend had immersed him in a relaxed and open atmosphere where a smile and a hello came more easily.

Nonetheless, he was surprised to find that a neighbor and casual acquaintance was a candidate for City Council. Paige Lee and her husband Jon lived only two blocks away, and she was especially active in many of the same civic groups that Ann had joined. Bob had played a few games of chess with Jon and had found him a clever player who made few mistakes. Ann and Paige had hit it off immediately, and she had seemed to him a fit combination of levity and seriousness, but did she have leadership qualities?

Watching the video of the forum sponsored by the Civic Association had given him an important perspective. He saw Paige under the hot lights and in front of strangers, and she held her own. Giving thoughtful answers to all questions, she was calm when she needed to be and showed passion when it was called for. When he had seen her a few days later in The Meadows, he commended her performance and heard her confess that she had actually been "really nervous". He was pleased to tell her that it hadn't shown.

Shortly thereafter, he received a call from a polling agency wanting to record his thoughts on a few local matters. Usually he deigned to participate in polls, but since he had just registered and planned to vote, he was intrigued at the opportunity to express his opinions in advance, hoping he knew sufficiently what they were.

However, when he was asked in how many of the last three local elections had he voted, he answered truthfully – none. The interviewer bruskly thanked him for his time and hung up. Bob was a briefly disappointed, but soon was called to dinner and forgot the conversation.

Just after lunch with a depressingly enthusiastic supporter, James McCanna found a bit of unoccupied time to make a call to San Francisco. Outwaiting the automated phone system and one snippy secretary, he was at last connected with David Horving who glad-handed him over the phone. The expected pleasantries flowed back and forth between the men before they got down to the meat of the conversation.

"David, that recent survey . . . what have you to tell me?"

"Well, James, we have some good news, but your campaign has a few hurdles to clear before we can cross the finish line. The undecided are making up their minds, and you are harvesting your fair share of them, and your support with them is firm." Here he hesitated.

"But . . ." the Mayor prompted.

"Yes. It seems that your opposition is picking up a proportionate share of support." He paused again.

"And . . ."

"And the outlook has not changed materially. At this point the race is too close to call."

"You mean to say," growled the Mayor, "all this time, effort, and money down a rat hole for no result?"

"Well, James, I wouldn't say for no result. Uh, we have done extensive testing on the public's perceptions of you, and you score high in the esteem of many individuals. Leadership and executive bearing, for example."

The Mayor was gritting his teeth as the consultant went on.

"People seem to think that if something needs to be done, you are the man to turn to, and you have a core of support which remains strongly committed to you."

"Do you want to tell me why I haven't been able to convert these obvious positives into a run-away victory?"

"James, there is one issue, a thorny, little knot, which won't go away. It hangs over you like a dark cloud."

"Let me guess, would it be Turner Canyon?"

"Yes, James. There is some development project a man named Keller is pushing, and a lot of people are very stirred up over it. I don't know all the details, but this whole business is weighing down your campaign. For every potential vote you gain, you loose one other because of this one issue. I don't how else I can express this to you, but James, you have to put a lid on this one – postpone it if you can until after the election. Anything. Put the fire out. Your victory hangs on it."

The conversation trailed on over less distressing details of the campaign and A & D Enterprises' efforts to mold public opinion in McCanna's favor. They both made an effort to put the best face on it, but after hanging up, the Mayor grimaced.

Damn it! Damn that man Keller and his bull-headed approach to everything.

He knew that a postponement was no simple matter. State law required a public hearing of any application within thirty days of the City receiving it. A postponement would have to be approved by the applicant, and he certainly would never do so.

A continuation is possible . . . to obtain additional

*information . . . but for what? Some sort of demographic study?
No. Can't be geological . . . that's done already. Maybe an
infrastructure report? Perhaps. We have the necessary utilities,
but it could take quite a while to reveal that fact. Shaky, though.
Got to find something that would kill two months!*

He was running over the skimpy possibilities in his mind
as the intercom buzzed. His next appointment had arrived and
was waiting. Was he ready to receive a deputation from the
Chamber of Commerce? The Mayor fluffed himself up and took
command of his outward appearance. He had to give every
appearance of self-possession and authority.

He rose to meet them as they entered.

"**B**ut why can't you be here for my birthday? What
meeting?"

In these few words Tracy's voice rose from inquiring
through irritated to angry. The emotion poured into her as her
face grew flushed, and she spit out the last few syllables through
tightly drawn lips.

"I will be there, Tracy, but we will just celebrate one day
later, on Friday."

"WHAT meeting?"

"It's the City Council meeting I told you about. You
remember, don't you?" He knew surely that she had been told of
this meeting and its importance, and just as surely that she had
chosen to remove it from her memory.

"I don't see why you have to waste all that time up there –
they don't need you. You aren't even involved. Aren't you going to
sell that place?"

"Yes, Tracy, of course I am, but first I have to protect my
investment. I can't just walk away."

She was silent, scowling at the floor for a time. As he
looked at her, he wondered where the spark had gone, the warmth
he had known. Every relationship is put under stress from time to
time, and it is how the couple rides out these times of difficulty
that proves the bond. Tracy and he had met and overcome their

share of these rocky times, but now . . . at length she spoke, not looking up at him.

"Jason, if you can't be here . . ."

"I can be here, but we will just have one additional day in anticipation before we celebrate your birthday." The thinness of this remark was apparent even to him, but with some coolness she seemed to accept it.

"Alright, if that is how it has to be. Can we eat where I like and go dancing afterward?"

"Of course. Whatever you want. It will be your night."

He found it difficult to interpret the look in her eyes. Was it resignation, acceptance, or resolve. Tracy was a woman who was accustomed to obtaining her preferences as specified. The warmth of their relationship had made up for a lot of her demands, and rarely did he have to insist that a thing had to be done otherwise. But to all appearances she seemed to relax and accept his words.

Their weekend together unfolded pleasantly enough from that point on, dining together, talking intently about subjects that intrigued each of them, lovemaking. Another crisis in their relationship had been averted, Jason thought. Things would go better from here on.

H oward Keller had one more call to make. He huddled over the telephone as a raptor bird mantling a newly caught prey, trying to ward off prying eyes. The secretary quickly made the connection and a familiar voice was in his ear, the voice of David Horving.

"Howard, I was just going to call you . . . "

Chapter Twenty – Two

The City Council meeting was well attended – far too well to suit the Mayor. It was bad enough that he had been forced to endure a harangue in his office from Howard Keller, a corrosive exhortation full of demands, promises, and threats. When the Mayor had raised the suggestion of a postponement, the vehemence of the response had obliterated that possibility. Keller apparently had no perspective but his own – the fact that the Mayor might have problems to solve, an election to survive, was irrelevant. As he took the center seat on the dais, he noticed with some irritation that most of the audience seemed to be residents of Turner Canyon.

Embedded in the group were two local citizens whose presence was more the result of curiosity than passion or economic interest. Standing at the back of the hall near the door was Frank Wells, who felt that his attendance would allow him to give a better report to the Civic Association on the results of the meeting. Not far from him was Bob Hurley. His wife had planned to be present with their son, but at the last minute young Brian had run a mild fever. She had insisted that he go without her and that she would be able to watch the proceedings on the local channel. Both men felt buffeted by the currents roiling through the audience even though the emotions of the moment did not affect them directly.

The Mayor's mood was in a slow burn as he mechanically called the meeting to order. How was he to reconcile the diverse forces tugging on him? No sure way seemed clear. The other members of the Council couldn't help notice the snarl underlying his words as he guided the meeting through the consent calendar and the first two items. With perceptible acidity he called for the reading of the title of the third item.

The audience developed a restless edge as the City Clerk

complied. Will Hansen followed, reading the staff reports which described the project and its administrative history. Brief mention was made of "some access issues" that would have to be solved, and a wave of alarm passed through the crowd as glances and whispered words passed between the Turner Canyon residents.

The final point he covered pertained to Ruskaya Bend's slope/density ordinance, and the Planning Director was clear that the application was in violation. As the steepness of any property increased, lot size was required to enlarge, reducing the number of residences per acre. Howard Keller had submitted a plan which would have been suitable for flat land. A petition for relief from the ordinance had been filed with the City on the grounds that the applicant was being denied a substantial benefit granted to other developers. Strict enforcement of the ordinance would require a reduction of the number of units by one third.

At a nod from the Mayor, Howard Keller rose, turning his back pointedly to the audience as he spoke into the microphone. When he gave his address as Ruskaya Bend, someone in the audience jeered, "You mean Santa Rosa." A self-satisfied smile whisked across Keller's face as he anticipated the level of contest promised for the evening. After all, what was a victory without a struggle. Let them mouth off all they wanted, as long as they lost.

He continued, pandering to the Council with each word and phrase. They had the opportunity to lead the City into the future, and they alone could make the right decision here. They had the duty to expand the tax base responsibly for the benefit of all of the City's residents. This was the right project at the right time.

Someone behind him hissed. Unperturbed, he shifted into high gear.

"There has been mention of access requirements, but I tell you that often it is necessary to make sacrifices for the greater good and to secure progress. In fact, this is one important reason why you should approve this project as submitted. The additional density would counterbalance any minor losses which would occur."

At this point the audience erupted into boos, and the

Mayor was forced to use the gavel to reduce them to silence. The applicant smiled and fawned over the Council in his last few sentences and then regained his seat, exuding complacency.

After the murmuring died out, the Mayor called for any other supporters of the project to make their statements. He waited for a prolonged interval, giving every opportunity for someone to rise from their seat and make their way to the podium. A few members of the audience fidgeted and rocked in their chairs, as if they were preparing to rise, but no one did.

Suddenly Dee Carella stood up and walked purposefully forward to stand before the microphone, looking playfully at the Mayor and sporting a large smile.

"Ms. Carella, do *you* wish to speak in favor of the application?"

"Oh, dear me, no. But I knew that we could all grow very old waiting around for another supporter of this project to show up. I just thought I would save a little time since you have such a busy agenda tonight."

The laughter which broke from the audience was a much needed relief, and all present settled into a more relaxed frame of mind. Only James McCanna and Howard Keller did not share in the levity. The gavel came down abruptly as the Mayor barked at the audience.

"There will be a fifteen minute recess."

Dee turned unperturbed and marched down the aisle to rejoin her compatriots. She addressed their worried and confused looks with a reassuring calm.

"Don't let this bother you. He is just trying to break our momentum. Now, this is what I want you all to do when he reconvenes the meeting . . ."

Mayor McCanna dawdled for as long as he could manage. *Damn those people. I'm in charge here.* He stayed in his office for twenty minutes grumbling to himself and when he returned, he assumed the center chair with all the presence he could muster. Looking up, he saw Dee Carella already at the microphone with about eight of her neighbors in a line behind her. Glowering at them for a moment, he leaned forward to fill the hall with his voice.

"The meeting will come to order. Any individuals wishing to speak in opposition to the project may now address the Council." And then, motioning diffidently toward the crowd behind Dee, he added, "There will be only one person at the podium at a time."

"There is only one person at the podium. My name is Dee Carella, 247 Turner Canyon Road. It is my privilege to address the Council this evening."

Damn her!

"I wish to speak in opposition to this project and I urge you to vote against it because I feel that approval would not be in the best interests of the citizens of Ruskaya Bend. I also feel that granting it would create a bad precedent which would reflect unfavorably on the judgment of this body."

Dee continued, outlining in skeleton form the major arguments against the project. As they had planned in their discussions about strategy, each subsequent speaker was to expand on a single point, using the two minutes alloted to best advantage.

Second from last in the line behind her, Jason Brandt waited his turn to speak. He watched the members of the Council carefully as each neighbor expressed their opposition, looking for some indication of rapport. Two, Len Williams and the Mayor never met the gaze of the speakers, busying themselves with the papers in front of them or staring aimlessly into the audience. Two others, identified by their name tags as Laura Goetz and Gene Ryan, allowed the speakers a respectful gaze, the former obviously in accordance with what was expressed, and the latter at least making careful notes. The fifth member, Patrick DelOstro, seemed to look into the speaker's eyes or not as the point expressed influenced him. *This is the one to win over. Didn't Dee say that he was an accountant?*

The first speaker after Dee was a middle-aged woman named Marsha Cassell whom Jason had met at Cynthia's quinceañera. She gave primarily emotional arguments to support her opposition, speaking warmly of the longevity and historical significance of the community which would be squandered and the families which would be disrupted. She asserted that the development was not worth this human cost. The Mayor thanked her graciously as she sat down.

Henry followed and he paused briefly before he spoke, knowing that circumspection was called for. He was certain that one reason why some of the Councilmembers favored Keller's plan was to facilitate the demolition of a majority of the homes in Turner Canyon and seize the properties by eminent domain. This would make the City a majority owner of the water district and, tearing up the contract negotiated by Ted Brandt, all the water could be appropriated at no cost. This undercurrent, of course, could not be mentioned.

"Members of the Council. I am sure you are all well aware of the controversial nature of this project. The benefits to come to the City are marginal, and the costs would be great. If this were a routine matter, like the subdivision of an additional parcel from my grandfather's farm, there would probably be little to say. In that case, the gain for the City and its citizens would be obvious, and only a few gophers would face a loss. The central question here revolves around whether or not so many should have to sacrifice so that only one individual could benefit."

Jason noticed that Patrick DelOstro was staring intently at Henry.

"I don't envy you for the decision you will have to make on this matter. However the decision may go, it will likely result in a lawsuit. So I have to ask you: would you rather be sued by several dozen of your neighbors, or by him?"

At this he pointed toward Howard Keller who squirmed in his seat and assumed an expression of distaste. The applause from the audience was strong and lasted long enough to compel Mayor McCanna to restore order with the gavel. There were no thanks for Henry as he regained his seat.

At this point, after a sharp glance from Howard Keller, the Mayor resolved to slap down this insurrection before it could get established. His voice echoed throughout the hall.

"The item before the Council is a subdivision proposal. All

speakers will confine their remarks to that one issue."

"Excuse me."

All eyes turned to look at the Councilmember sitting on the far left.

"Excuse me. I would like to inquire about a point of order."

After an exaggerated delay, the Mayor finally deigned to acknowledge that someone had spoken.

"The chair recognizes Laura Goetz."

"Mr. Mayor, I have before me a copy of the staff report to the Council. It clearly states on page . . . what is it . . . yes, page seven that to provide lawful access even to a scaled down development on the subject property, Turner Canyon Road would have to be widened. On the next page it states that this improvement would necessitate the 'removal' of some thirty homes. Another reckoning puts that number at around forty.

"Since it is obvious that the project could not be realized without these demolitions, they are inextricably linked, and it would seem proper that both would have to be legitimate for discussion at this time."

"I would have to agree with that." Gene Ryan spoke quietly but firmly.

Mayor McCanna stared at the back wall briefly.

"Next speaker."

"Excuse me, Mr. Mayor. I would like a ruling from you on whether or not these citizens will be permitted to discuss any matter presented in the staff report."

McCanna had to think fast. The pungent aroma of potential lawsuits was already in the air, and the last thing he would need splashing into the news before the election was a civil rights action against him and the City.

"Mr. Mayor?"

"They will. Next speaker."

This time the applause was colored by a measure of laughter, the kind which comes from relief. As Jason approached the head of the line, he noticed that Aurelia and her family were all sitting in the second row. Several of them seemed surprised and pleased that he was waiting to speak. Outermost on the row was

Cynthia who whispered to him as he passed, "*Golpealo, guey.*" At this he covered his mouth, not wishing to appear inappropriately mirthful. Connie gave him a smile and a nod, and Luis did the same. Then it was his turn.

"Ladies and gentlemen, members of the Council, I am Jason Brandt, 215 Turner Canyon Road.

"I am new in this neighborhood, and I hope that will not be held against me. It is truly a unique experience to live in an area where longevity is measured in generations, and I believe that this continuity is to be cherished."

For an instant Jason considered mentioning his father's years in the community, but thought better of it.

"In most cases, the business of development is a cut-and-dried matter. The past must yield to the future. The community at large is to be benefited – this is the way of life. But in this particular case I believe you have a situation not of the normal cut. Further, I believe you do not have the information at your disposal which you would need to make a fit decision.

"It is no longer even controversial that ordinary residential development does not pay its way in taxes. Housing tracts do not yield enough revenue to pay for the cost of services."

Several members of the Council found their attention focused sharply on Jason's comments.

"In most instances any city wishing to remain solvent must use the surplus of revenues which comes from commercial and industrial land use to subsidize the bedroom communities. This is the normal way of things. However, in this development proposal, not only is there no counterbalancing revenue source apparent, but also it would be necessary to destroy part of the City's existing tax base."

At this point, all of the Council were staring at Jason, carefully weighing each word as it was spoken.

"It would seem that by approving this project you would inevitably require the public to subsidize the profit of a private developer through their taxes. Your action could well result in expanding the gross tax base while shrinking the net tax base, at a cost to everyone."

Several people in the audience gasped.

"I believe that you lack the necessary information to decide whether this project would be a benefit or detriment to the citizens of this town.   That would have to be supplied by a thorough economic analysis, but you have none. I believe that none was ever requested.

"I don't wish to presume to tell this body what to do, but I would hope that any vote you might take on this matter would be conditioned by the best and most complete information possible.

"Thank you."

He stood away from the podium amid exuberant applause. As he turned to return to his seat, he caught Connie's eye and smiled at her. Henry and Carl clapped him on the back and shook his hand while Dee gave him a big hug.

The Mayor looked to Howard Keller, who shook his head and made a dismissive gesture with his hand. *Control this* was embedded in that gesture, and McCanna winced at the task. There was only one more speaker, and he motioned her on.

"Good evening, my name is Ruth Frazee. . umm . . 194 Turner Canyon Road.

"You know," she giggled, "it's not so good going last, and I just want to say that I agree with all the previous speakers . . . except for the applicant, of course . . . and it all goes double for me."

She got an even bigger applause than Jason had, which surprised her as she hastened to sequester herself among her neighbors. Public speaking was not in her nature, and she would be a nervous wreck for a few hours despite the assurances of her friends that she had done a wonderful job.

The Mayor closed the public hearing and focused his attention on the governing body. From this moment he shut the audience out of his mind and acknowledged only the four people sitting on either side of him. This was time to draw up the wagons and direct the fire. Comments from the audience were a burden which the law required him to bear, and now it was lifted. All their words could safely be forgotten. Now the blade would descend as the Mayor made his best effort to shove the matter along.

"The chair will entertain a motion."

Several members of the Council looked startled at this obvious haste. Len Williams shuddered to activity.

"I move that we . . ."

"Excuse me, Mr. Mayor. Before we make any motion, I would like a ruling from the chair on a matter of customary procedure."

Patrick DelOstro had a tone in his voice which could not be ignored. Much about the course of this meeting had troubled him, and now was the moment to raise his concerns before the issues were obscured within the dense fog of political machination. In the silence following his words, one could have heard a termite gnawing on the building's innards.

"What is it, Councilman DelOstro."

"As you are aware, there is always a preliminary time period for discussion to allow the council members to explore the different issues which could have a bearing on the final motion. I believe that in this case, such a discussion period would be especially critical and necessary, and that it's lack would be unprecedented."

The Mayor shot a glance at Len Williams who was staring into the distance vacantly. No help would come from that quarter.

"The chair recognizes Councilmember DelOstro for discussion."

"Thank you, Mr. Mayor." Patrick could appear very gracious when he thought it appropriate.

"All the speakers raised good points, but the young man who spoke second last made several which I found particularly incisive. I have to regard this project as an investment in the future which we would be called upon to make on the City's behalf."

Dee found herself smiling at this.

"As in making any other investment, it would be our fiduciary responsibility to ascertain the costs assumed by the City and weigh them against the benefits obtained. At this point, we clearly lack the means to make such an evaluation. I, for one, could not vote in favor of this project until we have a fully qualified economic analysis to give us perspective."

"I couldn't agree more." Laura was quick to reinforce Patrick's words.

Gene Ryan just smiled at the Mayor.

"Any other comments?"

Len Williams gave a short and pointless endorsement of the project, issuing the usual platitudes about the future and growth. No one else seemed inclined to speak.

"Well then," bustled the Mayor, "Do we have a motion now?"

Patrick was quick on the uptake.

"I move that we continue this hearing until such time as we have a competent economic assessment of this project in front of us."

"Seconded!" Laura was quick to jump in.

The Mayor surveyed the disarray of the evening. Howard Keller's face varied from pale to livid as he glared upward at the center of the dais, boring into McCanna's eyes.

"I am going to waive public comment and go directly to Council discussion of this motion." He stared at the audience, daring anyone to object. No one did.

"Mr. Mayor," Patrick began in a level tone, "I know this motion will result in a delay, but I believe a short one. Although my firm cannot offer its services due to conflict of interest considerations, we routinely prepare such reports in two to three weeks. I am confident that the City Manager has at his disposal a good selection of firms capable of having the report done and the results to us before, say, our meeting a month from now."

All eyes swung to bear on Jeff Heit, who nodded absently.

Howard Keller rose into new life. One month. He could live with that. He would have to grease a few skids, but it was certainly feasible. He started to line up his plots in his head.

"Very well," intoned the Mayor, "we have a motion and a second. All in favor . . .

There were four ayes – even the Mayor voted for it. Len Williams was the only dissenting vote.

McCanna called for another fifteen minute recess to collect

his thoughts and rushed out. Four weeks. Not enough time. He had to delay the vote until after November fourth. He started making his plans.

In the meeting hall the Turner Canyon residents and their supporters swirled and gestured, savoring their moment of joy. In the back of their heads each one knew that this was only a delay, a partial victory, but yet it was sweet.

As the crowd spilled out onto the street in front of City Hall, one man watched them go. In his hand was a pencil.

Tap, tap, tap.

Chapter Twenty - Three

Jason wished to avoid the highway construction on the inland route to San Francisco and so he steered toward the coast to meet up with Highway One. At this time of the year the air presented a marvelous clarity, allowing sweeping views down the coast as he drove through the drowsy communities along the way. Most of the grasslands had dried out during the usual rainless summer, and where cows were free to graze, it was reduced to stubble, a golden fuzz on the rolling hills. The highway's meander inland near Bodega Bay took him briefly through a landscape twenty degrees hotter, but soon the road turned him back toward the ocean and the coolness of the onshore breeze. Jason thought to stop at one of the vista points to enjoy the tranquility of a perfect day, but he pressed on, anxious to be in the City as soon as possible. On the seat beside him was a small box wrapped in a pink bow.

Jason saw that most of the traffic on the Golden Gate bridge was comprised of escapees pushing northward out of the City toward weekend destinations. He breezed across the famous span, paid his toll and found an easy route to his apartment on Pacific. The noonday sun highlighted a parking spot almost in front of his building, an auspicious sign, and he edged gratefully into it. Bounding up the stairs, he entered the apartment knowing that Tracy would not be arriving from work for several more hours. His plan was to tidy up – Tracy had many virtues, but none of them was domesticity. The sheets would need changing, a window or two to wash, perhaps some dishes to clean up.

As he entered, he paused at the entry, sensing a subtle difference. No, he knew Crash, Oso now, would not be there. The drapes were shut, which Tracy always preferred; he would usually leave them open. That was not it. The furniture was still in the same places. He mused about it for a moment and then brushed

the thought from his mind.   Plenty to do before she arrived.
He wanted everything perfect so that this night would be special.

The tasks he had chosen for himself flew to completion.   In
a few hours the apartment was immaculate, and not long after,
Tracy made her entrance.

Their embrace was close, but not long lasting, and Tracy
noticed immediately the subtle improvement in the apartment's
appearance, only chiding Jason mildly for leaving the drapes open.
Quick to list the efforts she had made to prepare for his arrival, she
complained that she had found items of his clothing in various
places around the apartment.   She had to hunt under the bed,
behind the couch, everywhere, but now everything was washed
and in his dresser. Jason tried to show suitable appreciation for
her thoroughness.   She spoke rapidly of her day and its
complications, pausing only to drink a glass of spring water.   She
did not ask about the Ruskaya Council meeting, and he did not
volunteer any details. Soon a small box with a pink bow was in his
hand.

"For a special woman on a special occasion."

She delighted at the sight of it, and presently the contents
were in her hand, an elegant set of earrings of silver and jade.

"There is a jeweler in . . . that I know who does fine work. I
hope you like them."

"Jason, I love them. I will wear them tonight."

"Where were you thinking to have dinner."

"There is a new place, Lucia's. I have eaten there a few
times already. It is in a complex out on Geary. I am sure you will
like it. They have a beautiful dance floor."

"It sounds wonderful."

"Let's get ready. I wish we could go right now."

"I think I had better jump into the shower and freshen up
first.   I don't want to smell like some sweaty horse on your
birthday celebration."

"Yes, but hurry. Oh, I must change."

They both moved swiftly to make ready for their evening
together. After his shower, Jason was rummaging through his
drawer for a fresh pair of socks when something caught his eye,

something an unexpected color. He lifted it up, examining it carefully, and turned it over. Seeing what was there, he paused for a moment and then pushed the object into his rear pocket.

It took little time for him to finish dressing, and Tracy was waiting for him. She was already running through the evening's agenda, savoring the events to come.

"I think that I will have the filet mignon, you know? It is so good there. And of course their Italian food is superb – I am sure you will find something to like."

He only smiled.

The restaurant was all she had said – elegant décor, illustrious clientèle, an atmosphere saturated with exclusivity. With food of the highest quality, this could prove to be one of the top-flight restaurants in the City. A portly, middle-aged woman greeted them at the entry; this certainly was Lucia herself. She expressed a manner accustomed to command as she selected tables for the entering patrons. Catching sight of Tracy, she greeted her in a tone surprisingly familiar, but then she had been there before.

"And who is *this* gentleman?"

The expression in her eyes made Jason feel slightly uncomfortable. What was there? Surprise? Amusement? She accepted Tracy's introduction graciously and personally escorted them to their table, set in a secluded location. They settled in to some appetizers and started on a bottle of Pinot Noir.

The main course was all he could expect from an establishment of this caliber. He chose seafood sandeman – shrimp, scallops and calamari in a nearly sinful cream sauce, and Tracy selected the filet mignon, as planned. His own meal was perfectly prepared and seasoned, and the quantity was just perfect, leaving only enough room for dessert. She ordered tiramisu and he the spumoni, and they shared bites of each.

Jason had covered the bill and they were resting briefly to prepare for the evening's promised continuation into dancing when a nagging recollection bubbled to the surface of his mind.

"Tracy, you have told me a lot about the people you work with, and even though I haven't met any of them, I feel I know them already. Your office partner, what was her name?"

"Oh, that's Jane. Jane Hansen." Tracy smiled as she recalled an image of her inter-office ally.

"And your office manager . . . ?"

"Yes. That is Richard Kendal."

"Richard Kendal."

"Yes."

Slowly Jason reached down and withdrew something from his back pocket, a handkerchief. Placing it before her, he let her wonder about it for a moment before he turned it over, revealing the monogrammed initials, RK.

"You might like to return this to him."

There were perhaps a half dozen reasons why this man's handkerchief would have appeared on top of his own in his drawer.   Some would be plausible, others unlikely, several incriminating. Tracy offered none of them. Neither one spoke for several minutes before he broke the silence.

"Perhaps we had better go."

Nothing was said as they drove back to the apartment. The silence continued as he got together his possessions and packed them. All the time her eyes followed his movement with a hollow resignation. He was surprised that there was so little to pack, but then, most of his day-to-day items were in Ruskaya already. He searched his mind for something to say, but it had all been said before now. As he started for the door, she broke the silence.

"Jason, you shouldn't have left me here alone."

"I understand." He slowly turned and looked back at her. "Happy birthday."

He put his key on the entry table and closed the door behind him.

"What do you mean you can't tell me who it is!" Howard Keller was not in a mood to be understanding. "I'm going to have to pay for the damn thing, aren't I?"

"Howard, its the appearance of the thing. For reasons of propriety, the contractor is only named when the report is filed."

"James, whose side are you on here?"

The Mayor felt his mood cooling toward this man. "Yours, Howard, of course."

"And you still believe in the project, don't you?"

"You know I do."

"Listen, if it's a question of a campaign contribution . . . "

This suggestion seemed to displease Mayor McCanna a bit.

"No, no, of course not. You have been more than generous. I couldn't . . . "

As he spoke, the Mayor's hand seemed to move of its own accord, sliding a small pad forward and scratching one line on it with a pen.

" . . . couldn't tell you anything. You understand my position. I would ask you to respect that."

He rotated the pad and pushed it into Howard Keller's view, who glanced down at it. His face resolved into a smirk.

"Well, I guess if you can't, you can't."

McCanna tore the sheet from the pad and crumpled it up, putting it into his pocket for later disposal.

"I wish I could help you, Howard."

"I understand, James. That's the way things are. By the way, how is the campaign going?"

"Couldn't be better. I'm looking forward to a great victory."

"Terrific news. Well, I must go. My best to your wife." He turned and strode out of the Mayor's office with the attitude of the cat who not only ate the canary, but who also knew where all the rest of the canaries were hiding.

Before Keller was through the outer office door, McCanna was making a note to call his contact at the accounting firm which had been contracted to do the report. Whatever that pushy schemer now slinking out of City Hall could hope to accomplish would need to be neutralized in advance. Leave nothing to chance, have no regrets. Such policies had brought him to where he was, and no pipsqueak developer was going to upset his plans now. This fool had lost his respect and would need to be taught a lesson. Yes, he would eventually prove useful in getting back at his enemies in Turner Canyon, but he would need to squirm a bit first. Even a friend needs to feel the pain once in a while so that he would appreciate the pleasure at having it removed.

The phone jumped into life.

Anna Ferrier was in the middle of straightening out some purchase orders, cross checking requisitions against deliveries, when her phone rang. Marking her place in the listings carefully with a penciled tick, she picked up the receiver.

"City Clerk's office. Anna Ferrier here."

"Anna, this is Carmen at the County Registrar's office. How are you?"

"Oh, I'm fine, dear. How have you been?"

"Busy. What is happening in your town?"

"Whatever do you mean?"

"I am just buried in new registrations."

"Yes, I know. I have had quite a few in my office, but how many are we talking about?"

"Nearly nineteen hundred. There are the usual amount of questionables, misspelled names, faulty addresses, and the like. We even got half a dozen who reregistered exactly as they did before – same name and party affiliation. We have discounted all of those. Anna, usually it is a big election year event if you get a few hundred new registrations. So what gives?"

"Well, there is one controversial matter, a development project, but I didn't think that the motivation level was quite that high. Several of the local civic groups have run big registration campaigns, but they do every election year, not with these kind of results."

"Well something is on. I will be sending you the new voter rolls for the precincts, and it is a big package. I didn't want you to be surprised."

"Thank you so much. By the way, is this upsurge county

wide?"

"Not at all – just Ruskaya Bend."

"Well, thank you for the heads-up. I certainly appreciate it. Goodbye, dear."

Anna set the phone on the cradle and began to ponder this news. It was well known that only about half of eligible citizens would bother to register, much less vote. Of those who could, rarely more than three quarters would actually go to the polls. This meant that about one third of those eligible would cast a vote, and a majority of them, sometimes as low as fifteen percent of the adult population, would decide the community's leaders. Ruskaya had about fifty-five hundred registered voters, and that number had just increased by a third. What did it mean?

Sometimes the civic groups would set loose particularly aggressive registrars, head hunters, they were called. Besieged citizens would sign the forms just to end the harangue, and then never vote. Would this uptick in the count result in a lot of no-shows? This had happened some six years ago and caused quite a stir. Was the Cliffs development raising up so much dust? Was that Turner Canyon business resonating so strongly? The proposed project seemed like a purely local matter, a sleeper for most folks -- something that generated a lot of talk which was then rapidly forgotten. Still, someone may need to know about this.

She lifted the phone and speed dialed a number.

Chapter Twenty – Four

Derek Crowley didn't mind the pressure – welcomed it, in fact. It was his stock in trade to produce a quality result while the heat was on. Having served four years as a forensic accountant, he was used to having some hot-blooded assistant District Attorney breathing down his neck while a hostile CFO did his best to fend him off. His reputation of steady and accurate results while working in a pressure cooker had landed him his present, sweet job at the firm of Gournatieff and Case. The work he did there had allowed him a moderate degree of satisfaction but it had not presented the intensity he had been used to, at least, not until his current assignment.

At first he didn't even know where Ruskaya Bend was located, somewhere up north was his best recollection. Consulting a map he was surprised to recall that he had actually driven through the town once or twice without even noticing it. The job seemed straightforward enough, though, an economic assessment for a proposed development. It was complicated only by the need for demolition of existing structures to provide access. He had done jobs like this one before, and this seemed more routine than most. He should wrap it up in no time at all. Then the phone calls started.

The first was from a very irritating individual named Keller, who turned out to be the developer. Derek was used to the type and was prepared to listen patiently to his unrealistic demands. He first had to suffer through an extended denunciation of the owners of the properties which were to be demolished. To hear it told, they were nothing but a bunch of anarchists, living in a slum of flea infested rat-traps, and the town would be better off without them. Next the man launched into a tirade about the City's slope/density ordinance and assured Derek that his project would be approved as drawn. Last, he stressed the importance of completing the report in a timely fashion, and came very close to offering a monetary incentive in return for a swift result. Derek hastily brushed aside this suggestion and thanked the man for his input, ending the conversation as abruptly as he could manage.

He began to write out a list of people to call and subjects to cover – the City Manager's office for the particulars of the slope/density ordinance and the County Assessor for values of Turner Canyon properties, but his telephone was not silent for long. The next call was from the Mayor of Ruskaya Bend.

It was rare for a public official to call attempting to lobby him, and Derek listened with some interest. The man, named McCanna, spent an inordinate length of time heaping praises on the firm he worked for, and obliquely on him, before he came to the point. He spoke of the need for the report to be "deliberate" and "measured", and as the conversation commenced, Derek got the strong impression that this man supported the project as fervently as the previous caller, but had a vital interest in the report being completed and delivered sometime after November fourth.

This took Derek by surprise. To be asked to massage the figures, to downplay or emphasize certain aspects of a study, to overlook a critical detail, these he was used to. To be asked to take his time was a first, but he knew from experience that politicians had a private ethic and unspoken reasons for their intentions. He politely buttered the man with vague assurances and brought the conversation to a close.

Derek gave a brief pause, allowing his telephone another opportunity to jump up at him before turning his mind to the report he was to prepare. Of course, it was hardly ethical for anyone to attempt to "encourage" a particular result in his work, but it was done all the time. Handling this sort of persuasion was assumed to be part of the job, but there was something about this particular assignment which aroused his concern. He took up his pen and added the name of his supervisor to the list of calls to make. Although he didn't usually feel the need to consult the higher-ups, this project might be a prudent exception.

He looked over the other tasks which would require his

attention this day and arranged the paperwork associated with each carefully on his desk before breaking for lunch, after which he would consult Aaron, his supervisor.

Cynthia knew at once that something had changed when Jason revealed that he would not be going to San Francisco for the weekend. She had dutifully been caring for the newly rechristened Oso and had developed a strong bond with the rascally cat, looking forward to each upcoming Saturday, but there was something in Jason's voice that made it clear to her that her assistance would not be needed further.

They both did not mention anything about Tracy. Even though she was surprised and pleased that her prediction about his relation with his distant flame had come to pass, it was obvious that the subject should be avoided.

"Well then, I hope I can come to see Oso."

"Of course you can. It's obvious that he really likes you. Over the last few weeks he has almost gotten civilized. Hasn't broken hardly anything."

"So . . . do you think that this is your home now?" Something impelled Cynthia to ask a question which probably she should not have. He did not answer right away.

"Perhaps so."

There was something in his tone which suggested that a choice had been forced upon him and that he was accepting it with difficulty. Sensing a change of subject was indicated, she skipped over to something which she hoped to raise his spirits.

"By the way, Dee has been singing your praises after the City Council meeting. She thinks that statement you made was brilliant and had a big effect on the Council decision."

"Well, I don't know about that."

"I had a chance to see it again on TV, and I think she is right. Even that bum McCanna was unable to look away while you were talking. Where did you learn to speak like that?"

"I don't know. I just tried to present points that nobody else had covered and make them as clear as possible."

"It sure worked."

It was Jason's turn to change the subject.

"How has school been going, your new classes and all."

"Aw, OK. But I hate Algebra II. The teacher, Miss Collins, is a slave driver and she started us off right away with factoring."

"What's wrong with that?"

"I hate it. I look at those dumb equations and I just don't know where to start. And the teacher has the attitude that if you need help, you are beyond help already."

"Well, you know, I was always pretty good at those kinds of problems. Maybe I could help you. There are a couple of tricks I could show you."

"Would you?"

"Sure. It's the least I can do for your good care of Oso."

Cynthia beamed at his offer, and in the brief pause which followed, Cynthia considered telling him about how Connie had obtained a superior job, but thought better of it. His old relationship might be dead, but the body was still twitching. Plenty of time later.

They covered a few items of neighborhood interest before she left. She had shut the street gate when the quiet settled over him, and he began to think about how his life had suddenly been reorganized. As his mood seemed ready to take a turn into darker areas, he felt a movement beside him. Without a sound Oso had moved to sit beside him. He slowly raised his hand to rest on top of the cat's head, and a loud purring began immediately. Raising his eyes to consider the house around him, he contemplated his father's gift to him.

"Did you get a call from him too? Howard Keller, right? Oh my god, what a steamroller job that guy is. How did he even get our number?"

Derek had not waited to consult with Aaron Walachinsky on the Ruskaya Bend assignment. He was not only his immediate superior, but also was the firm's political advisor. He was sure to find the right path through the land mines.

"Aaron, I think your impression of him is the correct one. The question is how do I interpret the signals I am getting."

"We never bend the data. That pressure you will ignore."

"Of course."

"Now, from what you say, this clown Keller wants a hurry-up job and the Mayor wants you to sit on it."

"As far as I can see."

The older man contemplated this tangle for a moment before speaking.

"Our business is not with either man, but with the City Manager. Was there any indication from his office about when he wanted this report?"

"No."

"Well then, do your usual thorough job, pull no punches, sugarcoat nothing. Don't waste any time getting it together and send it to the City Manager with no fanfare. Let him decide whether to sit on it or not. If either of those other fools call again, discuss nothing with them – cite professional ethics or something. Get this tangle out of your hair as soon as possible." He hardly took a breath before changing the subject.

"How's the wife?"

"She's fine. The due date is in five weeks."

"Be nice to her. She is entering a very uncomfortable time. Remember that your paternity leave starts when she enters labor. You will have a month off."

"Yes, I know."

As the supervisor left his office, Derek turned with a smile on his face to place a call to the Sonoma County Assessor's office. Many calls to make.

It turned from summer to fall with no preliminaries, no announcement. Suddenly the cool, dry wind blew through town, and everyone knew that the season's heat had ended. The sense of relief was twofold. The locals felt that now the town was their own once again – school had started, and the vacationers had headed back to their own homes. Now each morning had that crisp, refreshing coolness which prompted a corresponding quickening in spirit, a lightness in step. A person could think clearly, get things done, and even find a parking place downtown. It was a good time.

Jason was surprised at the sudden change in the weather. Living in a big city, he had scarcely paid the climate any mind, especially since it is consistently so temperate in San Francisco. The many square miles of pavement and buildings generate their own weather, and, except for times of rain or fog, it was difficult to know what time of the year was at hand without glancing at a calendar. Ruskaya was a small town surrounded by open space, more subject the whims of the natural world such as temperature changes. He had already noticed that, even during summer, nighttimes presented a welcome coolness, which was quite different from the balmy air of San Francisco evenings he was used to. The characteristic of a valley, the locals told him.

The change of season had the same effect on him as it did on everyone else. He became more active, spending increasing amounts of time repairing and improving his house, and his thoughts clarified as the air above him did the same. The few moments spent ruminating over his relationship with Tracy became rarer; his image of her became faded a bit. He adjusted.

As the time spent renovating his house decreased, he took on more work with his employer, Shaw and Ricchetti. The quality of his production still earned high praise from the two partners, and the concept of working at home was spreading. Two other associates had likewise abandoned their offices to be near their families during work hours. A broadband internet connection and a weekly visit to the office seemed to keep the wheels turning smoothly. To compensate for the decreased amount of social interaction, John had insisted upon more events, dinner parties chiefly, to retain the bonds between the individuals at the firm. It was during one of these, a spectacular feast at John Ricchetti's own home, that the change in his romantic status was noticed when he arrived alone.

"I never liked her," John confided to Jason. "What was her name . . . Lacy?"

"Tracy."

"Yes. It seemed that she was always looking over your head for the next opportunity. Well, never mind. The right girl will appear for you, you'll see."

It always impressed Jason that, as a gay man, John Ricchetti could be so thoughtful and understanding when considering the problems of his heterosexual friends. Perhaps this was to be expected in San Francisco, a community where tolerance was easy to come by, but Jason had always admired this man because he seemed more than merely tolerant.

Jason moved easily into a new rhythm of life.

Each weekend Cynthia arrived with her algebra books, and Jason taught her the intricacies of factoring. She was a quick study, making rapid progress. When her class got into word problems, her difficulties with them were quickly addressed and dealt with. On the day when she earned an A on the weekly test, they both celebrated by quaffing a mug of root beer at Rosie's restaurant.

She had just been discussing Connie's new job, and as she peered across the foam at him, a playful tone entered her voice.

"Say, what are you doing next Saturday evening?"

"Nothing. Why?"

"Oh, my family is having a little get together, and it would be nice if you came."

"Does anyone but you know about this yet?"

"Well . . . not yet. But if you are interested, I'm sure it would be no problem."

"Oh? Now let me guess . . . your cousin would be there."

"I have lots of cousins." She simulated an innocent look.

"You know who I am talking about."

"Well, she might be."

"Listen, Cynthia. Your plot is pitifully transparent. Connie and I scarcely know each other. We might not even get along."

"What's the matter? Did you and she have a fight?"

"We haven't been close enough to have had a fight."

"Well, that's a good start."

"Cynthia, you can't force these things. It is tough enough

to make a relationship work without being muscled into it by an insistent fifteen year old."

Her frown had a slightly pitiful aspect to it.

"Yeah, but you have to eat somewhere on Saturday night, don't you?"

"You may have me there. I've been known to eat somewhere on Saturday night."

"Then why not at our house? My whole family loves you."

Jason was searching for a way out, but not very hard.

"Alright. If I get a call from your Dad inviting me, and if it sounds that you haven't just conned him into it, I will come."

"Great!" A sly look crossed her face. "I never have to con my Dad . . . he does whatever I say."

Chapter Twenty – Five

"You say it has already arrived? Where is it? What does it say?" Dee felt her emotions passing from surprise through confusion to anger. "Who is holding it up?"

"First of all," began Laura, "Jeff Heit had it on his desk. Laurinda, my friend who works in his office, saw it when it arrived. She didn't have any time to read it, so it could say anything. We don't know who else knows about it or whether Heit has chosen to sit on it. She said that it disappeared almost immediately."

Dee took a moment to weigh the risks and potentials involved in these revelations before speaking.

"Howard Keller needs this report before he can commence. If he knew what it said and it favored him, he would be screaming bloody murder to get it presented before the Council. Either he doesn't know it is here, or it doesn't favor him. McCanna looks as if he is working toward avoiding any controversial decision before the election, regardless of what the report might say. Bringing it out now would force his hand and upset his timing. Hmmm."

"I think you are right, but what angle would the City Manager be playing?"

"As always, his own angle. Does he have anything to gain or lose either way?"

"I don't think so."

"Laura, could you call Gournatieff and Case and request a copy?"

"They would never give it to me. Their contract is with the City Manager."

"Damn." In an instant she had another idea. "Could you call them and find out whether or not the report had been delivered?"

"Dee, they might tell me that."

"Then do it. We have nothing to lose by trying. We might

regret it, but I think that the odds are greatest that we will be benefited by getting that report out in the open. If we can prove that it is here, and if Howard Keller finds out, he can be relied to do all the dirty work for us."

"I'll call right away."

After the hang up, Dee started to have second thoughts. All their moves were critical now, had she acted precipitously? She called Henry.

"Dee, I think you did just right. We are just probing at this time; the decision to act is in the future. Personally, I think that the report has the highest probability of making Keller's project look economically unsound, but either way, McCanna won't want to vote on it before the election. We have an excellent chance at a situation where they would wind up at each other's throats. You should rest easy, my girl. I believe your strategy was perfect."

Calmed by this evaluation, Dee settled back into her chair to contemplate the possibilities. What does the report say? Do we really need to know what is in it? If we use Howard Keller as our attack dog, how do we drop the dime without letting him know it was us? Is there any mischief Jeff Heit can raise? Would he even care to do so?

Very slowly the situation untangled in her mind, and she allowed herself a reserved smile.

"Yesss."

The dinner at the Salgado residence was everything Jason thought it would be – convivial, light-hearted, with delicious food, and totally engineered by Cynthia. She hardly let him get in the front door before she started working on him.

"Don't you think she looks particularly nice this evening, Jason?"

"Aurelia?"

"Connie."

"Everybody looks very nice this evening."

"But don't you think she looks especially beautiful?"

"Tell me, do you have any of those little, really hot chillies you served here at the quinceañera."

"I think so. Why?"

"I want to stuff two of them into my ears."

"Ooooh." Her mock wince was followed by a fiendish smile.

As Jason mixed with the family, he tried his best to be relaxed and unaffected when he happened to speak to Connie, and immediately it was clear to him that she was not in on the plot her cousin was hatching. He was not very surprised when Cynthia determined the seating, placing him next to Connie and herself directly across to keep an eye on them both.

As they all sat for dinner, he couldn't help noticing the alluring perfume Connie was wearing. He kept thinking that soon his olfactory senses would acclimatize and the scent would fade from his consciousness, but this never happened.

The meal was simple, but elegant. A variety of vegetable appetizers followed by a superb *mole rojo* over rice. A local Shiraz was made available, and Jason had half a glass with the main course. The dessert was flan, and this as well as the *mole* had been produced by Aurelia's hand.

Connie and he chatted during the course of the dinner, covering the usual topics – her new job, neighborhood matters, the coming of fall. The end of his relationship with Tracy never came up; she may not have even known of it. At each turn in the conversation, Jason could see Cynthia's dark eyes following their every word and gesture. An abbreviated smile remained on her face throughout, and several times he looked right at her and gave a diminutive shake of his head as if to say, "don't get your hopes up", but she only smiled the harder.

Jason had to admit that it was a wonderful evening, the food, the company, the surroundings. Even Cynthia's attempts at manipulation, which had escaped everyone else's notice, were available to provide a source of amusement for him.

After the meal, Louis was his usual animated self and launched into a series of humorous stories about the childhood of himself and his siblings. As Jason watched him speak, he had the impression that this man had seen a good deal of grief in his days, but chose to remember the happy times and accentuate those moments as he lived his life.

The group gradually congregated around the fireplace, where a moderate blaze fought off the growing evening chill. Cynthia couldn't manage to seat Jason with Connie this time, but they were immediately across from each other. He could no longer smell her perfume at this distance, but couldn't help noticing the shine of the firelight in her eyes. From time to time those eyes looked distant and sad, but not often. They lit up with a humorous remark and seemed to glow with the remembrance of a treasured memory.

As he was leaving, Cynthia's mother gave him a hug and said, "*Me gustaba mucho que veniste*".

"*Igualmente, señora. Muchisimas gracias.*"

Connie offered him her hand, presumably to shake, and he lifted it up as if to kiss it, but then merely held it up in front of him. He looked across it at her and said, "Very nice to see you this evening, Connie." She seemed pleased at this and murmured her appreciation. In the corner of his eye he could see Cynthia, her arms crossed and her head cocked to the side, with the same sly, half smile gracing her face. *Have to set that girl straight one of these days.* His thoughts were bold and assertive, but he knew that he probably wouldn't have any better luck in these intentions than anyone else.

H oward Keller usually did not waste time scanning the local periodicals, but the leader for an article on his project sat on the lower left corner the front page. He condescended to peruse it for what scanty news he might glean, turning with a flourish to continue on page ten. There he found a line which he read, and read again.

". . . the requested economic feasibility study which currently is under review at City Hall."

Slamming his fist down on the page, he raced through a number of thoughts rising up to assault him.

Why had he not been notified of this report's arrival? Who

was sitting on it? Surely someone's head needed to be thumped, but who's? This looked like McCanna's doing – he had been far too preoccupied recently with his reelection chances. Perhaps a call to the City Manager's office could pry up a few rocks, or one directly to the Mayor for a saccharin blast. Of course the conclusion of the report is important, but that is just a question of slant. If staff can be counted upon to present it correctly . . .

He rode these conflicting tides for a few moments before deciding on a course of action. A successful strategy at this point demanded accurate information, and this he had the means to obtain. He dialed David Horving at A & D Enterprises.

Keller was constrained to indulge in the amenities for a few minutes before getting down to the matter at hand.

"Well, Howard. Of course, the information I give you must not go any farther . . ."

Keller sneered unseen at the customary admonition and disclaimer. He was paying this man too much for him to hold out now.

". . . and must never be traced back to me."

"Naturally not."

The consultant paused to take a breath.

"The Mayor's candidacy is presently facing severe crisis. His favorables have declined slightly, but the unfavorables have risen significantly. There is also one local issue which throws considerable weight on the equation."

"The project."

"Yes. With it out of the picture, the election is too close to call."

"And with approval?"

"With approval, he would be defeated, but it is within the margin of error. With denial, he would be reelected by a narrow but significant margin."

So this was it. The work of the past year and a half and all the money he had spent was hung up on a few percentage points.

"David, let me ask. Is there any chance that your evaluation could be significantly changed before the election?"

"Only in the details."

"Has he been notified of these latest results?"

"I will be speaking to the Mayor on this matter later this afternoon."

"Is there any chance that you could . . . improve on your data. . . to give him the best possible impression?"

"Howard, I can't alter the information in my hands . . ."

A cold, hard silence issued palpably from the phone at his ear.

". . . but I could increase the margin of uncertainty."

"That might do. I would appreciate that. Now tell me, is there anything else about this election that I should know?"

"No, not really. There has been a surge of newly registered voters, but we are confident that we know how they will fall. Don't be concerned about that."

"Well then, on your say so, I won't." He laughed dryly. "Thank you, David. As always, your wise council is invaluable."

After the call ended, David Horving contemplated silently in his office. He hated to have to work with this kind of man, but Keller had put a lot of business in his lap, and there was bound to be an ample gesture of appreciation to come for this work. This particular job, like much of his business, was a precarious balancing act; but in the past he had always avoided the pit on either side of the tightrope. As this election was shaping up, his firm was likely to look good. If McCanna won, they could claim the victory. If not, it was Keller's project that had dragged him down. Either way, A & D would win.

"Darling, please come and help me prepare the meal. I know you are tired from work, but it would help you to relax after a hard day."

Aurelia Salgado had always produced the meals from scratch – to her it was a sacred purpose. Since her husband's passing, the effort of caressing the food into sustenance for her family had developed a higher significance. During these times came the opportunities for frank conversations with the other members of the family, especially the women.

Connie had not assisted her for some time now, and Aurelia had been concerned about her state of mind. The marriage had ended. The bad memories were still there but were no longer being added to. The divorce had been difficult, more for religious than legal reasons, but that too was over. Her new job in the insurance office seemed fulfilling, but there was still something lacking in her spirit. But never mind, there was nothing like peeling chilies to bring a moment of clarity and ease all doubts.

"*Si, mi Tia.*" Connie rose from the couch, setting aside the magazine she had been reading, glad of the chance to do something with a result which was sure to be appreciated. The recollection of many pleasant hours in the kitchen with her aunt quickened her step.

Aurelia began to bring the ingredients for the supper from the refrigerator, setting each with a delicate touch upon the large cutting board in the center of the kitchen. *Jitomate, cebolla, tomatillo, chile jalapeño,* beef for *carne asada, queso,* some fresh *cilantro.* The *masa* for tortillas was nearly ready, reposing in a small bowl and covered with a cloth. The *arróz* and *frijoles* were done and keeping warm at the back of the stove, and on the cutting board all the ingredients for her renowned red sauce were ready in small containers. The two women took up their tasks.

Connie undertook to cut up the many ingredients as her aunt prepared the tortillas. Always she had patted them out by hand, easing each adeptly into the correct form and thickness. Perhaps a bit old-fashioned, she considered tortillas slammed into shape with a hand press to be unacceptably artificial. "Factory tortillas" she called them. They lacked quality.

"Tell me about your new job, darling. Does it please you?"

"Well, I do like it, but there is a lot to learn. The insurance business is very complicated. I spend most of the day filling out forms on the computer, but Bob, the boss, seems a good man. He is very patient with me."

"That is good. Is there much chance for advancement?"

"Probably not, but the pay is good and I will have health insurance after another three weeks."

"As long as you feel you are accomplishing something."

"It is as if I work in a small factory where the product is piles of paper decorated with the proper words and figures. It is satisfying, but I don't think it would ever provide life-long satisfaction.

"Yes, I see."

They paused from their work to have glasses of lemonade, welcome for allaying the drying heat of the kitchen. Aurelia smiled at her niece in a knowing way.

"Have you met any new friends there."

"Well, I know everybody in the office, but most of them are twice my age. There is one person near my age named Sajida who is quite nice. Her family comes from India, and she has some interesting stories to tell. She has been a great help to me. She is better at explaining the intricacies of the computer system than Bob is."

"Are there any young men there?"

Connie put down her empty glass and started to cut up the tomatoes. She didn't say anything for a while.

"None my age, if that is what you mean."

"Well, of course, you wouldn't need to look so far away for fine young men who seem to think well of you."

"One in particular, perhaps? Tell me, *Tia,* did she give you notes?"

"Who?"

"Cynthia, of course. Every time I see her she is trying to push me toward that man. Now it is you doing the same."

"I believe his name is Jason, and he seems very nice and polite."

"They all seem so at first. That can change." Her bitterness gave Aurelia pause. She finished removing the skins from the chilies before attempting a continuation.

"I know you have been hurt, but not all men are like that one was. I only know that my Enrique made me feel like a completed person. Every day with him was a gift from heaven, my life has not been as full since he has been gone. I accept this as how it will be, but you are too young to do the same. I only say that you should not turn your face away from this man without giving him a chance to prove himself."

"Perhaps he already has. Almost the first things I learned about him is that he has a career and a woman in San Francisco, and that he plans to fix up his father's house to sell it. To me, he seems like a *mariposa,* a butterfly, flitting from flower to flower, from town to town, woman to woman. I just was married to someone like that."

Aurelia cut up a bunch of green onions before responding.

"He no longer goes to the City for his job, but works here instead, and . . . his relationship with that other is over." She looked up at her niece. "You heard how he spoke for us at the City Council meeting. You saw the sincerity in him. He is truly the son of his father, and Ted was a good man to us all. *Mi Sobrina,* I am not telling you to propose marriage to this man, but merely leave the door open and give him a chance to express his true nature."

Connie sensed she was running out of arguments.

"*Tia,* you can't be serious. This man is an Anglo."

"Yes, that is true. But you know, that doesn't seem to be so important any more. It is the heart that counts. And besides, he speaks Spanish."

"Well then, adopt him as your nephew because I hardly speak it at all."

"If you spend time around this family, you will surely pick it up."

"Oh, Aunt Aurelia!"

Chapter Twenty - Six

Balance. James McCanna contemplated the forces at work around him, the pressures, the demands, the personalities. Balance was all he needed to obtain. To match one push upsetting his equilibrium against its counterforce, to set one individual clamoring for action against another demanding the opposite, to let all swirl around him while he remained standing, this was how he had always survived. Balance.

The economic feasibility study for the Cliffs project was on his desk. He was not surprised at the conclusions, but how could he use it? The statement was clear. Demolition of homes in Turner canyon would represent a substantial cost for acquisition which would have to be financed through a bond issue. This would be coupled with a long term loss of tax revenues. On the positive side, development of the project would bring a brief gain of permit fees enhanced with long term tax revenues. Even with the increased density demanded by Howard Keller, it would require nearly a generation for the City to break even financially. If the slope/density ordinance were enforced, a net surplus would never be obtained. Where was the balance?

Deep in his heart he thirsted for a chance to watch the bulldozers ripping out the homes of those canyon rats, even if that weasel Keller would make a profit by it. The only thing sweeter to the Mayor than victory was revenge, but this little cauldron of hate simmered for him alone, and it looked as if he could not draw more than one other Councilmember into it. Patrick DelOstro would never overlook the import of the economic study which he had requested. Gene Ryan was in the throes of an attack of conscience, and although he might come around with the right combination of threats, it would require all the political capital McCanna could muster, and still his vote would be unsure.

The election. He now knew from David Horving that his

own ambition for a sweeping victory and a continued mandate was in peril. Too many eyes were on him and his work, too many tongues wagging, too many ears turned away from him at a critical time. The moment for the triumphant gesture, the convincing act, to win away the last few votes to his side was slipping past him. He had to get this thing back on track, neutralize the peril and balance the equation in his favor.

Keller. That insignificant flea. If only he would stop clawing away at McCanna's vitals. A delay in the vote on the project could make all the difference for the election, but Keller kept yapping his demands for a quick decision, one which would favor him. The fool left no room for subtlety, for maneuver. Once the man knew that the report had been delivered, the Mayor had known no rest. This man's pressure could not be balanced out since he refused to consider that the struggle could not yet be resolved in his favor. Amateur!

Slowly a plan formed in his mind which could restore equilibrium and shunt aside all the competing forces pressing on him. His first priority was, of course, to sweep up an election victory. To be a winner he had to act like a winner, to relieve the public tension with magnanimity. He had to offer the anxious voters what they wanted, or the illusion of it, to placate the herd and get them out of the calculations. Once he was safely restored to his seat, anything could happen. Whatever pressure he could bring to bear on other Councilmembers would then be irresistible with four more years of his abuse to anticipate. The only catch was the developer. Keller would have to see the wisdom in the stratagem, but would he? He continually acted like a man who was urged on by a bayonet jabbing him in the back. Would he, indeed?

He would have to.

Mayor McCanna lifted up the telephone and speed dialed the City Managers office.

Dee was composing a letter to the Editor of the Ruskaya View when the telephone rang. She didn't mind the interruption since producing a pithy yet persuasive written statement was not her strength, and a brief delay could only help the effort. Her computer would wait patiently for her.

"Dee, things are happening!"

"What is it, Laura?"

"He has made his move. The project is on the agenda for the meeting ten days from now."

"Which item is it?"

"The first. I wondered about that. You would expect him to put it last to wear down the opposition over the course of the meeting."

"I know. That doesn't make any sense. What about the report?"

"Several people came in after the article in the View was published requesting copies, but staff had been instructed to say that it was still under review and hand out nothing. None of the other Councilmembers have seen it either."

"How can he do that?"

"Dee, there is a rumor circulating at City Hall that the report will not be revealed until the last minute. He's obviously trying to keep it under wraps while he tries to round up the votes he needs. This will not help him with Patrick, but he has been working especially hard to bring Gene around."

"And Gene is . . . "

"Uncommitted so far."

The silence from Dee's end of the line lasted for an uncomfortable length of time.

"McCanna's running true to form, Laura. All through this he's been like a vampire following a trail of blood. He wants nothing more than to see this project rammed down our throats, but what is the reality he is facing?"

"He might know that he lacks the votes to pass it, and he does seem more than a little nervous about the election. Dee, I think he is trying to save his seat. Or possibly he does have the votes and is trying to lull the opposition to sleep and pass it quietly. The swing vote seems to be Gene, but he won't talk to anyone about his thoughts on the matter."

"He generally doesn't express his convictions in advance of public Council deliberations. He's always been like that, but imagine the hammer blows falling on him."

"Dee, I think we cannot take anything for granted and we should prepare for the worst."

"Yes. I'll call out the cavalry. We'll be ready."

After their goodbyes, Dee returned to her letter, but all had changed. Methodically, she erased the text already written and started again. Her previous effort now seemed like an attempt to bring down an elephant with a popgun. She would have to bring out the howitzers.

She started to type.

Mayor McCanna had picked a quiet corner of the dining room in the Plumb Branch for his conference with Howard Keller. It was secluded enough for the conversation to remain confidential, but public enough to constrain Keller from starting one of his usual high-volume tirades when the Mayor sought to acquaint him with the realities of life.

McCanna seldom wondered how the individuals passing through his life came to be as he saw them. This developer seemed to be motivated by more than just lust for a profit, but the reasons for this never troubled the Mayor. This man was just a force to be channeled and used, like using fire to cook a meal. At this moment he served a purpose, and there would be plenty of time later to claim a pound of his flesh. The path ahead was clear, and all that remained was to load up the baggage.

Howard Keller slid his pudgy bulk into the chair opposite.

They both were all smiles and charm, drifting though the customary empty forms of greeting. Presently they came to the business at hand – the project.

"I know, James, that you have everything lined up for the meeting . . ."

"Howard, that is the very thing I want to discuss with you." He hunched closer to the other man as if he were passing on sacred information. "You know that I continue to believe fully in your project. I know how important it is to this town and for the future.”

Howard Keller's eyes narrowed as the Mayor continued plying him with honeyed words.

“And you know I would want nothing more than for you to walk away from this upcoming meeting with the permits in your hand. But I think there will be a slight delay.”

Keller felt his face becoming hot.

“James, you said that it was in the bag.”

“And it will be. But we have to plan our moves carefully here. I have to be frank with you. I don't yet have the votes that we need.”

“You said . . .”

“Yes, yes. I will have them, but at this moment I don't have the leverage I need to force the issue. I am in an awkward position now, right before the election, but my hand will be considerably strengthened soon. Then I can call in chits without fear of . . . rebellion.”

Keller could not reveal what he knew about the Mayor's reelection chances, but he definitely didn't like the way this conversation was shaping up.

“Listen here, the matter is going to be up for a vote in nine days!”

“Yes, of course, but I think you need to look at the big picture. I must get reelected. This project hangs over me like an anvil, waiting to drop. I must neutralize the public sentiment over this to clear the way to our victory. I can get you what you want, what we both want, but you must be patient.”

As the Mayor looked at the other man simmering, he wondered if it would have been better to have met in a place where Keller would feel less constrained about screaming. He seemed to have more than a few in him at this moment, though he spoke softly through clenched teeth.

“Go on.”

“I have in mind a maneuver, merely a maneuver. It will seem . . . “

“James, I don't care what methods you use and I don't care

what your problems are – just get me the votes. I intend to walk away from the meeting Thursday after next with an approval. Do you understand? Do whatever you have to do, kidnap somebody's children, assassinate somebody, I don't give a damn. Get me the votes!"

The Mayor glanced around to see if any of the patrons had heard these words, but none had. He tried his best to lower the tenor of the conversation and regain control of the situation. His most soothing tone of placation was barely enough to bring an illusion of calm to the other man. McCanna was trying to restart his sales pitch when Keller interrupted him.

"McCanna, there is only one thing you need to know. I have the dirt on you, and if you don't give me what I want, I will give you what you don't want."

At this he rose slowly and towered over the Mayor.

"Clear?"

He glided out of the Plumb Branch like a shadow fleeing the light.

As the Mayor sat alone in the near dark, he considered Keller's threats, but not very seriously. Many men had threatened him, and where were they now? Making this man squirm later would be worth every unpleasant moment like this one, and he intended to enjoy it fully when the time came. He took a lingering sip of his coffee and settled back into his chair.

October was perhaps the best month of the year if the rains didn't come early. There were those in Ruskaya who maintained that April held the measure, but even those folks thought that October was not far behind.

In October the heat of a long summer was gone, and the temperate days complemented the cool nights. Those days still had enough hours in them to illuminate any task undertaken, and the clarity of the nights put a wealth of stars nearly within reach of an outstretched hand, or so it seemed. The local pace of life geared down to a more comfortable level, and all felt better for it.

Bob and Ann Hurley had developed the habit of visiting

the downtown of Ruskaya most afternoons after work. They drove to the edge of town and then parked, strolling with young Brian through the residential and business areas of their community. Here an elderly woman pruning her flowers would set down her clippers to chat with them, admiring their son. There a teenager walking his dog would greet them.   Merchants nodded, a restaurant hostess smiled. They had no trouble feeling at home.

On one of their forays, they came across Paige Lee handing out election leaflets. A tall young man doing the same across the street was called over and introduced as her nephew.   The neighborhood talk transitioned into a discussion of the election four weeks away.

Lacking the resources for polling, she had to gauge her acceptance from the people she had met. So far, she thought , so good. Her personal approach to campaigning seemed to put her in good stead, as well as her grasp of the issues.   There was one matter that Bob had been curious about since Asian Americans were rare in Ruskaya. He summoned the pluck to ask her, and her response was immediate.

"Well, I do see a look in the eyes of some people from time to time. But think of it from their point of view. Here is this . . ." She ticked off each word with her fingers. ". . .tiny . . . Chinese . . . woman . . ., whom they don't know, asking for their vote. But most of them will stay to discuss some issue or ask questions, and after a few minutes that look mostly disappears, and they are just talking to a person from their town."

"That sounds good."

"But I still don't know if they will vote for me. I do have a pretty big hill to climb."

"I have this feeling that you are almost to the top."

Paige just smiled at this evaluation and hugged Brian by way of thanks, taking her leave to hand out more leaflets with her nephew while the Hurleys continued their stroll which was graced by the setting sun.

Yes, October was probably best.

Chapter Twenty – Seven

Howard Keller was alone in his office. It wasn't much, this office of his, a small space with a desk and a telephone, one restricted window peering out on a desolate street, a bathroom in the rear. For a year and a half he had maintained this nondescript space for the front it provided him. With it, he had an address in Ruskaya Bend.

So the Mayor had a plan, did he. That fool couldn't whip up a plan to escape from an unguarded sandbox. No, nothing could be left to this man, and fortunately it didn't have to be. Keller's own researches had born fruit, the results from the probing inquiries of several adept private investigators. In his experience, everyone had something to hide, and professionals could always find it.

Laura Goetz maintained the strongest opposition to the project. She was on her second marriage – the first had ended in divorce twenty years before when she was twenty-two, and she had lost custody of her young son. There were claims of drug use and infidelity, all steadfastly denied, with no proof either way. She had had a "gentleman friend" for six years. Currently she had a strong relationship with her son. Hmmm. Not much to work with.

Len Williams was a willing fool. His support for the project was unconditional and unthinking. Keller couldn't resist a sneer for a man who required neither threats or a bribe. This idiot plowed on ahead like a driverless tractor with a stuck throttle. No problem here.

Patrick DelOstro was another matter. This man thought too much and asked too many questions. Keeping the disorder he sowed from spreading was paramount. The investigations had turned up nothing more damning than possible college pot smoking. His professional career was unassailable – he had turned down clients whose dealings looked a bit suspicious to him.

How disgusting. The only thing worse than a lawyer with integrity was an honest accountant. Where do they get people like this? His marriage was frightfully boring, a loyal wife whom he loved, no flings, no children of unsavory report. Nowhere to start grinding this man down. He might come around if City staff could be persuaded to present the economic report in the most favorable light, but this was grasping at straws.

The Mayor was acting a bit balky right now, nothing a few good slaps to the head wouldn't cure. The man was indebted to Howard Keller up to his eyeballs; he just needed to be reminded of the debt from time to time. Elimination of the viable alternatives would guarantee his vote.

This left Gene Ryan. He had remained non-committal so far, but this meant that he could still be turned one way or the other. He was not up for reelection for two more years, so it was necessary to find something else to beat him up with, perhaps something he would not want revealed or some way to pressure him indirectly.

And here it was, right in the report. He read the line again. His employer was . . . Keller knew that name from somewhere. He had seen it several years before in association with . . . what? Wasn't there someone with that name a few years ahead of him at U.S.C.? A member of his fraternity? Of course.

He started to grin.

Yes, this would do, but how should it be used? How to administer the medicine.

He jumped to the telephone.

Lucinda Ryan could see at a glance that something was not sitting well with her husband. A long, hard day would leave Gene tired and ready to relax, but this was something more. Fourteen years together had provided her with an insight into his movements, his gestures. She knew that something weighed heavily on him, and she would hear of it in due time, but not right now. She kissed him and removed herself to see to matters in the kitchen.

Shuffling over to his favorite chair, he changed shoes for slippers and settled in. When Lucinda offered him a glass of wine, he was staring out of the window absently. A glassful of Chablis probably would have brought him some benefit, but he demurred. Not good, she thought, but dinner will surely help.

The meal passed without any conversation. This evening offered simple fare, but Gene ate the pot roast with little of his customary enthusiasm. The occasional clink of silverware and rustle of napkins provided the only breaks in the silence. When he pushed his plate away and sighed, she knew that he would unburden himself presently.

"I was called into Ted's office today."

Lucinda knew that in the Real Estate business it was not unusual for agents to be summoned for a conference with the manager on a pending sale, especially one of some weight.

"He started out with small talk, patting me on the back for the Huston sale, but then he changed course and brought up the Cliffs project. I mentioned that I couldn't discuss a matter before the Council except in a very general way, but he waved me off."

Gene had been looking downward but raised his eyes to emphasize his revelations to her.

"This project, he said, would be supremely important for a prosperous future. Without putting it so directly, he indicated that its approval could result in an exclusive contract for our firm to market the properties. He was very clear that to let such an opportunity slip by would be bad for the company – and for me."

As the implications presented themselves to Lucinda, her shock was deeper for the fact that Ted Fordham had never before tried to influence Gene's vote on any matter.

"Brace, if you did what he is suggesting, vote for the project, wouldn't that be . . . "

"A conflict of interest? Yes, of course. A criminal offense. And even if I were not prosecuted, especially if not, he and that developer could hold it over my head forever."

"But if you vote against it?"

"Well, it's obvious that my job would be forfeit, and Ted could make it very difficult for me to work for any other agency in this town."

They passed a few more exchanges wrapped in resentment and dismay. The implications were all too clear, and Lucinda found herself staring downward at her plate.

"Luce, when we started out, life was pretty thin for us. There was a lot we had to do without for many years."

"But I . . . "

"I know. You were game, and tough. But now we are in a much better position – comfortable, and you don't have to work full time. We could lose all that and have to start over somewhere else. We are not young any more. I couldn't force you . . . "

"Brace, don't even start with that. Since I first met you, you have always had a measure of integrity which has made you what you are. Unlike many people, you knew how to choose between the right path and the wrong one, even if your choice landed you in trouble with your peers. I know your co-workers consider you a "boy scout" because you wouldn't get involved in deals which seemed a bit shady, but I admired you for it. Whatever you decide to do now, I will be with you. I will live with you in a tent in the park or come to visit you in jail, whatever."

For a moment he was stunned.

"Was that supposed to be funny, Luce?"

"I was hoping for funny."

The moment of humor came and went, and Lucinda could see from the look in his eyes that now it would be best to leave him with some time to think, to weigh the options and consequences. She rose quietly and went into the next room, leaving Gene sitting alone, looking out the window.

Dee was in a bad mood, a rare thing for her. Usually she could maintain the sparkle and wit she was known for, but with the Council meeting approaching, her disposition had turned sour. Her best attempts to gauge the possible outcome were frustrated at every turn. It looked like a two/two vote with one undecided, and all her efforts to lobby Gene Ryan were politely rebuffed. In fact, he would no longer answer her phone calls.

All campaign efforts had taken a secondary position to the upcoming Council vote as the dreaded day approached, and Dee made her preparations grimly. They would easily pack the meeting hall and dominate the assembly of speakers, but it might not be enough.

The economic report was rumored to be unfavorable to the project, but that fact could be ignored by the Council. Howard Keller was prancing around town as if he owned it, gracing the locals with a smile which said "it's in the bag." The Mayor was wrapping up his campaign with an air of invincibility, refusing all comment on the Cliffs or Turner Canyon as being too pedestrian to bother with. Dee's temper was not the best, and it showed. Even Dodger kept his distance whenever she walked down the street to get some papers from City Hall.

Finally, one afternoon she came to the realization that all she could do was to load up the cannon, aim and fire it. If the target went down, it would depend in great part on the qualities and actions of others. After much soul searching, she decided that she had confidence in those people. Thereafter, the cloud which had been following her around thinned out a bit, and her work went easier, to the great benefit of those who were often near her.

The clock ticked down.

On the day of the Council meeting an early rain threatened, but none came. The few clouds, menacing at dawn, thinned out to reveal a clear, endless sky; and a brisk north wind coursed through the streets of Ruskaya, playing with the dust and leaves in the margins of the streets.

The residents of Turner Canyon rose early and went about their daily routines, school, work, home; but all of them carried a thought tucked away in their heads, persistent, like an alarm bell ringing faintly at a great distance. *This is the day.*

At noon the sun had that sizzle which stings the skin in warning, as the air stood still and lightly on the earth. For those who dared to glance at it momentarily, the sun had a faint blue cast, seeming more a star for another planet, and not this one. People bustled about, doing the tasks which their lives required, but tended to keep to the shade.

Afternoon brought the cooler, oblique light characteristic of fall which was shepherded by a mild breeze going westward, lazily seeking a rendezvous with the sea. Shadows languidly edged across the streets to touch the buildings opposite as the sky assumed a deeper shade of blue, then almost indigo. One by one the street lights in downtown Ruskaya surged into illumination, each struggling in the twilight to brighten its restricted section of pavement. A faint crescent moon hung in the west, its horns pointing to the zenith, promising soon to leave the sky to the stars alone for the remainder of the night.

People started to collect in small groups along Turner Canyon Road, gradually turning their steps southward toward the bridge into town. As they passed through the one hundred block, they found Dodger on station in the street. As the separated groups passed him, he addressed each with a forceful exposition of barks, his throaty voice reverberating from the canyon walls. Some thought this was odd behavior since he never barked at the residents. Perhaps he was just wishing them well. Perhaps he was surprised to see so many of them together. Perhaps . . .

This irregular army closed on City Hall.

Chapter Twenty - Eight

The meeting hall was quiet, with only a scattering of early comers in the audience. City staff and the Councilmembers had not yet arrived, and the Turner Canyon residents entered and sought their seats as if moving with awed silence through a vaulted tomb. They chose to locate primarily along the aisle leading to the podium and the microphone used for public comment, correctly anticipating that here would be the locus of the night's activity for them. As other groups and individuals drifted into the hall, the seats began to fill just as raindrops gradually fill the extent of a dry and dusty sidewalk at the onset of a storm.

From a side door Will Hansen and Don Colesco strolled casually into the arena, preceding a flock of City staff members. The Planning Director and City Attorney were pursuing a casual conversation, which was lowered to hushed tones as they noticed the swelling audience. They and the others slipped into their customary seats and began purposefully to distribute and arrange papers relating to the evening's agenda on the workspaces before them .

Dee and Jason both noticed Howard Keller at the same time. Perhaps it was a small motion he made which drew their attention, perhaps some subtle mental cue. Jason observed that the agent of so much anxiety was sitting completely alone in the front row, and as the hall filled, no one took the seats near him. Keller happened to catch Don Colesco's eye and nodded vigorously in greeting, but the City Attorney was appropriately sparing in his response.

Since the door behind the dais was out of the strong general illumination, no one saw when it opened. Abruptly, City Clerk Anna Ferrier walked into the light, followed by the five members of the governing body and the City Manager, Jeff Heit.

As they assumed their seats, Keller's silent but enthusiastic greeting received an abundant response only from the Mayor and a diminutive nod from the City Manager. As they took their seats, the stage was set, the players were in their places, and the presentation would soon begin. Prefaced only by a small click as the microphone was switched on, the Mayor leaned forward and filled the air with the imposing thunder of his voice.

"The October eighteenth meeting of the Ruskaya Bend City Council will come to order." He slammed down the gavel with a purpose. "The City Clerk will call the roll."

During these moments Dee's head began to ring. Perhaps it was the accumulated tension of the last few weeks catching up with her, perhaps it was the dinner she had been too nervous to eat. During the presentation of the consent calendar, she retreated to the water cooler for a cupful, thinking that she might not have been maintaining proper hydration in the season's dryer weather. From this vantage she could only see backlit heads and shoulders of the audience set against the glow of light from the dais. Voices droned on from the Council, decisions were made, preliminary items were disposed of.

After a time she felt satisfactorily recovered, made her way back to her seat and rejoined her friends.

After the first regular agenda item, the Cliffs project, was introduced, Mayor McCanna made a show of ordering copies of the previously requested economic assessment distributed to the Councilmembers. Five additional copies were casually laid on a table next to the podium for public distribution, and they were quickly taken up."

"Mr. Mayor." Patrick DelOstro was quick on the uptake. "I have to object to the late date that this report was presented to us. None of us have had an adequate opportunity to go over its contents."

"Councilmember DelOstro, You and the other members are due an apology, but this was caused by factors beyond our control. Nonetheless, a thorough assessment of the report will be presented to us by staff."

"Yes, I'm sure. But I can and will read it myself and make

my own assessment."

This pointed barb gathered no response from the Mayor who was busy representing himself to his admirers in the audience as still supremely in command. Dee thought to herself that this man certainly did have the all the moves down pat, and she was surprised to feel herself amused by his stereotypic posturing. She found herself relaxing a bit.

Once the report was introduced, the meeting was a near echo of the one six weeks before, with a few notable inclusions. The staff analysis of the report was delivered as the audience and Patrick DelOstro were still pawing intently through it. During the sonorous murmur of the staffperson's delivery, pages were flipping frantically, but to Dee's practiced ear, it was clear that the fix was in. The positive results of the project commanded disproportionate emphasis, and the negative impacts were relegated to footnote status. Howard Keller visibly puffed up as these analyses were read into the record, and he turned to sweep the audience coolly with his eyes. They're ready for the meat grinder, he thought.

Displaying obvious deference, the Mayor then introduced the applicant. He rose and with every step and gesture expressing ultimate confidence he assumed the podium. With sweeping gestures he made exaggerated claims of benefit to the City and its citizens to come from his project. All good things would accrue from its approval. This time there were no gratuitous potshots at the Turner Canyon residents – they were now too insignificant to bother over. He ended with a flourish and regained his seat in dead silence.

The neighbors from Turner Canyon one by one took the microphone and read their objections into the record. Most statements were replays of what had been said at the previous meeting, some with shifts of emphasis. She noticed that Jason put more weight in his statement on the question of cost versus benefit, drawing heavily from the report he had just hurriedly digested. As her friends spoke, she carefully watched the expressions and body english of the Councilmembers, trying to glean some indication of how they were affected by the arguments presented. The Mayor was undisguised in his indifference and Len Williams stared absently at the back wall. Laura observed each speaker carefully, giving nods of encouragement when any of them stumbled over their words, but Patrick looked to the side with a somewhat disgruntled expression. Not necessarily a good sign, Dee considered his manner with a bit of anxiety. More worrisome, Gene Ryan seemed a thousand miles distant, wrapped in his thoughts.

The time for public input drew to a close.

The Mayor hastily rushed the issue along to bear fully on the other Councilmembers. Here was his opportunity to press and squeeze those almost-decided or faltering, a skill he excelled at. Using his authority as commandant of the Council meetings, he carefully selected the order in which each member would speak. Laura was ordered first to march along the gangplank so that the splash as she fell would scarcely be remembered.

"I believe that the facts are very clear in this matter. No matter how the data are construed . . . " She shot a glance at the staffmember who had delivered the obvious puffball analysis of the economic report . . . "this project cannot ever be good for this City. It makes as much sense as burning your jacket to keep warm, which is no sense at all. I cannot support it."

McCanna did his utmost to muffle the applause erupting from the audience and progressed swiftly to the next speaker. Len Williams said his piece, and it was exactly what Dee had expected. She was amused to note that it was almost word for word the same homily he had delivered at the previous meeting, a masterwork of pro-growth cliché mongering.

The vote now stood potentially at one to one.

Patrick went next, and the source of his irritation became obvious with his first words.

"I want to thank the Mayor kindly for my copy of this report." As he held it up, Dee noticed that he gripped it so tightly that it was rippled like a fan. "To me, this is a telling document. Reading it, I can only come to the conclusion that this project is not a sound venture for this City, and it could never be under any circumstances."

The Mayor hastened to interrupt and press on to the next speaker, but Patrick would have none of it.

"Mr. Mayor, I have not finished my statement. If I may continue . . ."

McCanna grimly looked away by way of assent.

"The figures are clear. This project would generate costs to the City which would never be recouped under any ordinary circumstances. Only if a special dispensation were granted to the developer, would it ever break even on its costs, but not during the lifetime of most of the people in this building. No other development has ever required so great a loss to satisfy the desires of a single property owner. I would consider granting this project to be an economic blunder and an action heedless of the public trust, and I could never support it."

Two to one against!

This time McCanna had serious difficulty reining in the crowd. These were the words Dee's neighbors had hoped to hear, and they celebrated them fully. Finally, after much wood pounding, the Mayor's demands for order were heeded, and he motioned to Gene Ryan.

Gene stared at McCanna for a moment and then shook his head and sat back in his chair, saying nothing.

The audience responded as if from a body blow. Dee felt her head begin to ring again, but fought against it. The thoughts raced through her head. Did he have something to say but did not want it on the record? Was he trying to stay as minimally involved with a controversial vote as he could? Did he not care? Was he ashamed of something? What?

Her train of thought was broken as McCanna started to speak. She scarcely gave any attention to his words, knowing fully what they would contain. True to form, he expressed all the same platitudes which Len had uttered, but put them into a slightly more eloquent form. Toward the end of his discourse, Dee watched him more closely, dismayed that he seemed to be a man supremely confident of the outcome. A great many uncomfortable thoughts started to race through her head, only halted by the words then uttered by the Mayor.

"The chair will entertain a motion."

Laura leaned forward in her chair to speak but her words were swept away by the Mayor's stifling tones.

"The chair recognizes Len Williams."

The shock on Laura's face was underscored by a groan from the audience. McCanna had the rudder in his hand and was fully intending to turn the ship his way. Len Williams was suddenly the focus of all attention, and after a moment of surprised inactivity, he shuddered into action.

"Yes . . . I move that we approve the variance request for higher density and that we approve application 11751, called The Cliffs project."

"We have a motion on the floor."

No one dared to breathe for the next few seconds, and after an agonizing pause Gene Ryan leaned over his microphone and murmured one word.

"Seconded".

Laura shot a dismayed glance at him.

"We have a motion and a second. All . . . "

This time Laura was like a lightning strike.

"Mr. Mayor. I would like to request a role call vote on this matter." She was anxious to remove any opportunity McCanna might have to "mishear" the result of a voice vote and throw approval to Howard Keller. McCanna was not pleased at this turn of events, but he had no choice. Legal procedure was clear.

"Very well. The Clerk will read the title and call the roll."

With scarcely concealed pleasure, Anna Ferrier complied with the first part of this instruction, then called the name of each Councilmember. They pierced the still air with each single-word response.

"Councilmember Goetz."

"No."

"Councilmember Williams."

"Yes."

"Councilmember DelOstro."

"No."

"Councilmember Ryan."

Gene paused for an instant before he spoke.

"I wish to abstain for reasons of a potential conflict of interest."

The crowd issued a gasping moan. Swiftly the implications of this turn of events became clear as Dee's thoughts raced ahead. The best Keller could hope for was for McCanna to vote no, causing a tie vote and no decision at all. Then the project would become a prime election issue with almost no time to reach the electorate. It was not clear whether she and her neighbors were any better off. The election was a gamble. It was all a gamble.

"Mayor McCanna."

Dee snapped to attention, anticipating the Mayor's one word, but it did not come. What is he thinking now? What scheme is he rolling around in that head? How long can he hold this off?

"Mayor McCanna."

Dee could not identify the expression on his face as he leaned forward and spoke.

"No."

The silence was so loud that is fairly hurt the ears. The audience was drifting through the many levels of shock as the City Clerk started to speak.

"The motion fails, three to ... "

That was as far as she was heard. The remainder of her statement was drowned out by the rising tumult from the audience.

Even as she and her neighbors rose to cheer, Dee was troubled by the vote. The obvious hypocrisy of arguing passionately for a motion then voting against it did not sit well with her. What was McCanna's game here? He would probably have risked far more than a difficult election to secure revenge against them. He clearly didn't want to vote the project down, but it gained him something. What? They had not seen the end of this.

Despairing of regaining order, Mayor McCanna called for a five minute recess, and strangely, the disappearance of the Council took the spark out of the audience's rejoicing. After much back slapping and hugging the neighbors started to drift out of the back door, aiming their steps toward home. Dee, pausing at the exit, glanced back at Howard Keller who had not stirred from his seat.

He sat immobile, and the tension in his shoulders indicated to her that he was gripping tightly the arm rests of his chair. She stood there watching him until he was the only person remaining in the audience, then she turned away.

T he shouting was not witnessed by many in City Hall. Howard Keller had sat through the remainder of the Council meeting, staring at the Mayor. After the last item was disposed of, he followed McCanna into his office and started in on him. To the few who heard any of their discussion, it was very one-sided.

"Just what the hell is going on, James?"

"Howard, you saw that I didn't have the votes for you. That damned Ryan spooked out on us. What could I do?"

The answer to this question departed from politics and more concerned what McCanna could do with various parts of his anatomy.

"Listen to me, Howard. What good would a tie have done you? The swing vote had effectively removed himself from any 'persuasion' we might work on him if we voted again. The rest had made up their minds."

The volume of the next outburst from Keller went stratospheric.

"Howard, Howard. I can get it for you still. Do you think I would give up so easily. I can get it for you, but just not yet."

Keller seemed to be descending in volume, so the Mayor continued to lay out his scheme.

"I had to vote against your project, it was the only way. Now the issue will be removed from the election. After I am reelected, I will have all the cards – no one will dare stand in my way. Don't you see? I had to vote on the winning side, against you, so that I could later bring the issue back for reconsideration."

At this Howard Keller stopped shouting and glared at the

Mayor intently.

"Reconsideration, eh?"

"Yes, don't you see. It's the only way. After the election I will be able to bend and mold the new Council to my will."

Keller considered these words as the scarlet color of his face faded a few shades.

"James, you better hope you know what you are doing. Because if you are wrong, I will ruin you. You need to know one thing about me: I never forget an enemy or a friend, and I destroy fools who cross me."

The remainder of the conversation faded below any ready overhearing and seemed to conclude peaceably enough, though there was a perceptible stiffness to Howard Keller's stride as he left City Hall.

Safely alone in his office, James McCanna sat considering his campaign of destruction – first, the scum in Turner Canyon, then the swine who had just left his office. He contemplated the impending misery of his chosen targets with a secret joy.

"**D**odger sick." To Edie, young Nick's statement seemed so matter of fact that she almost paid it no mind. Dodger had been up to his usual duties since the Council meeting, barking at newcomers passing by, calmly approving any residents within his purview, caring for his canyon. Edie had taken water and some kibbles for him just the night before, so she had no reason to be alarmed. Dodger had a few sick days each year when his stomach would bother him, but a day's rest would bring him around again.

"Dodger sick, Mommy."

The repetition left her with the thought that it would be best to visit the big dog and perhaps give him a few words of encouragement. She could check the water and food.

Edie found Dodger lying in his lean to, stiff and cold. During the night his heart had given out. With sudden concern, she thought of her son and how this must affect him and, mumbling something about getting some of the neighbors to help her, took the boy up the street to Henry's house.

In late afternoon Henry, Carl, Luis and Jason used an improvised stretcher to carry Dodger up the canyon to a selected spot near the spring. There, where the soil was deep, they dug a grave, wrapped Dodger in a sheet, and lowered him down to his final rest.

"Nick," Edie began as they put the earth over the dog, "We won't be seeing Dodger again after today. He was an old dog and he has lived out his whole life. He will be gone, but not really gone. He will be here now." She touched his chest. "Here in your heart and in your memory. Whenever you think of him, he will still be with you, and you don't ever have to forget him. You see?"

The young lad just looked up intently into his mother's eyes.

"And when you are grown up and have children of your own, you can tell them about your friend Dodger, about the good times you had together, and he will be there with them, too."

Nick blinked twice and reached up to touch his mother's arm.

"OK, Mommy."

For a few days after that he visited the lean to, as if checking to make sure his companion was really gone. These were difficult days for Edie, concerned over her son's state of mind, but presently Nick slid into his new routine and seemed well adjusted to the changes which had swirled around him. From time to time he would say that Dodger liked this or Dodger would do that, but never to people who had not known him.

He would go on to have many childhood friends, but never forgetting the dog who had stood strong at his side.

Chapter Twenty – Nine

Election day brought the beginning of the rainy season, which had been periodically threatening its renewal for several weeks. It was not the sort of storm which arrives like a giant wave, smacking the unready ground with a wind driven deluge. It was more like a rising tide, scarcely noticed at first. A few early, scattered clouds slid in from the northwest, scouted the dry landscape, and continued inland, replaced by a steadily massing blanket which had obscured the deep blue of the sky by the time the polls opened.

The first few voters could safely ignore the gentle drizzle squeezing out of the overcast which was thickening by the hour, but soon an umbrella in hand seemed a worthy precaution. The dribble of voters turned into a rivulet, then a stream, and by noon had progressed into a river, backing up through the doors of the polling places. Those caught without umbrellas found grateful shelter under those of their neighbors in line. Some made new acquaintances, others found old ones. Each waited patiently for the opportunity to express their choices.

Various groups of the Turner Canyon residents walked across Rosie's bridge into town, seeking out the Fire Station to cast their votes. The mood was generally upbeat since the memory of their victory in the Council chambers was still fresh, but each passed Dodger's accustomed station in the one hundred block in silence. They knew that he surely would have been there to oversee them, even in the rain.

The boundaries of their precinct threw them in with a group of merchants who lived in apartments over their shops in the business district. Normally, these two groups remained apart on election days, often finding themselves on opposite sides of current issues; but somehow the rain enforced a camaraderie, transcending the customary mutual aloofness. Before long the

Firemen found it necessary to put one of their trucks out into the rain so more voters could shelter inside the station. Several pots of coffee and a tray of breakfast rolls appeared in the hands of two Paramedics, and the morning passed easily for all. Following the local tradition, no one talked about politics.

Toward the end of the day, Bob and Ann Hurley gathered up their son Brian with a few, selected toys and drove through the rain to the Middle School where they were registered. As first time voters in Ruskaya, they were not recognized by the precinct workers, but young Brian was a hit. More than happy to watch over him while his parents voted, they gushed and cooed as the lad carefully explained about the important and secret characteristics of all his toys. From time to time he would turn a concerned glance toward the cardboard booths draped with plastic curtains where his parents were doing something, but as long as he could see their legs, he was unworried.

After voting, the Hurley's found it difficult to extract their son who was enjoying fully the abundance of attention falling his way. After lengthy goodbyes, they were able to make their exit into the rain. Their places in the booths were rapidly filled.

The precinct workers had their hands full. The anticipated large turnout collected and surged into the polling places for nearly the whole day. Rain had often been a deterrent in the past, but this time as the storm slowly picked up momentum, the voting activity did also. Those workers with the most experience had to admit that they had never seen such a turnout.

James McCanna voted as he did most things, with style and flourish. A photographer from the Ruskaya View had been alerted and was encouraged to take a carefully posed shot of the Mayor entering the voting booth. Once inside his cardboard castle, he surveyed the list of candidates and carefully bullet voted for himself alone. With another smile and a wave to the flock of admirers, he was gone, unassailably confident of the outcome. Leaving the polling place, he was swallowed up by the increasing rain.

Howard Keller spent the whole, gloomy day in his office. He had been registered to vote, but some civic activist had been alerted and had made a complaint that his address was not one of an actual residence. It was not that he would have voted anyway, a habit he considered a witless exercise appealing only to little people; but it was an irritation to be removed from the rolls. He had little to do but sip at his Scotch and plan retribution for injuries suffered, real and imagined.

The Lee family voted early. Jon knew his wife well and interpreted the listless silence as the initial symptoms of an attack of nervousness. Paige was devoted to action and waiting didn't work well for her. Needing to go to his job, he nevertheless made a point to call her each hour, trying to soothe her jitters. By two o'clock he begged off with his employer and returned home to provide some distraction for his fidgeting wife.

"This is worse than just losing," she complained.

"Darling, that could happen too."

"Well, you are no help!"

"Paige, no matter what happens, I will be proud of you. You raised a lot of important issues and got everyone thinking. You earned a great deal of credibility with the people you spoke to. You have done nothing you should have doubts about."

At these words, she settled a little.

"I wish it didn't have to take *all day*."

"Here, let me brew a pot of oolong for us. You know that will relax you. The hours will pass quickly, you'll see. And I believe that when the news comes, it will be good."

She watched her husband glide into the kitchen to prepare the tea and appreciated that he always knew how to calm her down in a moment of anxiety. Glad again of the choice she had made almost twelve years before, she moved into the kitchen to join him.

Outside the rain beat an increasing tempo on the roof as an occasional gust of wind rippled through the leaves of the oak tree in the backyard.

Despite Jon's assurances, the hours passed slowly.

As the hour of sunset approached, the rain began to falter, withdrawing almost apologetically from assailing the saturated earth. Gaps opened in the cloud cover, revealing a still, blue sky; and the remaining Ruskaya voters glanced upward at the promise of drier weather, shaking the droplets from their umbrellas. By the time of darkness and the closing of the polls, a crisp, clear sky offered a wealth of stars and a crescent moon to citizens hurrying toward their homes seeking refuge from the increasing cold.

Ruskaya Bend no longer tallied its own ballots since the change in County procedures made three years before. The conversion to electronic voting had obviated the need to collect hundreds of pounds of paper at City hall for counting of the votes. The same, ample cardboard boxes which had contained the ballots were still in use, however, making the small, plastic card in an envelope at the bottom look ridiculous. Twelve of these boxes full of air were scrupulously collected in the entry of City Hall and nervously protected by two uniformed police officers. After the last arrived, all the cards were to be removed from their envelopes and inserted into a special, lockable card case and sent to the County Seat for tallying.

The thirteenth box was mistakenly brought into Anna Ferrier's office from a precinct in the Meadows. The poll worker had parked in the rear lot and entered City Hall by a back door, not realizing that his cargo was not to be left in the empty City Clerk's office. As Anna was getting a data sheet from her desk, she noticed the box and considered its contents for a few minutes.

The County had already issued card readers to the cities in anticipation of the next election. At that time each municipality would tally its own votes, but the machines were not to be used yet. Noticing that someone had plugged the reader in and had connected it to the adjacent computer, she opened the box and took the card from its envelope. It was nondescript, slightly larger than a credit card but thinner, made significant only by the precinct name on one side and a metallic strip on the other. She thought of the many hours of campaigning, thousands of dollars spent, the diligence of hundreds of voters, all condensed into a bit of plastic between her thumb and forefinger. She inserted it.

Squinting against the glare of the overhead lights, Anna

scanned through the ballot issues and other offices until she came to names she knew well. Looking down the column on the right, her eyes became wider as she read down the list of figures.

Standing stiffly upright, she yanked the card from the reader and restored it to its original condition in the box. As she started to move toward the door, she noticed that the contents of the card were still being displayed on screen. Quickly turning off the computer, she hurried to the entry of City Hall with the box. The sooner she could send the cards off to Santa Rosa, the sooner the results would return. They would know by midnight.

D ee was trying to keep busy. She had vacuumed, dusted, washed the dishes, and rearranged the stock in her pantry. Throughout all of her activities, she kept an eye on the computer displaying the Ruskaya Bend municipal website.

In previous years, before the internet and electronic vote tallying, a nervous gaggle of citizens would huddle before a large blackboard at City Hall as each precinct reported its count. A new entry could bring hope or dread, and always there was a flurry of calculations as the spectators judged the odds of eventually seeing their favored outcome. Through the night, part of the assembly would become subdued and resigned as another group would become progressively more upbeat. In the end, however the vote might go, there was a natural culmination to the tension, a release which would permit all to retire to their homes with their normal mood restored somewhat.

But this modern technology had changed everything. Dee wondered if society was fragmenting into units defined by the presence of computer monitors, anxiously watched for hours. She missed the old days.

She was dusting everything for the second time when she noticed that something had changed on the display. Half the way down on the right side was a button which had not been there previously. It was red and two words were flashing within it – ELECTION RESULTS. She attacked the button with her mouse and another page opened. On it were buttons for each precinct and one marked TOTALS.   Clicking this showed Countywide offices and ballot propositions, and scrolling down brought her to Ruskaya Bend Council candidates.

At first her heart sank as she saw that the topmost name was James McCanna. But wait, this listing merely followed the order of names on the ballot. She looked down the column of figures on the right and shrieked.

Racing for the telephone, she knocked over a floor lamp but deftly caught it before it smashed into the floor.

"Oh, oh, oh!"

The number was busy, and again later. *Never mind, I can always call to congratulate her tomorrow.*

Dee settled into her favorite chair, turning off the room lights with the remote. As her eyes got used to the dim light maintained by the glow of the computer monitor, she noticed that the crickets outside seemed especially vocal in spite of the recent storm. She smacked the ends of the armrests with her palms.

"Sweet!"

In the end, it wasn't even close. Patrick DelOstro and Laura Goetz were clustered closely at forty-seven hundred votes, with Paige Lee one hundred and twenty votes behind. Sixteen hundred votes below her was James McCanna, followed by the remainder of the candidates. The size of the landslide diminished somewhat when the absentee vote brought another three hundred to McCanna. No one noticed this glancing mitigation to his loss.

A & D Enterprises had made two serious technical errors. Noting the increased registration, they assumed that these newly franchised citizens would either not vote at all or would march in lockstep with the rest of the established voters. Further, they made it impossible to learn otherwise by concentrating their only polling efforts on "likely voters," namely, citizens who had voted in several previous elections. They never saw the backlash building up which smacked McCanna out of office. He rewarded their short sightedness by withholding their last payment.

Three days after the election the rain started to fall in earnest, but no one seemed to mind. The downpour lasted for a week, scrubbing the town clean and raising the river level by several feet. The renewal of the soil moisture would soon bring new life to the hills and canyons around Ruskaya, and the wildflower bloom promised to be spectacular. During a pause in the downpour, someone noticed that the door to Howard Keller's office was ajar, and inside was the unmistakable evidence of a hasty departure.

All the residents of Turner Canyon walked with a new spring to their step. Although they discussed the election only for a few days and then went on to other topics, the removal of so great a weight added a relaxed grace to their movements and an extra enthusiasm to their smiles for a considerable time afterward.

The normal routine of life slowly returned.

During the two month interval between the vote and inauguration of the victors, James McCanna continued to play his part as Mayor with the vigor of a well oiled automaton. The same captive flock of admirers applauded his utterances before the Council as if nothing had occurred to halt the flow of greatness.

During this time he paid an office call to Patrick DelOstro. His intent was to make a last effort to breathe life into Howard Keller's project. He was expounding the same tired lines heard before when Patrick stopped him.

"James, I have known you for some time, and you have accomplished many fine things for this City. You are a man with some admirable qualities, but counterbalancing those is the most pronounced streak of vindictive meanness that I have ever seen in anyone."

McCanna blinked and launched anew into his jawbone session undeterred.

"Excuse me, James, but I have heard all this before and I am not going to change my vote, so . . . was there anything else you wanted to talk about?"

The Mayor assumed the attitude of a molested puffer fish and soon found an excuse to leave. As Patrick would relate the events of the meeting later, McCanna had demoted himself from the status of lame duck to that of dead duck.

Toward the last days of November, Gene Ryan left Ted Fordham's real estate office. For some time he had been musing over the pros and cons of starting his own business, and the sudden eruption of coldness from his employer hastened along his decision. Two of his colleagues went with him, and although they were aware that the risk of failure was high, they all knew the town well and had good reputations. Many people suspected the reason for Gene's abstention at the Council meeting, and this did not hurt his cause.

The second major storm of the season commenced and ran its course, causing the river to rise high enough to cover half of Battle Beach. Grasses sprouted in the spaces between the trees on the hills and the many Ceanothus shrubs pushed out a new flush of growth to crown their deep green magnificence.

Winter sneaked into town insensibly as people's thoughts drifted toward the upcoming holidays.

Chapter Thirty

January fourteenth was the appointed day. At City Hall the new Council was to be sworn in as the first order of business; and the throng gathered in the meeting hall, overflowing into the corridor where loudspeakers had been set up.

Mayor McCanna stiffly called the proceedings to order and led the customary flag salute. For a time he seemed to be shuffling through the papers in front of him as if seeking the instructions on what to do next. Abruptly he turned to the City Clerk and requested that she read the results of the election.

Anna Ferrier went down the list of names and totals in order of votes received – Patrick DelOstro, Laura Goetz, Paige Lee, James McCanna, Paul Covarrubias, and Ronald Hale. A round of applause issued from the packed audience, and most who had been able to find seats rose for the ovation, joining those already standing.

McCanna evidenced a wince of irritation and was tempted to use the gavel one last time, but thought better of it, merely permitting the clamor to die out naturally. He then spoke his final words as Mayor.

"The City Clerk will swear in the new Council." At this, he set the gavel down and rose, moving off the dais and toward the door. The smattering of applause almost mocked him as he went. The sight of the back of his head passing between the spectators flanking the door was the last view many in that room ever had of him. Soon he would become an example, a reminder, a footnote, merely an unpleasant dream hardly remembered. Before long he faded completely from memory.

Laura and Patrick both took their oath with a relaxed polish conditioned by four years of previous service, but Paige seemed a bit tentative at first. She raised her hand with looks of excitement and apprehension flashing across her face, but as she spoke the words of the oath, her manner became more assured and calmly positive. She finished with a flourish to generous applause.

Moving onto the dais, she noticed that the only seat available was the one recently abandoned by James McCanna and she paused behind it.

"I don't think I can sit here."

"Sure you can," Laura remarked in a playful tone. "You can't vote standing up."

Paige settled her tiny frame into the great seat, looking spunky but out of place. Glancing down, she deftly slid the gavel to rest in front of Patrick who was on her right, as Laura raised her voice to address the Council and the audience.

"I would like to nominate Patrick DelOstro as Mayor."

"Seconded," came immediately from Gene.

Anna Ferrier called for the vote and quickly five voices made it unanimous.

"Do you want your seat now? whispered Paige.

"Not yet," was the muted response.

Gene wasted no time and nominated Laura as Mayor-Pro-Tem. Paige jumped in to second the motion and then shortly it too was passed unanimously.

At this point the Council rose to assume seats appropriate to their new position, all in motion except Len Williams. To Gene he actually seemed to be grasping the arms of the chair, daring any of these upstarts to displace him. The tide swirled around him briefly, and the renovated Council was seated.

The rest of the meeting was filled with routine matters, a zoning change, contracts for civic improvements, a report from the Planning Commission. There was nothing on the agenda to highlight the occasion; it was business as usual, but yet very different. There was a finality to this new beginning, a spring uncoiled and set aside, but there was one further thing for Dee and her neighbors to anticipate.

After the regular order of business, Laura made a motion to lift the moratorium on residential construction in Turner Canyon. The vote was unanimous, with even Len Williams in agreement, and it was done. The meeting was adjourned soon thereafter.

A short while later, the few townspeople still remaining downtown after the Council meeting heard an odd sound coming from the vicinity of Rosie's bridge. To those who were there it sounded like a few dozen people howling like wolves. But no, they thought, it couldn't be.

D ee had been down the street visiting a neighbor, Beth Courat, offering her a bit of comfort after minor surgery. Dee was masterful at turning a few kind words and an gift of home made spaghetti into the best of medicine, and she made a point of looking in on Beth from time to time since her family was all gone.

On her way home she happened to notice something on Jason's door, a thin, orangeish sheet of cardboard. A closer view showed that it was the inspection register for a building permit. To the right of the door she noticed a new doorbell button and tried it out. A muted "bing-bong" sounded from within the house, and presently Jason himself was at the door, covered with a fine, white powder.

"Oh, Dee, good to see you. Come on in. Sorry about all the dust – I'm putting up new sheet rock in the back rooms."

"What was on the walls before?"

"The same thing, but it had been stained and damaged by moisture when the roof leaked." He paused thoughtfully. "I guess my Dad found it hard to keep up with all the maintenance. Anyway, I already did the roof repairs and I'm working my way downward."

"I see you were quick to get a permit. What all is it for?"

"Several things. I am going to underground the electrical drop and upgrade the panel. Then I plan to remodel the kitchen and bathroom."

"My, my. Big improvements. Then I suppose you will be able to put it on the market and move back to the City."

Jason was halted momentarily by her abruptness and just

grunted in lieu of agreement.

There was a clatter from the hall and Oso burst into the living room, bristling with feline excitement. He froze and took a long look at Dee, obviously weighing the advisability of flight. Suddenly, his wide eyes adopted a more relaxed aspect, and he flopped over on his side on the carpet with an attitude of boundless assurance.

"So, is this the cat I have been hearing about? Cynthia talks about him as if he had mastered both telepathy and levitation."

"Hmmm. His one great talent that I can see is that he can make a colossal mess and be somewhere else when blame is being assigned. Watch out. He will probably bite you."

His warning went unheeded as Dee made appropriately high pitched greetings and approached the cat, extending her hand to scratch him behind his ears. He deftly turned his head so her fingers were working under his jaw, which was his sweet spot. He owns her, thought Jason, another captive human. Oso started to purr loudly, and the conquest was complete.

"What a nice cat."

"Some people think so."

She just snorted at him and stood up. Jason judged from her body english that she might be departing soon.

"Say, Dee, I am glad you came by when you did. I was about to take a break anyway and I was wondering if you would like to share a pot of tea. I have some Pekoe from Sri Lanka you might like.

"That sounds wonderful."

They drifted into the kitchen and as he drew the water, Jason described the improvements he planned to make to that room. He paused to consider the contents of his kettle.

"I used to disdain tap water for tea, but what we get here is superb, and I use it all the time."

"That is the water from our spring. We are supposed to be chlorinating it, but somehow we usually forget to. They say the taste is due to the minerals that it picks up underground. Our supply goes directly from the source to our taps without any exposure to the air. There is no better."

They both were relaxed by the ritual of tea preparation – drawing the water, bringing it to a boil, measuring out the tea, steeping it. Dee was surprised at how short a time was necessary for this last step, but a fine tea must not be overbrewed. She carefully parked her gum on the edge of the plate. Soon steaming cups were before them, their scalding contents gingerly savored. Both liked to drink it as it came from the pot without anything added to dull the flavor. Before long a second round was being poured. Jason looked over his cup at his neighbor and curiosity prompted his boldness.

"Dee, would you mind me asking you something – that is, if you wouldn't object to a personal question."

"I wouldn't object, but I might not answer."

He put his toe into the water carefully.

"You knew my Dad for a long time . . . "

Her raised eyebrows prompted him to go on.

". . . Were you two ever . . . "

"An item?"

"Well, yes."

"Now, that is certainly a forward inquiry – downright incriminating, actually."

"Umm, I didn't think . . . "

"Let it be enough to say that your father and I were friends – close friends. We each cheered the other when we were down, as friends do. We celebrated each other's triumphs as well. Good friends, and let's leave it at that."

"I didn't mean . . . "

"I am sure you had to wonder if this wanton woman from up the street ever led your father astray, but, silly boy, I won't tell you."

Her sudden laughter put just the right punctuation on her statement, and they both appropriated another sip of the fine pekoe from their cups.

"But you never married, did you?"

"No . . ." Her mood slipped into pensiveness. "There was someone, years ago, but he was killed in an auto accident about a month before we were to be married. After that, I didn't avoid the company of men, to be sure, but I never could see spending my life with any of them. The moment slipped away, and now I am just a busybody who frets over the lives of her friends."

Jason hadn't been expecting such a frank self appraisal and tactfully kept silent.

"Not much of a life, I guess," she concluded.

"I wouldn't say so. From what I have seen, you have been a powerful inspiration to a lot of people who might have lost their way in this recent business with the City. You have earned a lot of their respect."

"But . . . ? There surely is some qualification here. What is the rest of it."

"You are considered to be a trifle eccentric."

"Oh, is that all." She waved her hand in the air as if shooing away a fly. "Eccentric -- I can live with that." She took up the teapot and poured another round. "But how about you?"

"What do you mean?"

"A year from now, or ten years, where will you stand? You were strong before the Council and you are doing a fine thing with this house, but is that all we are going to know about you?"

He was a long time before answering.

"I don't know."

"Well, I know one thing." She jumped up as if pricked by a pin. "I have to use your bathroom. Tea goes right through me without even pausing to say hello."

As she disappeared down the hall, Jason was left alone in the kitchen with his thoughts. Presently he sighed and pushed the cup away.

His remaining conversation with Dee was about mundane things – neighborhood news and the like, and soon she was gone, leaving him in the empty house. Jason started ritualistically to prepare some dinner as Oso set up station in a chair to watch each careful movement.

The door opened after the second knock, revealing Henry in his usual plaid shirt, munching on an apple. He was a bit surprised to see the person on the porch in front of him.

"Well hello, Jason. What brings you by?"

"I wonder if I could ask a favor of you."

Chapter Thirty - One

In late December the river rose up on the strength of previous rains to cover most of Battle Beach. This apparent loss of terrain was decried by those inexperienced in the ways of the river, but most knew well that what the water took away, it would restore in due time. Besides, some snickered, it was a great discouragement to the tourists. High water was also cherished as an indicator of the passage of the seasons since the weather often would not provide a competent guide. Many of the overcast, late spring days were cooler and more gloomy than numerous mid winter days blessed with clear skies and warm sun. The rise and fall of the river was like the earth's respiration, and most of Ruskaya's residents unconsciously timed their annual events by its rhythm.

At this time of year bold individuals looked up the face of the Bear and dreamed.

The word circulated lazily through the residents of Turner Canyon – a jumper, on January twentieth. This seemed a bit early in the season; someone could be anxious to take advantage of the high water in the river or perhaps hoping to seize the moment while he still had the pluck.

The first guess was that it might be a senior in the High School named Kevin, a brash sort of fellow. It would be like him, they said; but Cynthia dashed that speculation with the news that he had been hurt recently while playing soccer and would not likely jump with a leg injury. Then the consensus was that it could be anyone since few jumpers would trumpet their intentions in advance in case they could not take that last step off.

Dee and her neighbors usually made a strong presence at such occasions, partly because they all lived so close, and partly because they had a lot of respect for anyone who would make such a strong commitment and face such a risk. They also regarded themselves as the unofficial custodians of the Bear, and anyone who made the drop was tacitly adopted as one of their own. But it may come to nothing if a storm were to arrive on the chosen day – good weather with no wind was the invariable requirement.

The Hurley family had heard about Bear jumping but had chosen not to take their young son to any of these events, fearing for an adverse reaction. But now he seemed that he might be old enough if they could give him a proper appreciation of the danger. A few calls to neighbors with a few more years in the community served to assure them that the injury rate was low, a broken ankle about ten years before was all anyone could remember.

They spoke to Brian, explaining that this was something that grown-ups sometimes did, and that occasionally they could be hurt. He thought about this for a moment and stated, "We can take some band aids . . . and peroxide." The matter was settled in his mind, and with some misgivings his parents resolved to go.

Paige Lee knew that she had a problem with heights, going back many years to her childhood when she had fallen out of a tree. She was even reluctant to look up toward another person who was at great height, and the idea of some young man jumping off the Bear gave her a queasy feeling. She and Jon talked it over and she resolved to be on Battle Beach on the chosen day, for several reasons. As a Councilmember, it might be considered part of her civic duty, and the young person on the rock might need the little bit of additional encouragement which she could bring. Further, she knew that she had overcome much to be where she was in life, and it irked her to let this ancient dread hold her back now. Yes, they would be there.

Roy Butler heard about the jumper through the usual channels. He had always taken pride in his ability to keep his finger on the pulse of the community, and scarcely anything was slated to happen in Ruskaya Bend which would escape his notice. It seemed a fairly routine matter, and at first he thought to send an underling to cover the event and get a few pictures. It was not the only potential headliner for that weekend, but the more he considered it, the more he thought it better that he should attend personally. He could take his beat-up and beloved Leica and mingle with the crowd, perhaps cover the event from the point of view of the spectators, develop a new angle. He put his feet up on the desk and settled into the idea. *Better get some film.*

The City Manager heard of the jumper from his secretary. Personally, he was indifferent to the fate of these lunatics, except for how it might reflect on the City. The Police department had the authority to prohibit anyone from jumping off the Bear, but it could be a risky power to use. This ridiculous event was a long standing tradition, and a Police officer who had tried to arrest a jumper twenty years before had been given an unexpected bath in the river for his trouble. Naturally, it was an accident -- of course it was -- but he knew the locals could be exceptionally feisty. He resolved to do what he had always done, to delegate a single Policeman to watch from a distance, ready to call an ambulance if needed, but otherwise, do nothing. Let them have their spectacle.

He turned his attention to the papers before him.

Frank Wells found out about the event when he overheard part of a conversation during his lunch at the Plumb Branch. He knew about Bear jumping, but he had never actually seen it. It was quite a civic occasion, by all reports, and perhaps he should take it upon himself to be a part of it. Of course, it was nothing he would ever want to try, but he had to admire anyone who had the resolve for it. He made a note on his calendar.

The dawn of the twentieth of January was clear with a light breeze coming from the west. The earth was still sodden from the previous week's rain, a deluge which had served to maintain the height of the river, and even add to it. Battle Beach still retained a slim crescent of sand on the south side, and the river's natural undertow at the base of the cliffs had scoured out the summer's accumulation of sediment, making the water sufficiently deep – all in all, a perfect day to jump the Bear.

At about eleven o'clock, the residents of Turner Canyon began to collect in small groups, chatting about the upcoming events and drifting downward toward the river. Dee fell in with Aurelia and her clan and soon Carl Fish was with them, but Henry was not to be found. Not to worry, he certainly would join them.

Most all paused in the one hundred block to bring up a favorite memory of Dodger whose raspy bark and firm stance had been as constant as the sun's light, but now no more. In a mass they crossed Rosie's bridge and traveled single-file down the trail leading to the beach. There they found nearly one hundred of Ruskaya's citizens already spread out along the strand, with more arriving steadily from the center of town. Dee and her neighbors interspersed themselves among these people, greeting their old friends. The narrowness of the beach forced everyone together, shoulder to shoulder, enforcing a fellowship, and although several people inquired, no one seemed to know the jumper's name.

Cynthia sat on the slope leading from the town down to the beach and chatted with a few of her school chums, sharing surprises and secrets. Connie and Aurelia took up station down near the water, talking about family business, and from time to time they were amused as the young children in the group tried to make a break for the water, only to be intercepted by their parents and turned back. Luis and Adelita Morales sat nearby, happily passing back and forth the shared glimpses of life important to a couple together for so long.

Off to one side stood Carl Fish, surrounded by a group of attractive middle-aged women. He was considered a worthy catch, and enough time had gone by since the passing of his wife that he might be be thinking about a renewal of his married life, or so they hoped. He was polite to all of them, favoring none. He certainly knew the intentions of these ladies and wasn't cold or remote toward them, but they soon would have to accept that he was not yet interested in ending his bachelor existence. Still they persisted for, after all, there was only so many ways a man could say no.

A hush spread through the crowd as if blown in by the wind. Dee could not see the river over the people in front of her – her short stature did not permit it – but she knew that the launch was approaching.

A well-used, ten foot boat with a rugged outboard motor was traditionally used by the second when someone jumped the Bear. Normally it was tied to a short dock near the bridge in the

Meadows, from where it occasionally it was stolen by pranksters for a joyride. Nonetheless, these rascals always had the good taste to return it intact. It was a bit dilapidated, but its wide beam easily permitted someone to clamber aboard over the gunwale without risk of swamping. Dee could now hear the ragged put-put-put approaching. Looking up, she could not yet see anyone on the Bear, but he had to be up there by now. The trail up from the Meadows was not that long a climb. For an instant the group of people in front of her separated enough for her to see the boat midstream, being maneuvered into standby position. She took this opportunity to work her way over to the Salgado family, and as she established herself next to them and looked out across the water, she finally saw who was in the bow of the boat holding an air horn. She started to say, "Look, there's Henry" when an anticipatory rumble issued from the spectators who were all looking up. Dee turned her head up to follow their gaze. As their eyes adjusted to the glare from the sky, only Connie spoke.

"Oh my god, it's him!"

He stood next to a short length of weathered hawser pinned with a steel spike to the brow of the Bear. It would allow him a safe and easy descent of a few feet to the nose, and he tried to remember all the advice Henry had passed along to him.

At first, look only at what is in front of you, not down or across the valley. It was if the air he moved through had stiffened into the consistency of molasses, impeding each movement; but he reached down and grasped the rope, swung around, and lowered himself slowly to stand on the nose of the Bear. Pausing there, he was out of view of the crowd below and he tried to put them from his mind and focus his attention on the rock beneath his feet. His leather soled shoes made a dry, breathy crunch as he walked slowly along the Bear's nose toward the edge. A mild breeze surprised him there.

When you are in position, set your feet and look across the valley to get used to the distance. The breeze played with his hair and tickled his face as he slowly raised his arms out away from his body. Across the valley a wisp of smoke was rising indolently from someone's chimney.

Search for your emotions. If you find no fear there, don't jump, because you are insane and will get hurt. He looked inside himself and found he was not insane, very not insane. He rotated his wrists to allow the sun to shine into his open palms, and its warmth spread through his body, calming him.

Some people go off without looking down, others don't. It's your call. He slowly lowered his gaze to look at the assembled townspeople – there seemed so many, standing in total silence with their faces turned up toward him. It was much farther down than he had thought. The river was a narrow band of bluish-green, curving in its route below him, sparkles of reflected sunlight dancing across the surface.

Don't become overconfident because you still won't be able to fly. Take a little fear with you; it will keep you safe. His arms rose up to a horizontal position and remained extended and still for an instant, as the breeze faded to a whisper.

He stepped off the rock.